Smother

LINDA INNES

Parts of this novel first appeared in a different form as 'The Root of It'
in *The Diva Book of Short Stories* edited by Helen Sandler (2000).

Lyrics reproduced by kind permission:
'Son of a Preacher Man' © 1969 Atlantic
'The Wombling Song' © 1973 CBS
'Love Theme from A Star is Born (Evergreen)' © 1976 Warner Bros.

First published 2001 by Diva Books,
an imprint of Millivres Limited, part of the Millivres Prowler Group,
Worldwide House, 116-134 Bayham Street, London NW1 0BA
www.divamag.co.uk

A catalogue record for this book is available from the British Library

ISBN 1 873741 61 8

Cover illustration and design by Andrew Biscomb

Printed and bound in Finland by WS Bookwell

Acknowledgements

Many thanks to the following people for their support and encouragement: Helen Sandler for her editorial wisdom, acuity and sense of humour; Gillian Rodgerson, Kathleen Kiirik Bryson and all at Diva and Millivres Prowler Group; my partner Annie Watson for her love, strength, constructive criticism and sustenance; my daughter Helena Innes Waller for being perfect and gorgeous; Carol Ann Duffy; Linda France; Jenny Roberts; Jane Reast and Mudfog Press.

To Annie,
with love

1

Tanya: No use crying

No milk had been spilt. Just thickened in the bottle from slow cream, through sickly curds, to thin green. Mum and me together, almost like it used to be when I was a kid. But entirely different.

Folds of skin at her neck ruched into feathery tree bark. She was working something around in her soft mouth, thoughtlessly.

'No milk yet,' I said, 'Can you wait for your tea?' She wouldn't have heard.

From this house, I had waded out from the limits of the living room then swum beyond even her reach.

A moan. I plunged back towards her.

Just a song at twilight... quivering... *When the lights are low...*

I crouched down beside her and held her hand. It was safe now.

And the evening shadows... Softly come and go...

She crackled into laughter, her mouth hollow, her shiny gums and tongue like newborn birds.

'Mum!' I tested. 'It's me – Tanya.'

She focused and crooked her finger towards me. 'Listen! Here!'

I smelt cheese; old dogs.

'Where's me teeth?'

I looked on the table where a stocking lay twisted over the yellow butter dish. No teeth. Draining board. Windowsill. No teeth.

Fridge. Teeth. The faded bubble-gum palate was speckled with something yoghurty, so I rinsed them. She bundled them back into her mouth and snapped them into a smile.

'Now then. Come here. I'm not going to bite you.' She clacked her teeth together and chuckled deeply. Then stopped. She bent her finger to her mouth and whispered, 'Listen to me. Listen to this.'

I stopped my breath to catch the wind of her words. I knelt closer.

'Never trust a wolf in women's clothing.' She sat back. Nodded. Arms folded. Fell asleep.

I looked out for the milk. Across the patch of front garden, long grasses swayed with the weight of seedy plaits. My hiding place. One of them. I remember playing in the back garden. Our next-door neighbour, Mrs Shimmin, was a white shock, a dandelion clock. Through freckles of privet and ribbons of blossom, she shook and couldn't stop. There was no end to it.

'I can dance the Dying Swan,' I had told her. 'Look!' I had pirouetted till I was dizzy and slid down the side of the shed.

'Lovely,' she'd said, and shivered into a round of applause.

Mild and buttery now, when my mother dissolved, what would I have left of *her*? Her bite mark smiling from my shoulder; the small scar she gave me when I was eight, like a splash of milk on my cheek; the knot at my wrist where the bones hadn't knitted together; the nights I'd still wake, mewing. And the time it took my lover to settle me, to skim me with her cool hands, to separate me.

I can't remember being a child.

'Your childhood was stolen,' Mary said.

'Report it on *Crimewatch*, then,' I said.

Mary took her hand away from my cheek and got up. Good. Now we wouldn't speak for a couple of hours and I would wait for her to apologise to me. Then we would drink wine and make love. And she would not hold me too tight, so that I knew that I could always escape.

And in the silver light through muslin curtains I would wake and see the slope of her hip, her milky skin, the gentle valley of her breasts, her sleepy nipples, and I would nuzzle and suckle there till her nipple came hard and alive and Mary stirred and clasped me to her and opened her legs to my plunging fingers and fist.

Mary, sweet and tender, all her gestures tinged with understanding, and I would choke on the gall rising in my throat and I would fight against the urge to hurt her. And mostly I would hurt her. I hurt her where the bruises would not show. Not where my mother hurt me, physically, when I was supposed to be a child, but in the secret places of the heart. I hurt her so that no one but us would know, until she left me for another lover. Then it would all show and Mary would know how it was and how it would be. It is a matter of fact.

She traces her soft fingers over my scars. At first that made me wince. Not from pain, I don't know what. Mary could give it a name, no doubt. She has lots of words for all occasions, all apt and evocative. She should be telling this story, not me. She would make it moving and beautiful and there would be a moral in it somewhere. Mary knows best and what she doesn't know will hurt her.

My mother still lives and I am learning tenderness with her. We are both of us bad teachers and worse students. Let Mary alone with us years ago and we would have dealt cruelly with her. But in age, my mother is the child she never had and I am learning to be mother. Mary is most fortunate to know us now. Mary, for all her gentleness, is a brick shithouse of a girl. Robust, ruddy, all fat and six feet tall. In bed she is all soft roundness like a fertility goddess, large breasted and juicy. I like to drink from her like a baby, like a lover. I do not like her to touch me. She smells of the countryside and of the sea. Places I know exist in a kind of mythology.

But enough of this, for I am a jolly, light-hearted character and don't like to go out of my depth. Let us be shallow, where it's safe.

I am a loud woman. I am the loudest librarian there is. I hoot with laughter if I am amused. If I want someone, I will shout. You can't be too sacrosanct about libraries. Or in them. Anyway, it hasn't held me back at all: I'm a branch librarian in a town we'll call Middlesbrough, because that's its name. Mary came into the library one lunchtime. We hadn't known one another very long but she was in love, eager to see me, to surprise me with smiles and a rose. I shouted. I told you I liked to shout – I shouted as furiously as I could, *'Get out!'* and she did. Too shocked to do otherwise. She brought up the matter in bed in the early hours of the morning. She never brought it up again.

Oh, Mary, soft as melting butter. And me – butter wouldn't melt.

At infant school I used to play with Debbie, who had skin falling off her face and cracks in her hands that bled. I played school and when she was the teacher, she had to cane me really hard.

'I don't want to,' she sobbed. But I told her if she didn't take a stick to me and beat me with all her might, I'd shake her so hard her face would drop off.

On the mountain stands a lady, who she is I do not know...
All she wants is gold and silver, all she wants is a nice young MAN –
And then you jump in and join the skipping. I didn't.

Back at home, mum would have her head in the gas oven again at 4.10pm. After all, high time I was home from school.

I panicked – screeched –- the first time. Screamed and ran, clawing her out, tore one of my fingernails inside out, blood-blistered, ripping her dress. I never did that again. The gas was sometimes on, sometimes not. That was the pain of it. The thrill of it.

If I push Mary to the point that she can't stand it, then she should go. She won't. I must be quite an interesting case. She must get a lot out of it, while I hold her tightly and whisper endearments: 'Doormat'. She says she needs me. I say she's too needy.

When I was two years old I packed a bag and left home. I toddled up the street, my auntie said, heading for my grandmother's. They smiled indulgently. But what does a two-year-old pack when she runs away from home? I am afraid to ask. I am afraid it was a knife, a box of matches, some rope.

Mary was unpacking the shopping. Lamb chops.

'Mary had a little lamb,' I observed, 'Its fleece was white as snoo-ow,' I shot up. Mary flinched, but I was marching across the kitchen at her. 'And – ev'ry-where – that – Ma-ry – went...' I grabbed her waist. She froze. 'That lamb was sure to go-oo.' I pushed my hand down the waistband of her jeans and bit her neck gently. She relaxed a little, so I turned her head towards me and stared her straight in the eyes.

'What are you thinking?' I asked.

'That I love you,' she said.

She only *thinks* she loves me.

I rarely visit my mother. She is hanging on to life and lucidity and so the community cares for her. I don't. Recently, her existence has become more problematic to me and I am forced to have her in my mind and in my life: I communicate with social workers, nurses, doctor. I don't communicate with her. Mary likes to press, to urge me to visit, to build a relationship before it's too late. It is. If Mary were to know everything she would be frightened, so I tell her little, but enough. 'Shutting her out,' she says. So I shut her out. If she can't accept me as I am, then I don't see the point in telling my past. Mary likes to build up stories, to know the details; she is hungry for the scraps of past that make up my history, my identity. I am endlessly fascinating. I leave her to her imagination. She wants to understand me. I don't want her to be understanding.

My forecast is this. There will be a fine crop of corpses this year, stirring painfully from buried stock, spurting white shoots and thready roots through grainy soil, sprinkled with bone. My mother lies restlessly, stirring heavy limbs in pain. Each night a war against the winding-sheet and the pull towards the earth. Her throat is dry, whilst others quench the air with light, wet laughter. She'll die before long, in her own time, and all we have to do is to wait. Patience is all. But I dream of pillows. Blackness. And pillow talk.

When I was seventeen I had a boyfriend. Many girls do, before they realise that they are lesbian, or to contradict the fact that they are lesbian. When I was seventeen I had sex with this boy. Many girls do. And who can say what pheromones or vibes I gave off or what aura I had? Who can say what womanly confidence I displayed or what a show-off I'd been? But, for some reason, my mother must have known. Soon afterwards I came home from school to find my mother having sex with this boy – my first lover. I'll leave it there. If you're anything like Mary, you can make up the rest of the details and accordingly believe what you like.

Mary is warm in bed. Mary is warm out of bed. I am cold. Mary feeds me warm milk at night and tucks the sheet around my shoulders and strokes my hair until I fall asleep or fuck her.

3.45am. A ringing sound crudely awakens me. I am annoyed but Mary passes me the telephone, whispering, 'The hospital'.

And I am driving one hundred miles through the night, alone, despite Mary's hysterical complaints. I don't want her. I am driving one hundred miles alone without stopping. You think it's the last chance, the once-in-a-lifetime, the deathbed reconciliation, the dying words. It's the end of a story you've been on the edge of your seat to finish. The one you couldn't put down.

I am driving through the night, sick with expectation. Visualise the scene.

I burst into the side room. My shrunken mother on a thin bed. She turns watery eyes towards me. I don't know what my face says. She uses all of her strength to wrench the oxygen mask from her face to cry, 'FUCK OFF!'

The nurse whispers, 'Don't worry – she's not in her right mind – she doesn't recognise you.' All too well, my dear. All too well.

By now, Mary is tidying up the patch of front garden outside the house. She crouches close to the earth. Her back is broad, a creamy ellipse of skin stretching between her jeans and her T-shirt. There is a fine vertical line of golden downy hair glistening there. Her fingers are unaccountably slender and strong, brushing earth delicately from the petals of the flowers she has just planted. The flowers are brightly coloured, almost cheerful. She has removed the rough patch of grass which I left to grow long and seedy, laid down some fresh green turf and dug out flowerbeds. Now she is settling bedding plants. She says she wants to make it lovely for us.

She can't.

2
Mary: Along came a spider

Tanya sleeps the sleep of the innocent. I watch her on the pillow beside me, soothed by her regular breathing. She falls asleep like someone crisply diving into water, leaving no apparent ripple, no trace. Like someone who'll never come back up for air. It's all so peaceful, so sweet, so comfortable.

My mum tells me you're never safe anywhere. Out crossing the road you could be hit by a car. You mightn't even be safe on the pavement, 'cause all it takes is a car to mount the pavement and you're dead. When I was a kid I wasn't allowed to cross the road. Crossing the road was dangerous: cars, wolves, bears, men. Maniacs everywhere.

These days my mum reminds me that if you're out driving, you could crash. Could be another driver's fault, or could be your mistake: a moment's wandering thought. You could be reaching into the glove compartment for a humbug, then get your hand stuck in the bag. Could kill you.

'I wouldn't drive into town,' she warns, brows furrowed.

'You can't drive, anyway,' I retort.

'Hmm. Best I don't drive into town then… Watch yourself. Town gets crowded. There are people there.'

There's no limit to my mum's disaster theories. I wasn't allowed to go to Brownies, 'cause my mum had been to Guides once and she'd fallen over and hurt herself. It's all dangerous. Take care out there.

When I was a kid, I used to entertain myself by thinking of all the ways I wasn't safe. The bookshelf over my bed could come crashing down in the middle of the night, crushing my skull. And I could be sitting looking out of the front window, watching the schoolkids walk past, when a lorry driven by someone with their hand stuck in a bag of humbugs could come smashing through the window of the front room and I could be killed. You can't trust anybody. Anything.

Does your life flash before your eyes at the moment of death? Our life was like this:

Saltburn. By the Sea. The Marine. An old bar. Two years ago. Kerry and Mary (me). Kerry is broad and slow with lank, light brown hair. I'm broad and quick and lanky, with mousy brown hair.

'Course it takes about ten minutes to pull a real pint.' Kerry nodded towards the Guinness in her hand.

I was turning my beer mat over and over from edge to edge while Kerry persisted, her eyes bulging in her red sweating face, 'You know, in Dublin they just pull it so far up the glass then leave it to settle, like,' she swirled the remaining Guinness around the glass, leaving a lacework of beige flecks on the inside, 'so they have all these pints standing on the bar in rows, waitin' to be topped up. It's true!' She nodded earnestly. Her cheeks and chins wobbled.

She drained her glass in one deep pull – 'Magic!' – wiped her mouth on the back of her hand and stood up. 'I'll get yer another one.'

Left alone, I used the edge of the beer mat to brush some spilt lager from the tabletop, then swabbed the table with it. Trying to watch the beer mat suck up the lager, I was absorbed too, when Kerry planted another pint in front of me.

'There y'are, lager lout. Not goin' down very easy this time, though. You're already one behind, ya wimp!' She pointed to my hardly touched first pint of lager. I smiled vaguely at the beer mat. Then I started to peel the damp paper layer off the beer mat, noticing the orange stain of the cardboard underneath.

'Mind you, it'd be better if you drank a decent pint!' Kerry held up her new Guinness reverentially. 'Something smooth and dark, like.'

'Like me!' The stranger was at my shoulder. A slim woman of about forty, with a cascade of wavy hair and a black floppy fringe that almost covered her eyes. But such penetrating eyes! She pointed towards the chair opposite: 'Seat free?'

Kerry shrugged and nodded. The stranger swept round and sat down, then drew out a tobacco tin from her black overcoat pocket. She proceeded to make up a cigarette, her thin darting fingers shredding and working the tobacco into a tidy line along the black Rizla paper.

'Ah, Guinness! Rich, dark, smooth and full of goodness... like myself!' said the woman. Kerry chuckled, slamming her hand down on the table so that the pint glasses rattled and the lager quivered.

'Laxative, though,' said the stranger and lifted the cigarette to her red lips, sliding the translucent edge across the tip of her tongue and gazing steadily at me through the strands of hair that masked her face. Then she balanced the thin cigarette on the edge of the ashtray, pulled another licorice paper from the box and continued with the same ritual.

I traced my finger down the condensation on the side of my lager glass. I looked at the bead of water on the tip of my finger, then sucked it softly. I glanced up and saw that the woman was watching me. I caught her eye again and blushed.

'You what?' Kerry turned her wide, shiny face to the stranger.

'I can attest to the laxative qualities of Guinness.' Her slim fingers deftly rolled the cigarette, while Kerry still frowned. So the woman added, 'Laxative. Gives you the shits!'

She grinned, then addressed me: 'Like licorice...' she hissed and held out the thin black cigarette to me. I took it automatically. I don't smoke.

'All good things in moderation,' the woman said, then with another, slower hiss, 'Excellent things to excess...'

She flicked her lighter and held the purple flame to me. I had to stretch just too far to reach it, my breasts brushing against the damp tabletop. My nipples were hard.

Kerry's dull eyes frowned momentarily, then cleared as she went on, 'Honest! It's dead good for ya! They give Guinness to pregnant women – my granddad had it on prescription!'

'Was he pregnant?' the woman queried, holding my gaze, and bared her teeth in a silent grin. I sniggered and she blew out a thin trail of lilac smoke into the hazy air of the bar. I watched as the smoke drifted, then dissolved. I watched the end of the stranger's cigarette glow fiery red as she took a strong pull of it and narrowed her eyes.

'And Guinness is filled with chemicals, as Christiane could confirm.' The stranger blew out the smoke, all the time looking at me. Kerry's brows knotted in a frown.

'So who's this Christine anyway?' Kerry asked.

'Christi-ane,' the stranger corrected, 'is the woman I love.'

'Oh,' said Kerry. And for the first time since the woman had sat down, I looked away.

The woman stared at me, flicked the ash and slowly sucked the tab to a red glow. She blew out a last thin strand of smoke, which coiled into milky grey wreaths. She ground the butt into the ashtray with a dying whisper. I looked down at my own smouldering cigarette.

'Don't burn your fingers,' said the stranger.

I gave a nervous smile and took a tentative pull at the cigarette. I held it awkwardly between my first two fingers, with my hand spread before me.

Kerry's voice was a background hum because I was completely taken by the woman opposite me who leant across the table, flicked back her fringe and said in a low voice, 'I can see you have some learning to do.'

My mouth was dry. I'd even forgotten the two pints of lager in front of me. The woman electrified me with a sudden, slow reach. She clasped my wrist, folded her fingers round my palm and smiled. 'Like this. Be gentle with it, as I am with you.' She drew away her hand and sat back, still gazing steadily at me.

I was conscious again of Kerry. '… in cans these days, but they're a bugger to open with fingers like mine.' Kerry held up her thick stubby hands.

I tried to swallow but my mouth was parched. Kerry went to the bar and I tried to concentrate on her broad back, the T-shirt stretched across it, the rolls of fat, the indents of her bra-strap, the damp patches of sweat under her arms.

'Incidentally –' the woman grinned and held out her hand again '– you ought to know... I'm Tanya.'

I took her hand. 'Mary,' I croaked then cleared my throat, trying to cover my mouth and pull my hand back again. But the woman – Tanya – held on to my hand, just until I started to feel uncomfortable. Then she dropped her grip of me and stood up.

'They call me Tanya Hide.' She smiled down at me.

'Oh, er, I'm Mary Connor.'

'No. You're not listening to me!' she cried. I swallowed hard. 'I said they call me Tanya Hide. As in I'll "*tan your hide*"? Yeah?'

'Erm...' was all I could say, with a nervous smile.

'I'll see you again,' she said as she left. It was a command.

The second time I saw her was by candlelight at a party at the house of a friend of a friend's and it was her hair that ensnared me. Long, dark, rippling and shining. She was like a dark angel. I couldn't help sidling over to her at the buffet table, but I caught the button of my jacket on one of her curls. I hadn't planned it that way, but it served its purpose. I felt huge and cumbersome against her delicate frame while we laughed together. The top of her head brushed my chin and I gasped at her nearness and my self-consciousness.

'It's you.' She smiled, her breath on my cheek. Hot with embarrassment, I struggled to free the lock of hair from around my button.

'Of course, now you're mine forever,' she said. My heart battered away in my chest. I was literally breathless. Once released, she swept away taking my breath away with her.

Big Mandy, Clare and Clancy bowled over towards me, whooping their greetings, 'Hey, Mary! Whasssssssssssssuuuuuuup?!'

I lost sight of Tanya across their flailing arms and the jostling groups. I slapped Big Mandy on the back, hugged Clare's skinny frame, rubbed little Clancy's shaven head in my usual way, then pushed my way through to search for Tanya. I went into every room, even queuing for the toilet for no other reason than to see if she was in it. My eyes strained for the sight of her. I could have cried. I investigated the garden, my anxiety growing with every breath of cold air that hit my lungs. She'd gone. Life wasn't worth living.

When I'd given up all hope of finding her, I asked around the party. I wanted to know more. Since that first time in the pub, I'd been desperate to see her again and now – God! So close! I could almost grab hold of my emotions. All my senses were blaring as if they'd out-grown my body and were monstrous, rampaging round the house. Uncontrollable.

Kerry, who'd been there with me the first time we'd met Tanya in The Marine, was no help: 'What? That weirdo? Dunno. I've seen her about.'

Big Mandy was usually vague, so she didn't know who I was talk-ing about. Clare shrugged her bony shoulders, tossed her ginger hair and sullenly said she'd seen her about, with Georgie and Robbo, but didn't really know anything about her. With a big grin, Clancy raised her eyebrows and pointed me in the direction of our pal Georgie, who might be able to help me.

'What d'you mean, Clancy? She might be able to help?' But Clancy put her little hands in the small of my back and pushed me towards Georgie, who was filling her glass with red wine.

'Hey, George!' Clancy called.

Georgie, looking very handsome in a dark suit, swung round and raised her glass to us, winking and saying, 'Hiya, Clance, me old mucker! Mary – wotcha, darlin'!'

I was shy. Clancy wasn't.

'Hey, George – Mary's got the hots for Tanya –'

'Clancy!' I screeched and covered my face with my hand. I felt like a teenager. My mate fancies your mate. I was 26 years old, for God's sake. I really could have died.

'Well, you do!' Clancy stated, eyes twinkling, her freckled face wrinkled into a mischievous elfin grin. She turned again to Georgie. 'Spill the beans, bud!'

'We-ll-ll… what can I say?' Georgie swept her hand through her fringe, down to the cropped back of her head while she frowned thoughtfully. 'She's always been a dark horse, our Tanya. Difficult to say. She's had a bit of a thing with this woman called Chris. She's not on the scene. Don't really know her. Bit snotty. Hmmmm –' Georgie took a swig of red wine '– but… hard to say if they're actually together…'

'*Together*-together?' From Clancy.

'Yeah – they were together, but I'm not sure they were together-together.'

'Aha! *Were* together, but not together-together! There you go, Mare…' Clancy nudged me in the groin with her elbow. 'Get stuck in, girl!'

I peeled my hand away from my eyes.

'Only Mary's like a bitch on heat,' said Clancy.

After the party, I became Clancy's project. After all, she was so blissfully happily married to Clare that she needed to get her vicarious thrills through me. Moreover, since she knew I'd never really taken such an interest in a woman before, it must be special! I'd had crushes on teachers at school but there'd never been anything sexual in it. They'd been pure and innocent. Like me.

But when I was young I just did what was expected of me: I went out with boys, even though my mum had warned me about them. And all they wanted. And how they wouldn't respect you afterwards if you had sex with them. And how sex was terrible… Awful… especially if the person didn't love you. And how the wrath of God would come down on you if you slept with a man before you were married to them. And sometimes you weren't even safe then. And she told me how a woman she'd worked with – Jeanie Scott – suffered irreparable damage after her wedding night, because the pain had been so dreadful…! Like a red-hot brand, like a red-hot poker, stabbing you. And the woman'd been torn inside – ripped – and it'd been excruciating. Ended up in hospital, she did. My mum had lots of old wives' tales to protect my virginity. I'm surprised I ever got round to losing it. I decided that if I ever had a daughter, I'd encourage her to be promiscuous. And not to believe in God. I'd bring up a pagan slapper and be proud of it. Anything but bring up a child to be frightened and docile like me. So my mum warned me about men, but not about women!

No women for me yet, though. When I first came out on the scene, people had thought I was bisexual, 'cause I'd only had relationships with men. But although I announced, 'I'm more interested in women now!', some people misunderstood me. Were suspicious. I wasn't experienced. Although I knew I was a lesbian, I hadn't slept with a woman at all. I liked to go out on the scene and had lots of lesbian friends but I'd never really felt anything strong – no matter how many women Clancy and Big Mandy had set me up with. Clare'd even made a pass at me – which nobody knew about, thank God. Much as I loved Clare as a mate, I didn't want to mate with her. Unfortunately – or perhaps fortunately for us all – I had a practically racist hatred of her type of red-headedness: her skin so pale it was marbled purple and so translucent you could see the very veins of it; her red-rimmed pale eyes and her skeletal figure… Besides, she was Clancy's long-term partner! And they had kids! It was just as well Clancy loved her to distraction.

'You're not a *real* lesbian!' Clancy would accuse. When I assured her I was, she told me to '*Prove* it!'

So far I was a virgin. I said I was asexual. Clancy told me I was a sexual volcano just waiting to erupt.

She said, 'You're not a *practising* lesbian. Remember – practice makes perfect!'

'Then I don't need to practise,' I would say, smirking.

And now that we'd spotted the woman to rock my world, there

was no stopping Clancy. She would ring me up: 'Target seen, twenty-two hundred hours. Britannia. Back room. Target with group of women but alone, if you catch my drift.' I could hear her winking even down the telephone line. She had spies, she said. Discreet ones, I hoped. There were Clancy messages on my answerphone every day. I didn't stand a chance. Neither did Tanya. Clancy had already told me Tanya worked in the library. Funny kind of librarian, I thought.

'Funny kind of librarian,' Clancy said.

'What d'you mean?' I spat, defensively.

But I couldn't just go into the library. I couldn't just stroll in, pretending to look at books. I wasn't a member.

'Pathetic!' said Clancy.

So I walked past a few times. Sat in my car on the double yellow lines outside the library a few times, round about closing time. Just on the off-chance. Nonchalant. Unfortunately, Middlesbrough library is next to the police station. I realised I'd turned into a stalker. I never even saw her. I could imagine her, though. Stamping books. Fining people.

One night, about two weeks after the party, Clancy hammered at my front door at twenty past eleven. She was jumping up and down with glee when I finally opened the door.

'Guess what? Guess what?' She grinned, waving her arms, her tattoos a blur. 'I bring Tidings of Great Joy!'

'Joy who?' I didn't tell her I suspected the word 'Tanya' might come into the next sentence. Or 'Target', more likely.

'I suppose you'd better come in.' I sighed, keeping an eye out for the neighbours. They already suspected I ran a house of ill repute. 'You have a lot of lady visitors... at all hours,' Mrs Archibald had said. I ushered my latest lady visitor into the house.

Clancy clasped my hands and bounced up and down. 'Mare – well, you're gonna think you've died and gone to heaven!'

'Yes, and it's you that's the death of me!' I smiled, ruffling her bristly hair and catching my finger in her nose-ring as she bounced.

I steered her by the head into the front room. She flung herself on to the futon, yelped in pain as she hit the slats through the thin mattress and waved her arms, saying, 'Just listen to this – you are not gonna believe what your old mate Clance has done for *you*, girl!'

Apparently, Clancy and Clare had invited a few people round to their house for drinks and things. That was nothing unusual. With the kids in bed, it was easier for Clancy and Clare to invite people over than to arrange baby-sitters. Clare was a great cook and they both loved having friends over to play games, musical instruments and anything that might be fun. There was a memorable night when Kerry brought her karaoke machine over. The night of the tequila slammers.

Clancy was full of it: 'It'll be just me, Clare, Big Mandy, Kerry, Robbo, Georgie and... *her*!'

'Who?'

Clancy tutted, 'Woman of your dreams! Woman of your sordid fantasies! Ya *eejit*!'

'So – just her, you and them. Aren't I invited then?' I smiled.

'*Mare*!'

I liked to exasperate her. 'Okay... when is it?'

'Next Saturday!' she said in triumph.

'*Awww*!' I was crestfallen, 'I'm not here! I'm at my mum's!'

'Shit! You *can't*! It's all *arranged*!' Clancy was getting angry now, her voice rising into hysteria, 'I've been sorting it *all night*!'

Over half a litre of Bailey's Irish Cream, we plotted and planned. With one tense but thankfully short telephone call the next day to my poor deserted mother... my fate was sealed.

Now I started to worry. How would Tanya like me? Did she like her women feminine? Butch? Should I get my hair cut? Should I grow it? Damn! In four days? Should I wear a skirt? And risk Clancy, Clare and Big Mandy really taking the piss? What was I wearing that night in the Marine? The night she captivated me, the night she never took her eyes from me, the night that possibly changed my life? It was a blue silk shirt and jeans. I couldn't wear those again! ...

Could I? She'd think I had no other clothes! Should I buy something new? And could I lose some weight? In two days, now? Damn! Life was complicated.

And was she bringing anyone with her? Oh, my God! I'd be devastated! I'd die!

'No,' said Clancy, 'George doesn't like this Christiane woman. Tanya knows she can't bring her.'

I could hear myself starting to whine.

'Or anyone else,' added Clancy.

Forty-five hours, twenty-five minutes later, I was standing bravely on Clancy and Clare's doorstep clutching a bottle of Rioja. And a bottle of Chardonnay. I didn't know what Tanya drank, but I'd drawn the line at bringing beer as well. I couldn't carry it all.

'Party time!' Clancy leapt at me when she opened her front door, wrapping her legs round my thighs and burying her face in my cleavage. 'Hmmm… you smell nice, Mare!'

I rubbed my hand across her prickly head. She disentangled herself from me, gave me a knowing look and tapped the side of her nose with one finger, whispering, 'Yes, she's here! Come this way – if you'll pardon the expression!' I punched her in the back to distract myself and followed her into the room.

I swallowed hard. Tanya sat in the corner, absorbed in a pile of CDs on her knee. I beamed around the room at everyone, careful to scan them all. Mustn't stare at her especially. She glanced up through her fringe and smiled briefly. Too briefly. Nina Simone was on the stereo, Clare's favourite. Tanya was joining in the lyrics, *'Ma baby don't caaaaaa-are who knows… it…'*

Then she lifted her face, tossing back her glorious hair to roar, *'Ma baby just cares for me!'*

'Oh, so you know Mary already?' Clancy grinned.

Although Big Mandy had brought her cocktail shaker and recipe book and despite Kerry bringing a carrier bagful of crappy old liqueur dregs from the back of their cupboard, that evening was not an entire success. Tanya appeared to be fascinated by everyone but me. I sagged with despair.

In the kitchen, over a dusty half-bottle of Parfait Amour crystallised around the lid, I hissed to Clancy, 'She's ignoring me!'

'She must really like you then,' Clancy said firmly, pushing the cocktail shaker into my hand. 'Shake it up, girl! Go and offer her a Screaming Orgasm.' I frowned. 'Sex on the Beach?' As I left the kitchen I heard her call querulously, 'Long Slow Comfortable Screw?'

Tanya barely caught my eye all night. But I spent all night looking at her, longing for a crumb of her interest. Everyone's attention was on Tanya. She was magnificent. She choreographed another session of 'My Baby Don't Care For Me', this time a capella. She started with the bass in the background. She told Big Mandy to sit with Kerry between her legs and play her like a double bass, singing: *'Du-umpy, dumpy, dumpy, dumpy, dumpy, dumpy, dum-peeee...'*

Clancy said that with all those Dumpies she sounded like Snow White and the seven clones. 'Seven clones... pheromones! Mary smells good, though!' she added, to my humiliation.

Tanya, oblivious, set Clare off with two paintbrushes on a biscuit tin, 'NO! The brush end! Not the handles!' she ordered, 'Or just say *"shoo-ca-shoo-ca-shoo-ca"*, if you can't manage that!'

'Cashew?' Clare tested sulkily, trying to stare Tanya out. Tanya was in control.

I marvelled at her, how she took charge of the situation and manipulated the group. With Robbo taught to go *'do-wap'* any place she felt like and Clancy shaking the cocktail shaker full of ice and all of us in tears of laughter, I couldn't wait to see what she had in store for Georgie and me. I strained with eagerness. I grinned and bobbed my head into Tanya's sightlines, trying to catch her eye.

'Mary smells really good – go and sniff her!' Clancy pointed at me with the shaker.

'Georgie, I dedicate this song to you, baby...' Tanya cooed, resting her fingertips on Georgie's cheek. The blood rushed to my face and I could feel it throb through the veins in my head. She had Georgie as her baby and would sing the words of the song to her, while Georgie responded in extravagant mime. Then Tanya lifted her arms and got ready to conduct. What about me?

'You can watch,' she said over her shoulder. Somewhere inside me something howled like a wounded animal. I was so gutted, I nearly burst into tears. Then I composed myself. I decided that I was in fact very privileged just to watch, as it happens. Watching her conducting with her slim expressive hands and counting them in with a *'One-two, a one-two-three-four: Mah Baby...!'* I could concentrate on just caring for her. Adoring her completely.

She was so stunning – so bright, so smart, so charming – she drew everyone into her energy. If I were being objective, I'd have to admit that she wasn't a great singer. But she'd got so much confidence – such *balls* – I thought her voice was the most fantastic thing I'd ever heard in my life. She'd got charisma. I could barely keep my gaze off her. She was enchanting. Commanding. Breathtaking. But there was Georgie, down on one knee gesturing like a mad woman, pulling the song in with her hands and such a raggle-taggle of do-wap dumpy cashews and shakes in the background, I was lucky to notice Tanya at all. She certainly didn't notice me. But her voice rang out, strident and powerful above it all. Then we all cried with hysterical laughter anyway.

'Honestly! Have you smelt Mary? She smells good enough... to eat!' piped up Clancy, just when we'd recovered.

Kerry was mixing a range of 40-proof drinks into one highly volatile cocktail. Then she ran out of 40-proof alcohol options and was stumped till Tanya shouted, 'Just add a couple of 20-proof ones – same difference! What is it? Molotov cocktail?'

'No... I've heard of that one, ' frowned Kerry and stood with one blunt finger on her chin, deep in vague thought. 'Hmmmm... it's...called... Kerry's cocktail!'

'Highly original,' scoffed Tanya.

'That sounds fine to me!' Clare said defensively. 'Without the aid of a recipe!'

'And without the aid of a safety net! Or a hairnet!' yelled Clancy.

'Not using a recipe! Whatever would Delia Smith say? All hail the Goddess Delia...' Big Mandy tried to bow, but ended up flat on her face. Clare stood on her hair and there was chaos for some time.

'Who wants to try it then, like?' Kerry beamed, holding up the pint glass full of cloudy brown alcohol. The silence spoke volumes. 'Aaaaaaaw!' she complained, then took a gulp and ran to the sink to spit it up. Then she had to go to bed.

In the kitchen, Clancy had it all planned. It was excruciating. She reassured me that she'd fixed the sleeping arrangements and briefed the others so Tanya and I would just have to sleep together. The only space left was in the attic: with a double bed. She was determined to persuade Tanya to stay over and share the bed – and her body – with me. This was all too much.

'No way!' I shook Clancy by the shoulders, so she took the opportunity to shake the cocktails extra-violently at the same time.

'God, Mare, it's all innocent! What's your problem? It's only a bed!'

To my relief and disappointment, Tanya insisted on calling a cab and Georgie and Robbo went too. They said goodbye, leaving the rest of us to a brief postmortem before I went up to be mad in the attic. I lay in my virginal bed with my arms folded, staring at the ceiling. I played over the events of the night, fuming with indignation. Then I replayed them and:

1. Made the air crackle with sexual tension, like it did the first time I met Tanya
2. Made Tanya, overcome with passion, declare her love and lust for me
3. Had us consummate our love on the living room floor, crunching CD cases under our writhing bodies

4.   Left tiny Clancy in a huge cocktail shaker, to be shaken by
     a giant.

The next morning I sneaked out of the house before anyone else
was up. I couldn't face any more of Clancy's strategies, Clare's snide
comments, Big Mandy's enthusing over 'what a great laugh that Tanya
was' and Kerry saying she was a weirdo but we should hang around
with her more often.

I was at home filling my coffee cup and getting ready for a day of
hangover and depression when the doorbell rang. I knew it'd be Shelly
from across the road, popping in for her caffeine high, so I opened the
door and was horrified to see Tanya.

'You look pleased... not!' she cried. 'Is this a bad time? Have I disturbed you with your lover?'

'N... no... I'm just surprised!'

'I do like to surprise!' She smiled, leaning against the doorframe
with her arms folded. So confident, her small chin thrust out. Staring
me brazenly in the eye, as if she hadn't blanked me last night.

I let her in but I was stuck for words. I took to the obvious: 'How
did you know where I live?'

'I have my spies.' She smiled again. I hoped they weren't the same
ones as Clancy's.

She sat on the futon. 'I had a good time last night!'

'I know,' I said. I'd noticed.

'I wasn't sure if you had a good time, though.' She stared at me,
challengingly. I was surprised she'd even noticed me. What was all
that about, then? I realised that I was still wearing the same clothes as
last night and the house was untidy, but I was too puzzled to worry. I
scooped the magazines off the armchair and sat perched on the edge,
clutching them to my chest.

'Oh, you know. I was a bit tired, that's all.' I gazed at the carpet.

'That's okay then,' she said, emphatically. I couldn't place her tone
of voice. Irritated, perhaps. I didn't want to irritate her.

'Want a coffee? Tea? Parfait Amour?' my mouth said without my brain knowing.

'I'm surprised you haven't suggested a Slow Comfortable Screw… *yet.*' She held my gaze. I went red and flustered, dropped the magazines and went into the kitchen to clatter some cups. I realised I didn't know what she wanted to drink, but I was too shy to ask her again. I made her a cup of tea and a cup of coffee and brought them through.

I held both cups towards her. 'You've got a choice!'

'Oh, I've made my choice,' she said. But she didn't want a drink.

For weeks afterwards, I held my secret so closely I thought I would burst. Yes, I was that volcano. There were fireworks, bells ringing, the earth moving. I was in love and wanted to shout it from all the god-damned clichéd rooftops in the schmaltzy rose-tinted world where I suddenly found myself. I'd never met anyone like her before! I was beaming so much my face hurt with it! I could hardly contain my joy – my lust! I was bursting! Mad with it! But Tanya forbade me from telling anyone. Her life was very private, she said. She wanted it kept that way. And if I wanted any part in it, I would live by those rules.

And I would live by those rules. Every moment with her – any chance of time with her – was precious. I wanted to see Tanya at every possible opportunity. I'd make sure I was available at all times because Tanya tended to ring me up and invite me over at a minute's notice, or she'd turn up at my house spontaneously. But my puppyish excitement was getting the better of me. I had to distance myself from people, especially Clancy, 'cause I couldn't trust myself to keep quiet. She'd guess. So Clancy still left messages and, when I did speak to her on the phone, it was to say I was really busy. Sorry. Thanks.

'Clancy, please don't bother with the Tanya tales anymore. She's not all that. You could tell she wasn't interested in me at your party. Really. I've gone off her. I really don't want you to talk about her anymore. It was fun, but… stop,' I told her soon after Tanya and I'd got together. And even Clancy, for all her cheek, could sense the seriousness of it all and stopped her teasing and scheming. But then, that was two years ago and, as Clancy says, we've all passed a lot of water since then.

In the dim grey light, I'm looking at Tanya's hair strewn across her pillow like black seaweed. It drew me; it entangled me first, and held me here, shipwrecked. And I thought my survival depended on holding on to her, but I was wrong. My survival depends on destroying her. But she's beautiful. Her hair ripples from her high brow. I've kissed every one of the tiny downy hairs there, tracing the line of her hair, her ears, and neck. Her eyelids glisten in the moonlight and flicker in her dreams. And then her lips... satin soft. Such a pity...

3
Tanya: How it is

I've always been fascinated by women, although I wouldn't let them know that. The sight of them, always. And, later in life, the touch of them, the taste of them. They amuse me. I amuse myself by counting up the number of lovers, but get lost in the nameless dozens that filled up times of nightclubs, discos, parties; crazy, wild, happy, high, drunken, lonely, low, sad times. Oh, I don't know – a boastful hundred, perhaps... I tease Mary with the memories of them. She gets sulky, tries to hide it with bluff, calls me a Don Juan.

'Donna Juanita,' I correct her, drawing out the guttural Hkhkhhkkhh-Juanita. 'Let's name our first child that!'

She melts, but I don't like kids and if she knows me at all, she knows I'm kidding.

'I wouldn't bring up a child in this world. My world,' I say with unquestionable authority. Mary doesn't argue. She knows better than that.

Mary would make a great Smother, I tell her. She is attentive to my every need and even to those needs that I do not have. She makes every attempt to anticipate my desires, is ever ready to please. '"Mary is eager to please," I bet they said that in your school report,' I tease her. With some embarrassment, she admits that her teachers did say that of her. Sometimes she buzzes around me so persistently that

I could flick her away, like a fly at a picnic. She won't let me get on with it. Life. She dances attendance on me. I get up in the morning and magically, there before my very eyes, is all last night's washing-up done, the kitchen sparkling, fresh coffee waiting for me.

'Who did this? The fairies?' I yawn.

'A gnome help... from the National Elf Service,' she says and I have to laugh. She amuses me. She's lucky her mind is quick and sharp, her ways gentle. I wouldn't tolerate her otherwise.

I am used to seeing to myself. Seeing to my own needs. I am not used to living with someone and still I tell her we are not living to-gether, although she stays all too frequently. We have been sleeping together for two years. I begrudgingly allowed her to keep a tooth-brush and some underclothes at my house. She is honoured. And she knows it, because I tell her. I am being serious. I do not permit people to get close to me. There is a danger in that. But somehow Mary has wheedled herself into my life, into my house. However, I do not want her to get too comfortable. Too cosy. I will naturally keep her at arm's length. She says that she loves me, so I am touched.

Ways in which my mother touched me. To shove me in the back. To push me down the stairs. To slap me. To punch me. To bite me. To kick me. To poke me. To scratch me. To pinch me. To beat me. To twist my limbs. To hold me down. To swipe me. Things I have been hit with: a plate of Sunday dinner; some brushes (name your cate-gory: broom, hairbrush, toilet brush, toothbrush); a book (mine – she didn't read); a pan of asparagus soup; a length of flex; a coat hanger; a kettle of boiling water; a can opener; a Beatles LP record. To hurt me. I don't remember my mother touching me with any-thing but hatred. But I remember longing to be held with love. Too sentimental. Strike that out. I sound pathetic.

My mother died. The funeral I arranged was quick, simple, quiet. A small affair. As elaborate as my affection towards her. I have no father. I have no siblings. My mother also had no relatives alive. Not even me. Relatives. Relate-ives. People you relate to, people you relate with. Hate with. Now we might be getting somewhere, with hatred. Now we are getting close.

I notified the neighbours. The professional mourners were: her home help, the district nurse, one of the nurses at the hospital and old Mrs Enderby, on her sixth funeral that year. I was not a mourner. Mary asked if I wanted her to come. I said no. Mary offered to come. I said no. Mary insisted that she come. I... said... NO! She said she wanted to be there for me, she was concerned how it would affect me. I said I wanted her to be there in my bed. Sexy. Down and dirty. I wanted to know I was alive.

I didn't even want Christiane there. It was something I wanted to face alone. After all, no one had been there for me, before. And I survived.

The morning of the funeral was bright and sunny. Joyously so. Not at all like the stereotypical funeral day of cold grey drizzle or a sharp white frost, as befits a day of death, a day of mourning: dismal. Grave. No – that day was a day to slap on the suntan lotion, get out the Ray-Bans, and smile, smile, smile, smile, smile. *The sun has got his hat on.* Hip, hip, hip, hooray. I drove down the motorway with the sun-roof open, my window rolled down and my arm leaning outside, catching the coolness of the wind in the palm of my hand, rejoicing in the air slipping through my outspread fingers and the breeze whipping my hair behind me. The stereo blared. I sang at the top of my voice. That was the life! That...was life. Life.

And so to Leeds. I relished the city now, and smiled at the new urban developments that had sprung up since I'd run away from it as a teenager. How prosperous it looked these days. I might even come back and live here now. Make it my own.

I parked the car a short distance down the road from the church in Armley, under the shade of the trees and composed myself a little while. Lit another cigarette. Put the sunglasses on my head, where they clipped back my hair demurely. I looked in the mirror and liked what I saw. Damn, but I was good! Shame there was no one there to benefit. I pouted out my lower lip and blew the smoke up into the air.

Maybe I would hang out in Leeds later, go to some gay bars, get the most out of my sharp new suit. It was not funereal. And dammit, I looked hot! Yes, I should get out there and have a good time! Impress the ladies! Live! Nodding my own agreement in the mirror, I got out of the car, locked it up and stood for a moment, taking long deep drags from my cigarette, enjoying the dapple of shadow leaves swaying on the roof of my car, the swish and shush of the bowing tree branches beyond. I took a deep breath, scenting the blossom and filling myself with the moment. Through the railings and beyond the trees, I could see the small dark huddle of people just outside the church door and, pleased with the clip of my heels on the pavement, I swung round the gateway and on to the short gravel path towards them. I flicked the cigarette butt on to the grass and looked keen.

I didn't know which nurse was which and it didn't really matter. They both stood with brave smiles, their heads inclined to one side, caricatures of sympathy. One of them looked a little dykey, which immediately caught my interest. Not my type though. Mrs Enderby carefully swivelled her head, which was heavily bedecked with a hat like a large black cabbage. She looked pained, which was no surprise at all. The home help snivelled into a sopping wet tissue, apologising that she was upset, but it was just that her own mother had died only last month and she probably shouldn't really have come at all, it was just bringing it right back, and oh – she hoped she didn't get too distressed – that'd be the last thing I would want – oh dear, she was sorry. I smiled and walked through to shake the hand of the vicar, who was hovering in the doorway. He said some words that were probably designed to comfort people. I smiled, said thank you, and looked at my watch.

I hoped I didn't have to stay for long with these dismal strangers now looking lost and lonely in the pews of the cavernous church. Mrs Enderby's Great Cabbage of Death loomed dark from the second row. Fortuitously, as I stepped back out on to the path, I saw the smooth glide of the hearse along the street outside, its windows glinting through the railings, the light stuttering through each bar. Epileptic. Hypnotic.

White flowers. Black soil. I don't remember any more. I didn't disgrace myself, I know that. Not at the church.

I know at some point I went to a club where the lights whirled in psychedelic frenzy and the music pulsated through my head and my chest and there were hot, musky bodies everywhere. Girls in skimpy vests, baby dresses, T-shirts, cargoes and gilets; hard looking women in shirts, with razor cuts and borstal tattoos on their faces. Women in full make-up and spangly dresses, brassy, glittering. Women with cleavages bursting out of their fishnet tops. Women in bra tops. Women in smart jackets. Studenty girls with wide eyes and cheeky faces. Sullen girls. Laughing, blustering girls out for a great time. Girls with long straight hair, hair in plaits, spikey hair, hair in bunches, afro hair, no hair. Alive. Shouting, grinning, drinking, laughing, kissing, fighting. And the throb of the music kick-starting my heart again.

The next morning I awoke early, my mouth dry as ashes, suddenly wondering where I was. I looked up at a grey wall with a poster blu-tacked on to it. Turned to see a hunched-up duvet. A couple of seconds to realise, to remember and to rise. I dressed swiftly, picking up my clothes from the floor where I had evidently ripped them off in drunken lust. I tiptoed out and left the woman in the tangled bed. I didn't even remember what she looked like, let alone her name. I stood outside in the tree-lined street, gazing from one end to the other of the terraced rows of houses. I tried to get my bearings and rake through somehow distant memory to recall where I'd left the car. I was dehydrated and headachey but I hadn't wanted to stay in the strange house even long enough to get a drink. I had no stomach for small talk, politeness, half-promises and half-truths. I appeared to be in Chapeltown. I vaguely knew the main road, so I set off, knowing that I could find a café for a desperate coffee and call a cab. I thought I'd left my car in the carpark near the university. If not – well, I was sure I'd come across it eventually. I always did.

When I got to my car I remembered that my mobile was still in it. I picked it up. Twelve missed calls. Nine text messages. Mary had excelled herself. I clicked to read them:

1   HI, THINKIN BOUTYA. HOPE U OK. AM HERE 4U. TAKE CARE, LUVU, CU L8R, YOUR MARY XX 1.12pm

2   HI, U OK? IT GO OK? LET ME NO, PLZ. LOOKIN 4WD 2 HUGN U SOON. BIG SEXY XX M XX 3.34pm

3   DARLING. CONDOLENCES. C X 3.50pm

4   TAN- WOT U WANT 4 T? PIZZA OK? PLZ LET ME NO WEN UR BAK, & IF U R OK. MISSIN U. LUVU M XX 6.21pm

5   WHERE R U? I AM WORRIED. PLZ CALL ASAP LUV MARY XX 8.05pm

6   TAN! RING ME! M XX 10.40pm

7   IT'S 12.15 & I AM REALLY UPSET. WILL RING POLICE SOON!!!! M X 12.18am

8   STILL WAITIN 4U. WHERE R U? DON'T DO THIS 2 ME M XX 1.54am

9   CALL ME. M 6.23am

I tossed the mobile on to the passenger seat beside me and started up the car to head home.

Not such a cheery morning. The same fine weather, but a note of coolness in the air. And for me, a dull headache. An increasing irritation and rising sense of foreboding with every mile closer to home. A rush of loneliness. I shut it all out. I sang loudly to the radio. Loud music. Loud lyrics:

'The only man that could e-ever reach me… Was the son of a preacher man!'

The irony was not lost on me, but I concentrated on Dusty and out-Dustied her till my throat was hoarse. Loud singing and loud music to fill my thoughts. Fill my head. Block it out. I made my own head hurt and lungs ache. Better that than… I bounced the palm of my hand on the steering wheel, hard. Good to feel it. Good to feel it smarting. Good to be alive.

I sped home to Saltburn. Saltburn-by-the-Sea. The place where people find refuge and stay. Christiane had said that she had heard tell of people who had come over to Saltburn one Saturday night for a party and had found themselves still there, six years later. Just couldn't leave. Saltburn drew people. She had said it's like *The Prisoner*, the cult classic TV programme, and I had nodded sagely because Christiane is older than me and I had not wanted to show my ignorance. Anyway, she had laughed at my moving to a quaint Victorian seaside town, at my animated retelling of the history of the smugglers of the Ship Inn and Henry Pease, the Victorian entrepreneur whose vision of Saltburn – 'like a jewel' on the cliff-top – gave rise to this Victorian watering hole with the railway line running into the Hotel, the Italian Gardens, the miniature railway, the water-powered cliff lift, the only surviving pier in the North East.

'Darling – you're a positive mine of useless information! You should get yourself a flat cap and work for the Tourist Board!' she had scoffed.

All I knew was that Saltburn was far enough away from Christiane, but not too far.

I drove on auto-pilot, losing track of the roundabouts on the A174. I just knew that I crossed them all to get there. The farmland became one green mass, one field indistinguishable from another. In a few weeks the blue linseed flowers would show, but mostly there would be a ripening glare of yellow rape. Rape! The sickly scent of it and its garish, eye-aching brightness, later mellowing to a dull mustard. The stables loomed to the right and I was there: the WELCOME TO SALTBURN road sign dripping with bright flowers ready for the 'Britain in Bloom' competition. As well as the hanging baskets and a cart being used as a planter, other tubs and containers were cropping up. A land-locked rowing boat, painted red, white and blue and filled with flowers. And an idiosyncratic touch: two scarecrow-dummies made of sackcloth and dressed as sailors, sitting

beside the boat, obviously added by the militant band of mad old
biddies who led Saltburn's bid for supremacy in the contest. They
looked like sorry rag dolls in their knitted clothes – the sailors that
is, although come to think of it, that applied to the women as well.
But as to the sackcloth sailors – Mary and I had planned to kidnap
them or, better still, place them in compromising positions, per-
forming acts of obscenity just in time for the 'Britain in Bloom'
judging. I'd like to see the women's faces then... These were the
same stalwarts who campaigned to keep the railway branch line
open and collected money for Saltburn's Christmas lights; the
women who dressed as Victorians each year in August for Saltburn's
Victorian Week; the ones who'd organised Saltburn's attempt on the
world line-dancing record and were only 11,500 people short. The
worthies, the pillars of the community, the good women of
Saltburn. Matronly, matriarchal, maternal.

No wonder Christiane thought they were all mad here.

I got back to an empty house. Good. The answerphone. Three
hang-ups and a terse message from Mary, 'Tanya. Call me when you
get back. Let me know if you're okay. Or not.'

I didn't call. I went straight to bed and slept the sleep of the innocent. After I had drifted through the flashbacks. The glint of a pierced
tongue. My mind numb but struggling to wonder how sexually grati-
fying that might be. Music. Flashes of light on hearse windows. A
frenzy of dancing. Heat. White teeth. Brown coffin. Another bottle of
Budweiser. Lascivious, moist lips. Glint of tongue piercing. A sopping
wet tissue in the hand of the snivelling home help. Head tossed back.
Tongue pressed against her upper lip. Small breasts filling my hands as
I kneaded and squeezed them, straddling her easily. The dykey-looking
nurse with her head cocked to one side. The slick of the wetness between her legs. A sackcloth dummy. Moaning. The trees. Music. Heat.
And the dark. The sound of her coming.

Black soil. White flowers. The Great Black Cabbage of Death.

4

Mary: Curds and whey

I looked after Tanya's house better than I looked after my own. I don't
like cleaning my own house – I'm afraid of turning into my mother.
But I did like to do things for Tanya. Never anything radical: just little
unassuming things to show I cared, to save her the trouble, to give her
pleasure: cleaning, cooking, offering flowers, plants, small gifts, small
delicacies, tidying up the garden. I'd never try to stamp my personality
on her house. It wasn't my house. And I'm not even sure I had a personality, except for what was brought out by Tanya.

In retrospect, I wanted Tanya to be pleased with me and with the
things I did. I wanted to be an asset. I wanted to be indispensable. I
wanted her to need me like I needed her. Like a drug. In retrospect, I
was a fool.

'You are only to come over to the house when I ask you. I don't
want you just turning up. I need my own time. My own space.
Privacy!' she said.

'Of course! I need my own time and privacy, myself!' I said
brightly. But that didn't stop me ringing her or staking out her house
once in a while.

'Tanya can't answer the phone right now. Please leave a mess...'
Then I'd hang up. It was just good to hear her voice, even if it was a
recorded message. But I couldn't ring too often. I knew she left the

answerphone on all the time and usually never answered at all. So she could easily be there. Doing what? Or with someone. Who? Or she could be out. Where? Who with?

It didn't stop me ringing her up every day. It didn't stop me parking my car in the street opposite her house and watching. Waiting. I didn't do that a lot. Just when I felt insecure. Maybe once a week. Twice, at most.

I was hardly ever in when Clancy rang or called by. I'd find little notes through the letter box: 'Clancy woz here. AGAIN!' Her answerphone messages got shorter. I rang back when I knew they were out and left non-committal messages with the babysitter or Chloe, their eldest girl. Just to say I'd called. It wasn't that I was avoiding her, just that... I couldn't tell her about Tanya. And 'cause my life revolved round Tanya, I couldn't tell her anything. I did miss Clancy making me laugh, though. Relaxing, having fun.

Being with Tanya was a challenge, but I was going to rise to it. I had to be subtle and feel my way, use my senses. She wouldn't tell me much about herself, her feelings or her past. I had to puzzle it all out from little things she said, things she did, how she behaved. I had to read her like one of her library books. My mum would expect me to wash my hands afterwards.

My mum didn't have many hobbies, but they were:

1. worrying about germs
2. worrying about everything else
3. washing things – especially with bleach
4. counting.

My mum worried, my mum washed, and my mum counted. Tins of beans, tins of peas. She regimented the rows in her cupboards in single file, labels facing forward. Neat. She might have been a good librarian, cataloguing things, if she hadn't been so afraid of the germs from library books. Or she might have made a good accountant if her interest in numbers had gone beyond muttering 'One, two, three, four.'

She counted the number of slices of cucumber under her breath while she made the salad. The number of tomato slices. Made it always an even number. Never an odd. She threw away the ninth slice of cucumber or the last biscuit, if they didn't fit. Even numbers are good. Four is best. Four slices of tomato each. Four slices of cucumber. Four pieces of lettuce. Or, failing that, eight. Eight is nearly as good. Eight slices of bread. Four rounds of salad sandwiches, each cut into four. Four in my family. My dad, who was a funny bugger, very much in my mum's shadow, quiet and sad. My brother, Vincent, who was four years younger than me. He was the apple of his mother's eye and somehow he got to live a carefree life. And me: an experiment in child-rearing.

My mum discovered that kids were messy and I guess her alarm with germs started with me. I wasn't allowed to mix with other kids: they carried germs. She didn't want them in the house. Kids or germs. I wasn't allowed to play in the garden. There were germs. I mustn't touch the leaves of plants outside. They might be poisonous. I must always wash my hands. My little hands were red raw. It was easier not to do anything. So daisy-chains, whistling with a blade of grass between your thumbs and – heaven forbid – mud-pies, were all a mystery to me. I read about them in books. As long as I washed my hands after them.

When I was a bit older, I went to the library for books. We didn't have any at home, except a family bible. So the library was a wonderful place and books were something marvellous and forbidden. I brought library books home and read them voraciously while my mum sat anxiously on the edge of her seat, watching me. I'd maybe shift in my chair and move to prop my head up with my hand or scratch my nose and she'd shriek, 'Don't touch your face! Wash your hands!' and when I put the book down, she'd pull me up from my seat and into the kitchen. 'Wash your hands!'

I read up in my bedroom a lot.

She said library books were filthy – you never knew who'd had hold of them and what they'd been doing before they handled them. I struggled to imagine what that might be.

If I bought a book she'd say, 'I don't know why you buy books, when you can get them from the library.'

When I bought more books she'd say, 'Another book! Haven't you got enough?' as if a book was something you only needed one of – like a house or a husband.

But if library books were filthy things full of germs, what about librarians? What would my mum say to that? Although she wasn't over the moon with my being a lesbian, she said she wanted me to be happy and she thought it was sweet, women together, like best friends. If I'd told her we slept together, she must have thought we slept like Babes in the Wood. Holding hands? Too dirty! Good job she didn't know what lesbians do in bed. And I didn't tell her Tanya was a librarian. Now wash your hands please.

Apparently my mum never touched door-handles with her bare hand. She mentioned it recently and laughed about herself, said she'd watched a TV programme about a woman nearly as bad as she was. I'd really never noticed that my mum opened door-handles with her wrists, grasping the handle with the heels of both palms or using her blouse or cardigan hem. How'd I not noticed? Were the doors always open at home? Or had I thought her hands were wet and she was try-ing to keep the handles dry? Or had I just come to think it was nor-mal, like her hovering over a toilet seat instead of sitting on it (the lid had still been down once... that was a disinfectant moment), the whisper of counting and her constant warnings we should wash our hands after everything. I didn't know otherwise.

I remembered her hands. The feel of them, their sandpapery whispering over my skin. Hands like harsh tweed, hands that were dry and calloused with long and constant washing. Hands that hand-washed clothes and dishes. Washing down the paintwork, the worktops, the cooker. Washing hands. The kitchen always smelt of bleach. I didn't realise. I thought it smelt of kitchen.

I was a bright kid needing constant stimulation. Attention.

'What can I do?' I would whine, tugging my mum's apron as she stood at the sink, 'I want something to doo-oo-oo!'

'Count these,' my mum would say, passing me a jar full of lentils, 'that'll give you something to do!'

I could only count up to four.

With my life filled with Tanya I never had time for anyone else. Eventually, Clancy confronted me. She came round to my house when I was expecting Tanya. I was always expecting Tanya. I was disappointed to see she wasn't Tanya. But I was a bit pleased to see Clancy, although I wanted her to go soon. Before Tanya came.

'Oh, Clancy!' I distractedly brushed my hand over her head for old times sake. Clancy raised one eyebrow. She was hardly smiling, which wasn't like her. She stood on the doorstep while I held the door half open.

'So... hi! Can I come in?' She squinted over my shoulder and scratched the back of her head with all her fingers bunched like a claw.

'Well... erm... for a bit... but I'm sorry – I'm... expecting someone.' This was a cue for her to leave, but I let her in and followed her, twisting my bottom lip nervously with my finger and thumb.

'Uh-huh.' Clancy nodded. 'May I ask who?' She stared me straight in the eye.

'I'd rather you didn't.' I stared at the carpet.

'Fair enough.'

'I can't tell you who it is,' I gave as explanation. I'd never kept anything from Clancy and it pained me now.

'Why?'

I shrugged.

Clancy bit her lip and steeled herself to speak, 'Is it Clare?' Her eyes began to brim with tears.

'No! God! What do you take me for? I'm your mate!'

'Really?' Clancy looked serious, then her impish face puckered as she struggled to stop her lip trembling, 'And would you say,' she rolled her eyes up to the ceiling, concentrating on steadying her voice, 'you've been – particularly – "matey" with me lately?'

I put my arms round her. She was so tiny. Smaller and slighter than Tanya. She stayed stiff and cold, just holding herself together. Her bristly scalp scratched my chin as I bent to kiss her forehead. I couldn't bear her brittleness, her pain. I felt so bad about avoiding her, lying to her all this time.

'Oh, Clancy!' I burst into tears. Her eyes were wet too, but impassive.

'What's going on, Mary?' She never called me Mary.

I cupped her face between my hands and bent to look her in the eye, 'Oh, Clancy, please promise not to tell... I... I have been seeing someone, but I've promised I'll keep it secret. Please... don't say anything. It's Tanya!'

Clancy's face flickered with hurt, shock, surprise, relief, bafflement, disbelief, bewilderment. She struggled to understand. 'What? Why the big secret? After all, it's –'

'Please don't tell anyone, Clancy. Or it's over for me.'

Clancy still looked puzzled. We sat on the futon while I explained, relieved to have someone to talk to, relieved of the strain on our friendship. And delighted to speak the love that dare not speak its name! I was suddenly gushing out all my repressed emotions while Clancy sat silently watching me.

She had hardly recovered from her own turmoil. She sat still, even her freckles pale. She frowned.

'So it's not Clare.'

'My God! Of course not! You're together! You're Mrs and Mrs!' I was aghast.

Clancy winced and tried to change the subject. 'Mare – but this can't be good for you!'

'What do you mean?'

'All this secrecy, all this cloak and dagger, lying to your mates, cutting yourself off from people who love you...'

'Oh, but just till she learns to trust me. Just while it's so new,

Clance. Then it'll be okay. We're fantastic together, but I don't expect it to be easy. She's volatile. Passionate. Turns my heart inside out.'

Clancy shook her head and gave a wry smile. 'You're mad. Can't be good for you, Mare.'

'It's the best thing that's ever happened to me. She's the best thing that's ever happened to me.' I beamed. I glowed.

Clancy studied my face. 'We'll see.' Then she slapped my shoulder and laughed. 'But am I the best matchmaker or what? Result!' She pulled in her fist, victorious. She refused to talk about herself and Clare any more. She put her anxiety on hold and took the time to celebrate my joy with me.

I did ring her more often and made a real effort to see her again. It was great to have Clancy back in my life.

A year later Tanya and I were still together, but I was disappointed that things hadn't progressed much. Our relationship hadn't developed. My feelings for her couldn't get any deeper, but I wasn't sure she felt the same way. I guess I was pissed off that she never talked about us in a future to-gether, but I was scared to push her. Just my insecurity. It was always women who rang her up. Georgie was fine, I knew her. But others. Francine. Sue. People I didn't know. Someone called Red left messages on her answerphone a couple of times. Nothing intimate or suspicious and Tanya was quite open and nonchalant about them – just another col-league from work or friends from her life before me – but my stomach still tightened with paranoia. I would always back down to avoid Tanya's un-accountable rages. And there was Christiane. Tanya said Christiane was in her life for good and I would have to get used to it. They didn't have sex, but were deeply close. I felt particularly threatened by her, but had to swallow down my anger if I wanted to be with Tanya. What I really wanted was commitment. I still felt like her 'bit on the side', even if she had no main course. So it was all the more bearable having Clancy to con-fide in, although her advice was what you might call… idiosyncratic.

'Christiane's still around. But not around,' I grumbled. 'They're together, but not together-together. It's driving me mad. I know it's platonic, Tanya told me –' I ignored Clancy's frown of disbelief '– but what can I do?'

'Well, you've got two choices…' I huddled closer to her to find out what I should do, hanging on her every word. I wondered if I should take notes. She continued, first raising one finger in the air. 'One – you kill the bitch. This Christiane woman, I mean, although it sounds like Tanya needs a good slapping too. And two –' she raised a second finger '– you get another woman, yourself. Two can play at that game. Or four.'

I didn't think either of these was the solution. However, we spent a jolly afternoon thinking up spectacular ways to kill Christiane, which made me feel much better.

'Are you a wimp or a woman?' Clancy asked, after I rang her to complain about another distressing scene with Tanya. 'Get a life!'

'I've got a life! She is my life!' I squeaked.

'Puh-lease!' said Clancy, then all I heard was the sound of retching.

Christiane's still around. But not around. They're together, but not together-together. Still, for discretion's sake, we're discreet.

One morning I made Tanya a cafetiere of coffee, 'cause she prefers that. Columbian, 'cause she prefers that. With hot milk, 'cause she prefers that. I brought it into her living room and snuggled up next to her on the sofa.

'What you fancy doing tonight?' I asked, hopefully.

'I'm going out!' Tanya said, flicking her hair to one side and taking a sip of coffee. 'Lovely coffee, pet.'

I frowned and felt a pain starting in my chest. 'Oh, where are you going?'

'Pictures.'

'Oh? Who with?' my voice said casually.

'Christiane.'

'Oh,' I said, the knot in my chest tightening. 'What are you going to see?'

'*If These Walls Could Talk 2*.'

'Awww! But that's the one I wanted to see!' My voice was suddenly high pitched.

'So?' Tanya snarled, banging her mug down on the table so a tidal wave of coffee flew over the arm of the sofa and the table. She stood up and I flinched.

'For fuck's sake!' She swung at me with a TV guide, the pages fluttering loudly. It didn't hurt me, just shocked me. She put her fists to her head and shouted through clenched teeth, 'Don't! Don't hem me in! Fuck off out! Go on!'

I looked up at her wild bulging eyes, the set of her mouth, her bunched fists. I sat very still, unable to move. She flounced out, slamming the door. I heard her stamp upstairs.

I sat for a while, wondering whether or not to wait out the storm. I'd said I'd cook us a risotto for lunch and I'd got all the ingredients ready on the kitchen counter. Should I get on with it and hope her temper had gone by the time she came down? Or should I follow her upstairs and apologise, try and make up with her? Or should I flounce out myself, never to return? As if! I picked up my coat and stole out quietly, so's not to disturb her. Oh, and I left a little note: 'Sorry. I love you. Can I see you tomorrow?'

I spent the rest of the day shopping. I ended up buying a new shirt for myself that I thought Tanya would like to see me in and a little cuddly tiger for Tanya and a handmade card with a rosebud on it that said, 'My love is like…', and some incense for Tanya's burner and some handmade chocolates I could take round the next day. I spent the evening with my heart aching with hurt, jealousy, injustice and anger. I checked the time of the film but stopped myself from going there. Instead I watched the clock and imagined Tanya meeting up with Christiane – kissing her hello and both of them delighted to see one another again and – who knows? Watching the film – my film – that I'd wanted to see with Tanya, holding hands. My bitterness built up till my head hurt and I sent myself to bed, hiding under the duvet. And now was she spending the night with her – despite me? To spite me? Or without a thought of me – because I wasn't even worth it? I rang her number – no answer.

Then I cried myself to sleep with long wracking sobs and howls.

'She's mesmerised you,' my mum said after meeting Tanya for the first time, 'I don't like that woman. She's like a witch!' She crossed herself. 'She's bewitched you and I honestly believe she's evil. I do.'

My dad frowned and nodded and chewed the end of his pipe.

'She's got you mesmerised!' Mum persisted. 'You can tell! You can't keep your eyes off her. She's got you under a spell. What are you doing, jumping to her every beck and call?'

Trying to make her love me, I guessed.

Then again, my upbringing was quite happy and normal compared with Tanya's. If I'd had to put up with Tanya's mother, Tanya's experience, I would have hidden under a duvet for the rest of my life. Or killed myself. You had to admire her. You had to stand back in amazement at her turning out so well in a family so dysfunctional. A blessing she hadn't turned out worse. I tried to make it up to her. Tanya needed me. Tanya needed to be shown love. She needed unequivocal, relentless, unbounded love. Unconditional love. Even so, her mum seemed so sweet and harmless when I knew her. No threat at all. Just like me. When Tanya was told that her mum was terminally ill, she was impassive. When the social worker said it might be a good idea for Tanya to go down to Leeds, Tanya was polite and said she'd do what she could. When she put the phone down, she told me there was no way she was going down to see her.

'But Tan, you're gonna have to…'

'Have to? There are no "have to"s with that bitch. There's no way I'm getting back into it now!' Tanya sounded determined but she looked distracted.

'She's just an old woman. An old dying woman, Tan. You need to see her for your own sake, if not for hers.' I felt inarticulate. 'Go and see her now, while you're strong. She can't harm you now…'

Tanya stood looking out of the window, her arms wrapped around herself.

'It's the end Tan, and you won't forgive yourself if you can't make your peace… She is your mother…'

I saw that Tanya's shoulders were shaking. I went up and put my arms round her. She was biting her nails and hiccupping to hold in her sobs. She stared out of the window, her eyes brimful of tears.

'Hey... hey,' I said softly and traced the line of one tear with my finger. 'It'll be okay. Shh now,' I wrapped my arms right round her, cupping her head against my breast and rocked her gently. 'Shh, it'll be all right. Shhhh, it's okay...'

Tanya's voice went shrill, 'You – uh – you... don't know!' She took a great staccato breath and howled. I held her close, muffling the cries that wrenched themselves out of her, her whole body convulsing. When she'd finished, she sagged like a rag doll. I led her to bed and she stood bewildered while I undressed her. Then I lay with her quivering in my arms till she had exhausted herself asleep. I lay with my arm round her all night. The next morning her eyes were bloodshot red, her face was bloated and my shirt was still damp with her tears.

It took a lot of coaxing before she relented and decided to see her mother again. It took a long time for her to trust me enough to let me go with her. I remember the first time we went. I was going with her to share the driving. We both knew I was only going because Tanya needed my support and love. But it was easier for her to take – and more acceptable for me to say – that I wanted to go shopping in Leeds and we could kill two birds if we shared the petrol and driving. That made it just a practical business arrangement. It took out the emotional involvement. I was the co-driver. If anyone asked.

She was silent all the way to Leeds until she pulled up outside a florist's and told me she was popping in for some flowers – did I want to come? Glad of a leg-stretch and pleased she wanted me with her, I followed her. I don't know why, but I expected her to grab the nearest ready-bundled bunch of carnations or something as a gesture, but no. She selected one exotic hothouse stem – with flamboyant, waxy, orange-red bugles and some spiky dark leaves.

When we pulled up outside her mum's house, I was wary. 'Do you want me to come in?'

'No!' she flashed. Then more gently, 'No thanks... well... I'll see how we go. Will you stay here?'

I would do anything. I sat and read the road atlas in the car outside the house and, twenty minutes later, Tanya appeared, looking sheepish and said if I wanted, I could come in – it was okay. And after all, it wasn't so bad: an old lady, even a bit frightened of me. A tiny wizened stick of an old lady unsure of herself in her own house, but I watched Tanya and took my cues from her. We stayed an hour, Tanya chatting stiltedly about work and the weather, me sitting politely admiring the garden, the china. Her mother looking at me from beneath her brows, when she wasn't looking at Tanya in bewilderment. When we got back into the car, Tanya burst into tears and I comforted her and drove us home.

Since the news that her mum was on her deathbed, Tanya had been strange and distant, but that was only to be expected. I trod as carefully as a deer near a sleeping lion. I was timid, waiting for her to come to me, just holding my arms open to her. She could accept me or reject me.

After the hospital race that awful final morning, I sat ready for anything, waiting for her to come back to her house in Saltburn. A week later I wanted to be with her at the funeral just to see she was safe, stop her going over the edge. It must have been doing her head in, I knew, even if it was a relief for Tan to know she was dead. It must be... what would Big Mandy call it? Re-stimulating? Clancy in her own charming way had told me I had to watch out for myself but then again, I couldn't put myself first. Not under these circumstances. Tanya was the important one.

Tanya – the evil one. She won't drown, but she'll rise like a witch to thrust pins into flesh and twist the knife. My tormentor. My sorceress. For Tanya, only burning at the stake would suffice. Flames licking blackened thighs, peeling skin like blistered bark, crackling flesh to charcoal. Would she feel, then?

And still I'd reach through fire to brush the ashes from her hair.

5

Tanya: How it was

It wasn't that my mother neglected me. No, far from it. She engaged with me all too well. I was at the core of her purpose in life. She existed only to make my life a misery, so my own act of revenge was to live and to succeed. You have to build up a certain resilience, a certain survival instinct or that's it, you're dead. And if people think I'm arrogant, self-opinionated, strong-willed, selfish, then I'm pleased. I'm glad to be! How do you think I got this far?

How do you learn to survive, when the beatings are the least of it? When your very being, your soul, your character, is chipped away in ways more subtle? When it's your birthday and Mother is being so nice to you that you're almost persuaded that she must have changed. That your birthday wish has come true. But you know it hasn't, really. You know something's going to happen, but you just don't know when she'll strike. And there's a party because your mother has decided that this is her one concession to normal family life and the family and the neighbours would expect it, and you're sick to the stomach, and everyone thinks you're sick with excitement because it's your birthday, but actually you're sick deep in the pit of your soul. Because when the kids are gone, when the mothers have thanked her and when everyone's left, when the last of the party-bags has been happily taken, clutched by your innocent, unsuspecting friends, then you know you have to pay for it.

On the mountain stands a lady, who she is I do not know
All she wants is gold and silver...

You either develop a keen awareness of your own self-worth or you die. I intended to live. So if I'm cocky now, I'm damn proud of it. I still hate birthdays. People laugh and think it's my fear of getting old. But no – it's my fear of being young. I still wake up on every birthday morning with the acrid taste of bile in the back of my throat. Tanya dreads birthdays. Joke, if you like.

I remember my thirtieth birthday, waking up with that sick, dreadful feeling again and it had been some poor deluded, short-lived girlfriend's idea of a nice surprise to throw a party. Whereas I just threw up. I spent the day in silence, my stomach in a tight knot, glaring at the girlfriend. She didn't even have the decency – or the sense – to ring everyone up to cancel. I was quite well behaved otherwise. I drank myself unconscious early on in the evening and slept face down on my bed for much of the night, with a bucket beside me. The party was great, I heard. Shame I missed it.

I've never spent a whole birthday with Mary. I say that without regret – there's only so much niceness you can take in one day. Besides, I am always invited over to Christiane's for dinner on the evening of my birthday. I generally accept the invitation. It is a fact of life. It is like breathing. Mary doesn't understand this, of course. Mary wants to be my whole life. Mary thinks I should not live without her. Mary thinks that I shouldn't breathe without her. Mary wants to be my respirator, my resuscitator, my lifeline. Mary likes to think that I would die without her. But the truth is – she'd die without me. As for birthday parties – Mary wouldn't dare. At least Mary knows not to take things into her own hands. Not to presume. Not to assume. She suits me quite well in that respect. She is very loving, very affectionate. Sometimes, that is good. Sometimes, bad. There are times when she takes me down that spiralling tunnel of love to the edge of myself, where I lose my bearings – almost lose myself – in her. I have to shake out my head to collect myself and remember. You always have to protect yourself. At all times.

Mary adjusts her manner to suit my mood. Mary-chameleon, camouflaging herself to the atmosphere around her – my atmosphere, my moods – so she doesn't annoy me. Sometimes that is the very thing needed. Sometimes it irritates me beyond words.

And yes, there are other women. I don't boast about it, but other women are important to me. I just haven't made a big deal of it. Haven't rubbed Mary's nose in it. To be frank, I couldn't stand the upset. Her upset, that is. Have I become soft in my old age? Maybe it's cowardice, I don't know. All I do know is that I do not want things getting out of control. Measured precise steps, not wild emotion. So I prefer discretion – or if not discretion, then distance and anonymity. I don't like unnecessary risks. And then there's Red... I don't know... she could be a loose cannon. This could be a mistake. I must beware.

But even the first time was easy.

'You know, you're honoured to have me,' I told Red, twisting and twisting a lock of her hair as we lay on my bed after making love. She looked at me askance, as if I were arrogant, which I am. I like her honesty – it's refreshing, since she makes no bones about showing her disdain. Down to earth disdain, not superiority like Christiane.

'I haven't even had you!' she declared and rolled on top of me – which I don't like, but she didn't know that yet. I rolled quickly over her and we managed to escape that one for the moment. I wrestled myself up on my elbows and sat astride her, pinning her wrists to the bed. We'd turned it into a joke and she laughed, 'You're so mistressful!' She tried to thrust her hips up but she's so slight, I was immovable.

This is so easy, this relationship. So fresh and fun. We have no investment in it. It's sex and laughs. Not like Christiane, which is angst, high drama, an intellectual challenge, a grand passion. Not like Mary, which is simple, basic emotion, sometimes painful, sometimes raw. I can't give her what she wants, which is the picket fence, the 2.4 children, the 'Hi, honey, I'm home!' One day I'll get up and Mary will be baking cookies, I know. Wearing a frilly gingham apron. A Stepford Wife, I wouldn't be surprised. And yet I'm in too deep now. But I'm afraid that she needs me. I'm afraid that I need her. Don't tell anyone.

I'm biting Red's lip and she's hungry for it, but as I move to her throat she winces and makes to push me away, 'No, no, please... Don't!' She's serious suddenly. She hasn't learned to trust me.

'It's okay! You know I don't do love bites –' I reassure her '– I don't suck!'

She laughs but she's still uneasy. I will use that again. It's good to have a little unease. For God's sake, don't let us be too easy. I don't like easy, too much.

But she's spoiled the moment for me now and I edge off her and lie sidelong, resting on one elbow, to view her long, thin, pale body; her nipples alarmingly pink, alarmingly small. The difference between women. A red-gold tuft. Sweet. I am sated. I close my eyes.

'I'd better get going, I guess,' she says and I open my eyes as she picks up her watch from the bedside table, puts on her ring. I like to watch these women and their little ways. She stands up and stretches for my benefit, the skin taut over her ribcage, her tiny breasts with their unaccountably bright pink nipples lifted higher, almost flat as she reaches both hands up towards the ceiling. The tiny triangle of clear space at the top of her thighs even with her legs together. She stops and looks at me. I wait. I'm not going to persuade her to stay longer. She shrugs, unaware that she's done it, turns away and sighs as she reaches for her clothes on the floor. She bends low, a calculated manoeuvre to give me a fine view. I say nothing. I am sleepy now. I have exerted myself. That's the problem with lovers. They are very labour-intensive. You can't just sleep with them.

'You have worn me out, ' I confess, and she seems happy with that. A job well done. She is a little more sprightly in her dressing now, a little less slow and recalcitrant. The next time I open my eyes, she is fastening the belt on her jeans.

'You're faster when you're ripping them off!' I observe.

'When *you're* ripping them off!' She puts her tongue out at me.

'Watch it with that tongue – or I'll have you!'

'Too late!' She pouts and walks out. I like that. No long farewells. With Mary, every goodbye is as if forever. She clings, she kisses, she half goes, comes back, kisses again. Has words to say. Parting words. Important words. I love you. You are the most important thing in my life. I will get some milk.

When we first got together, I was 42. Mary – I don't know – 25, 26, I think. Yes, I'm old enough to be her mother, but I was very clear at the outset that I am no mother-figure. Entirely wrong tree to bark up. I still feel uneasy when she snuggles beneath my arm, nuzzles at my nipple. She has tried baby talk, which makes my flesh creep. I am wary of her attempts to mother me too, stroking my hair, presenting her breasts for me to suckle. I can take it for so long, then I have to pin her on her back, get in control.

'You're passive-aggressive,' I've told her, holding her shoulders against the mattress.

'What d'you mean?' Her eyes widening in alarm after the sleepiness of cuddling up to me.

'You would have me believe that you are incapable of acting with malice, a victim of circumstance. When it's all just part of a plot…'

'What? You're mad!'

I dug my fingers into her shoulders and made her yelp, then leant a fraction of an inch from her face and hissed, 'I know your game, that's all. Think I'm stupid? You're not so innocent!' I peppered her with spittle. She blinked, terrified.

I flung myself off her and lay with my back to her, listening to her rapid breathing, feeling the rigidity of her lying in bed exactly where I'd put her. No more cuddles tonight. No more baby-play. No more Virgin Mary. I laughed.

Tonight I would make light of it all. The night was our canvas, water-washed with the past. Bold strokes of laughter shaped our present. The moonlight, amused, sharpened the tone, picked out the light in her eyes, detailed her wry smile too close to tenderness. So tonight I would turn out the love and make light.

Mary would have it that I have been bereft of love. She tells me that her friend 'Big' Mandy was talking to her about 'modelling' behaviour.

'I hope you haven't been talking about me!'

'No!' Mary is shocked; horrified. I know she wouldn't dare.

'You know that if you betrayed my confidence – that would be the end!' I affirm. She nods quickly.

'No, no…' she mumbles, then picks up the pace, 'But Big Mandy – she's into all this psychological stuff…'

'Bullshit.'

'Well, maybe… But, anyway, she was telling me about how you pick up patterns of behaviour from other people, like your parents.'

'What? And you're telling me I'm a psycho because my mother taught me to be?'

'No, no… not that. Just… well, it was interesting, that's all.'

'"Like mother, like daughter"? Is that what you're saying?'

'No… not at all…' she trailed off, weakly.

'Your mother must have been some goddamned whingeing door-mat, then!'

My mother didn't so much talk *to* me as talk over me. I had to piece through her hatred. If I try to understand her, it might human-ise her and I'm not sure I want to do that. Mary says I must try not to think badly of the dead but, frankly, there is little good to remember. I understand that, as an illegitimate child in the late fifties, I brought suffering upon her. Single parents did not exist and unmarried moth-ers were scum. They were not accepted. Part of it might have been that. She blamed me because I devastated her life. I know it wasn't my fault. I know it was unfair. I still cannot forgive that. I'm fairly sure when I was a tiny thing I never did anything to justify such malice, apart from exist. Her venom later was because I was a cocky little bas-tard. Isn't that what she wished for me? And when I was a teenager, yes, I did do things deliberately to annoy her, to exact my revenge. But I wasn't born that way. I don't think you can be a cocky little bastard when you're two years old and Mummy tells you stories of how she wishes you were dead and the ways she can kill you. Tells you every day that you're shit on her shoes, that you've ruined her life. So, now you've got to pay. I remember that I was scared because I had no money to pay.

Or, when you're three and you realise that it's your mummy who's taken to smothering you with a pillow till you lose consciousness. It wasn't nightmares after all. She never went too far, but sometimes I did wish she would go all the way. Even then, the blackness was bliss. First it was frightening. First you struggle against it. Suffocation feels scary the first few times, especially when you're small and can't fight back. Then the lovely things happen – coloured things float in front of your eyes slowly, soothingly: a vibrant neon-green triangle, a Day-Glo pink circle, a purple Mickey Mouse, other Walt Disney characters, and it's like floating with them. I learnt to go limp and surrender, because that's when she would stop and – I like to think – panic a little. But perhaps she didn't. Perhaps she simply thought she had won. But when she tried it when I was ten, I was ready for her and strong enough. I had to pay for that, but it was worth it.

I know Mary's in awe of me – frightened of me, even. All well and good. You have to watch out for yourself.

The other week, I rang her and she came over, bringing red wine and chocolates. She always brings something. She can never just bring herself, but she has to bring a prop every time. Even if it's just a carton of milk. She uses it as an excuse to come over, because she thinks I won't let her in by herself. Maybe she thinks she just isn't enough by herself. And maybe she's right. These days I'd be shocked if she came over to the house empty-handed. Insulted, even. So I opened the door and she stood there with an uneasy smile on her face and proffered the wine and the chocolates before she came over the threshold, like a pass, like an entrance fee. She stood and waited, examining my face. I played along, ignoring her querulous look and stayed in the doorway, leaving her on the step while I examined the label.

'Rioja,' she said.

'Never!' I said. 'It's a good job you're here – I'd never have been able to tell! Not from the label!'

Her brow furrowed. She knew I was being sarcastic, but she just couldn't tell my motive. I stayed in the doorway to see how long I could spin this out.

'It's 1997,' I read from the label. From the corner of my eye, I could see her chewing her lip. I looked straight at her but she couldn't meet my eye. 'That's no good. You should have brought a 1996.' She was jiggling one knee and biting her lip but still silent. This was getting boring so I sighed and said, 'Okay – it'll have to do, I suppose. Come in, then.' She stepped past me looking relieved: not obviously but subtly. She didn't want to look a complete doormat, I suppose. Just the bulk of one. Speaking of bulk, as I followed her down the hallway I added, 'You won't be wanting any of these chocolates, I hope? You're wide enough, aren't you?'

I threw them on the sofa and looked forward to an evening's entertainment, Mary-baiting. Beats masturbating.

Ah, but Mary's a sweet girl, a fine girl and she doesn't deserve this, I hear you say. Let me tell you, she loves it! Or why does she come back for more? So I oblige, of course. I meet her needs and she meets some of mine. Red, she is a distraction, a temporary solution. She is handy, she is different. But no more than that. And Christiane? All right, I'll tell you a little about Christiane. For Christiane is the only woman I will ever love. Yes, I love Mary in my way. That's right! I love Mary – and she's in my way! Whichever way I turn, she's bobbing in front of me in my face, there to serve. Like a loyal lap dog, no matter how much I throw her off she'll run up again, tongue hanging out, ready to lick me – even my boots – ready for more. See how faithful I am! Or she's more like Mary-lastic – yes, she's like a rubber band! Push her away, stretch her nerves to breaking point till there's a thin strand between us, tautened to its limits – and twang! She springs back – same shape, same Mary.

Whereas Christiane is less immutable. Christiane is as unpredictable as the wind or the weather, subject to change. Fascinating, intellectual, unattainable. She stretches me, she exercises my mind, she develops me. I admired her and I still do. She's an ice-blue, frosted autumn day, fragile as dried leaves, fallen. Crisp as an apple, bitten. Yet she retains a strong sense of her own identity. She doesn't need me. Our initial coming together was passion on a grand scale, made fluid with drinks. We kissed. We breathed the flowers of gin, one to another. Gin scorched our lips, gin warmed our tongues, gin fired our throats. Flames licked our bellies. Senses blazed into senselessness. Ah, my milk of amnesia. Our mouths the morning after, filled with ashes.

Christiane is accomplished in all things. She has an air of elegant ease, of poise. Not like lumbering Mary: awkward, gauche. Christiane has delicacy and is full of old-fashioned words, like decorum. She is older than me but her beauty makes her youthful. She has many admirers, but none more admiring than me.

Christiane says, 'I may take you momentarily – but I remain aloof.'

Mary says, 'Take me, take me! I'll do anything!'

Which one would you choose? I almost never choose the easy option. I do not admire the easy option. I have no respect for the easy option.

But sometimes it is necessary to be easy. Sometimes I do not have the strength for challenge, for stimulation. It is fatiguing. Sometimes I need a rest. In fact, there's many a time that Mary is more convenient to me. I am not a taker, however. She cannot make love to me, except in the most passive way. I will not be controlled. I will not be overwhelmed by anyone. I do pride myself in seeing that my women are satisfied by any means, however. I wanted it to be beautiful for her, sordid for me. That's my vanity perhaps, that I wanted her to want me. Unfortunately, she wants the picket fence, too. In Mary-land, we are a devoted married couple living happily ever after. Impossible. I have a terrible need to hold her at arm's length. There are times when I am close to losing control, close to losing myself. And that cannot be. Since my first relationship with Christiane, I have felt the end of something beautiful, fragile, impossible. So – all that remains is a pale hair on my pillow, a bruise on my thigh and in my mind, everything smells of her. I will not place myself in such a situation again. It's so easy to deceive. Frightening. So frighteningly easy.

You cannot allow anyone to take control of yourself or the situation you find yourself in. Best of all, simply never find yourself in a situation. Make all of your situations your own. It just doesn't do to be a victim, to be vulnerable. I speak from experience. What I am about to say is something that I have told no one before now. I will tell it as it is: as a matter of fact. My experience of sex began earlier than most so I am, perhaps, more cynical than most, but how I remember it is this way. I was coming home from Sunday school. Mrs Shimmin, the next-door neighbour, usually took me there, but on this day she wasn't able to. There were some weeks like that, because she was quite an old lady and frequently ill. I still wanted to go – it got me out of my mother's way and my mother wanted me to go too, so it suited both of us that I made my way across the park to the church and back. I was eight. Sometimes I stopped to watch the bigger boys playing football; sometimes I played with some girls from school but I was a loner, so I often dawdled by myself, playing house in a den in the undergrowth or doing handstands on the grass. Anything to delay going home. On this particular Sunday I'd already been to Sunday school, already taken baby-steps to the field, one heel carefully placed in front of the other foot, touching heel-and-toe, heel-and-toe, baby-steps to make being away from home last longer. I watched the football for a little while, then wandered away towards my den, singing the last hymn they'd played at Sunday school, *'Jesus Loves Me, This I Know…'* and I'd started to push myself through the bushes round the back of the toilets to my best den. It was an arc of strong brown branches: whippy, twigless ones, completely enclosing a round bare earth-floor room. My best den. Its vast ceiling was a vaulted cathedral of twigs with a much higher canopy of distant leaves. You couldn't even see the sky. It was a magical place, under a spell of protection woven by wildlife. Above were the songs of innocence and enchantment. Beneath you could hear the gentle scrabble of birds and if you sat really, really quietly and didn't move and held your breath, sometimes the birds would hop right up. Trusting and trusted. My best den. My sanctuary. I don't remember anyone being around. Anyone else. I'd hardly entered the tunnel of branches. I'd barely parted the leaves.

Jesus loves me, this I know. In the beginning. *For the Bible tells me so.* Eyes shine in sunlight. Hair blows like grasses. *Little ones to him belong.* Belt buckle... glinting. In the... bushes.

A chaos of feet and fists and eyes and teeth as the branches and floor whirled around me, a crazy tumbling. Then a heavy hand across my face, across my nose and mouth, trapping my breath. Keeping the air out. No sky. Couldn't breathe. Grinding my head into the ground. *They are weak, but he is strong.* Heavy on my chest. Hurting me! Hurting me so I couldn't breathe and then... excruciating pain!

Ran home, crying. Wanting someone – even my mother – to make it better. Ran out. Flashback. Black. Can't breathe. Sweat and heavy on me. Can't breathe. Heavy hand... face. No air! Pain and black. Ran home. Sunday school dress dirtied and torn. Blood on me. Face stained with tears. Ran up the pathway. Breathless. Hiccupping. Hysterical. Ran inside. Wailing. My mother took one look at me and smacked me hard and repeatedly, chanting in rhythm with every smack: 'Dirty! Dirty! Dirty bitch! Dirty little bastard!'

I must have done something very, very bad. That's what I thought, then.

And after the tears and the pain and the guilt and the fear and the years –

Jesus loves me this I know, For the Bible tells me... So?

The worst thing was – I couldn't bear to go near my den again. My best den. My sanctuary.

6
Mary: Pride in all we do

Clancy said she was sick of me moping round and it was about time I got a life and had some fun. 'Cause you're dull, dull, dull, dull, dull!' she sing-sang. 'How about coming to Pride on Tyne? It's next week and we're all going, y'know! It'll be a great laugh!' I was sitting in the pub with her and Big Mandy.

'Yeah – come on!' Even Big Mandy was getting enthusiastic, which was unusual.

'Hmmm... well, I'll see what Ta... erm... my friend's doing and let you know...' I still hadn't told anyone but Clancy that I was with Tanya, even after eighteen months, and I was sure she wouldn't have told Big Mandy. Mind you, Big Mandy was so full of discretion, confidentiality and 'personal boundaries' that she wouldn't pry anyway. She just wasn't the type.

Clancy gave me her best psychopathic glare. 'You will not! You'll make your own decision, all by yourself!'

'Well, I'll see...'

'You won't! You're coming, and that's that!'

'That's not me makin' my own mind up! It's you, ya bossy cow!' I pushed her off her bar stool.

'No really, Mary – why not let people work around *you* for a change, instead of you always making yourself available? It'll be good for you.'

59

Big Mandy was so sensible she made me want to slap her sometimes.

I thought about it for a few seconds: 'Tell you what – a compromise. I'll ask if… my friend… wants to come.' Clancy and Big Mandy exchanged eye-rolling glances. 'But if she doesn't… I'll come anyway!'

'A breakthrough!' Clancy raised her glass in celebration. Big Mandy just gazed at me thoughtfully.

After I'd known Clancy for quite a while and Big Mandy for a shorter time, I'd asked Clancy why Big Mandy was called Big Mandy. She was quite slim and shorter than I was – so not big in any way I could see.

'Oh, it's just so you can tell her from Little Mandy,' Clancy had explained.

I had nodded. I could see the point then. 'Who is Little Mandy?'

'Dunno.' Clancy had shrugged.

'Am I called Big Mary, then?' I had felt self-conscious of my height and stocky build.

'Nah – 'cause there's no Little Mary to get you confused with… Hmm… but I suppose if a seven-foot tall Mary came along, then we'd have to call you Little Mary…'

My mum had been alarmed to find me growing taller and taller. My mum was only five foot two, and shrinking all the time these days, and my dad was five foot ten. At six foot myself, I must have been a throw-back. My mum'd particularly made me feel a freak. If it turned out that I'd been found on their doorstep, if I hadn't belonged to them at all, it would have been a relief. I'd've been pleased to know I'd been adopted. That would explain everything.

'You'd better not grow any taller,' my mum said to me when I was twelve, self-conscious and only five foot nine, 'or you'll never get a boyfriend!' Funny to think I'd really taken that to heart. Wish I'd had the confidence then to know she was talking a load of crap, whichever way you look at it. But from twelve years old until about last week, I took to slouching a lot. I also did quite a bit of cruising for lads from my seat. At school I developed a crush on a lanky lad called Keith – or Kecky, as he was affectionately known. I fancied him just because he was gangly and lanky and the same height as me. He had no personality, no sense of humour, wasn't good-looking at all and wasn't even very bright. But he was tall and that was the main thing. One teacher saw Kecky and me talking together and told me later she thought we made a lovely couple. I was mortified, which should have rung alarm bells, but I still yearned for him. However, he was too shy to ever take the initiative. And my mum had told me never to be 'forward'. The men should do the running. But no one ran towards me. So my mum was right – I'd grown too tall to get a boyfriend. So apparently girls were my only option, but she never told me that. And it never occurred to me! I must've led a sheltered life... And that's the trouble with Section 28 – you just don't get to know the options!

But Pride on Tyne... okay, I relented and said I'd go. It would be fun going with the gang and, as Clancy pointed out, although I was a Pride virgin, at least I wasn't still a lesbian virgin. They'd let me in now, she said. It didn't stop me feeling kind of awkward when I next saw Tanya, although I tried to be upbeat. We'd just finished our tea and I'd just washed up and we'd settled down to watch telly for a bit. I'd been practising all kinds of ways to tell her:

'Tanya – I'm going to Pride next week. You coming or what?'

'Oh, er, Ta-an, sorry, but I've been told I've got to go to Pride next week. I know... sorry... I don't suppose you'd like to come, would you?... Yes? ...You would? Oh, but that's great! Oh, thank you! You don't know what this means to me!'

'Tanya – I'm not available next Saturday, okay? No – I'm not telling you what I'm doing. It's private.'

'Tan, it's Pride next week and I'd love us to go together. Will you come with me?'

'Hey-ha! You'll never guess, but I've been asked to go to Pride, now I'm a proper lesbian! Fancy coming?'

'Tan – wondered if you fancied a trip to Ikea next Saturday? We could get those CD racks you pointed out. Maybe go into Newcastle for lunch? Oh, and there's something on at the University, might be worth a glance...'

'God, I feel really ill... flu... migraine... Think I'm coming down with something. Tut! Bet it all takes a hold just in time for the week-end! Tut! Feels really contagious, too... Did I tell you they called me Typhoid Mary at school? Diarrhoea will probably rear its ugly head again...'

So I sat staring at the TV guide, thinking about which approach to take. I'd made us a nice tea, poured the wine, tidied up, made sure I didn't interrupt during *Who Wants To Be A Millionaire?* and now there were no excuses left.

I cleared my throat, 'Er... Tanya...?'

'Mmmm?' she said, flicking the remote from channel to channel.

'Er... Tan... are you doing anything on Saturday?'

'Not that I know of... I might be... why?'

'Well, a crowd of... us... are going up to Newcastle for Pride on Tyne. Do you fancy it?'

Tanya looked at me and frowned. 'A crowd of us? Us who?'

I cleared my throat again. 'Well, there's Clancy and Clare... I don't think they're bringing the kids, though... and Big Mandy, Kerry...'

'That idiot?'

'Erm... Georgie and Robbo... all sorts... There's a minibus from the Line... it should be good fun...'

Tanya snorted.

I carried on. 'There's workshops, and stalls, and performances – some singing, a drag show, a band. A big disco at night – and it's all free!'

'It'd have to be. Sounds like a complete circus!'

'Oh...'

'And you're going, are you?'

'Well, unless... you want to do something else?'

'No, no. You go – and have a good time!' She folded her arms and stared at the telly. Antony Worrall Thompson was wrestling with a dead chicken.

'Won't you come?' I wheedled, pushing my hand between her folded arms.

'Puh!' she said.

'Aw, go on, it'll be fun! Pleee-ease?'

'Mary –!' She looked at me hard. Antony Worrall Thompson's voice was whining how important it was not to overdo the spices.

'Do you mind if I go?'

She looked askance. 'Huh!'

'I won't go, if you'd prefer…'

'Oh, for God's sake! Have some respect!'

I didn't know what she meant, so I left it at that and sat quietly for the rest of the evening, watching Tanya out of the corner of my eye to try to judge her mood. She was quiet too and maybe a bit irritated, so I couldn't help wondering if it was because of me. We went to bed and I snuggled up behind her with my arm around her waist, hoping we'd be okay. I made sure I was extra nice to her over the next few days. I rang her up every night, even the nights I was going round to see her, just to reassure her that I loved her very much. See, I'd love someone to say that to me and I always treat people how I'd like them to treat me. It's a bit like that sign you see in toilets. Not 'Now wash your hands please' (that would be my mum), but 'Please leave this toilet in the state you'd like to find it in'.

Clancy rang me up to sort out details. 'Hey, wotcha Mare! Still up for it?'

'Yep!'

'And are you coming to Pride, as well?'

'Hmm…yes, that was the "it" I was up for…'

'Ah, well – I've heard you're up for anything!' She sniggered. 'And is your woman up for it, too?'

'Nah.'

'Thought not, miserable cow! But you're coming, yeah?'

'Uh-huh,' I agreed.

'Well, good on yer, Mare – that's a turnip for the books! It'll be grrr-and! Anyway – twelve o'clock at The Intrepid Explorer – very apt for *you*! We'll just ease you in with this small provincial Pride, then the world's your veritable oyster, me old dyke!'

I thanked her very much for her guidance, listened to her complaints about work, then rang up Tanya.

The answerphone cut in as usual, so I waited. '... message after the tone... bleep.'

'Yeah, yeah, yeah,' I said to the machine. 'Hey Tan! It's me, Mary – just called to say –'

'You love me?' Tanya picked up the phone. 'Yeah, I know that!'

'Awww, but I can always tell you some more! No – but I'm actually ringing to tell you the arrangements for Saturday.'

'Very fascinating, but what's it got to do with me?'

'Just in case you change your mind...'

'I won't.'

'No, but in case you do... there's a minibus from...'

'Look Mary – how many times do I have to tell you? I am *not* going!'

'Well, if you know the arrangements, you have a choice!' I squeaked.

'For fuck's sake...' she muttered.

'Okay, I was just giving you the chance...'

'Mary, are you ringing me up for any other reason or just wasting my time and your phone bill?'

'Erm... are you doing anything tonight... or can I come over?'

'Please yourself. You can if you want.' That was as enthusiastic as Tanya got these days, so I took that as an invitation.

'Am I just your bit of rough?' I asked from under her arm in bed that night.

'Yes, dear.'

'Thought so,' I said, not sure if she was joking or not. I lay and pondered. I recalled when we first got together, I couldn't even figure out this butch–femme lark. It had occupied me for ages, wondering if I was doing it all properly. Was I supposed to be the butch one? I didn't know, but I guessed it might be about more than dress sense. I was too embarrassed to ask Clancy, who'd probably just laugh at me, and I didn't know anyone well enough to talk about what lesbians did in bed! Did I look like a dyke? Did I act like one? Neither Tanya nor I wore make-up... so we weren't lipstick lesbians, then. Neither of us wore skirts, or dresses. So were we both butch? But then again, we both had longish hair – so were we both femmes? I did quite a bit of cooking and cleaning – was I a bit wifey? And Tanya liked fast cars and football... was that a bit blokey? She was quite petite and cute and with her long, dark curls, I'd guess she was a femme. Then why wouldn't she let me touch her in bed? Well, I could touch her but not... completely. She definitely liked to take control. She definitely liked to fuck me. Was that butch? Was she femme on the streets, butch between the sheets? Was I girly for letting her? But I would've liked to make her come, too... so was I butch? But I wanted it both ways! Blimey, it was complicated, this lark. Heterosexuals have it easy.

7
Tanya: The web

I have recently become very interested in the benefits of the internet.
The benefits of anonymity. The benefits of distance. The realms in which
it is possible to engage in all manner of activity, sexual or otherwise and
yet to remain detached. I am very taken with it. Very interested in the
possibilities. Fascinated. When I first connected, I found it possible to sit
for five hours at a time on the weekend without moving from the computer. I'd take five minutes to fetch some coffee, visit the lavatory and
then sit for another five hours or more. My telephone line is almost con-
stantly engaged, which some people – especially Mary – find irritating. It
is of no matter to me. I get my calls: Callminder takes messages and I
have a mobile. There are benefits, challenges and solutions.

I pick up the phone and hear the stilted tone which suggests there
is a Callminder message. I press 1571. The automated voice tells me that
I have six messages. I wonder who that could be? Not. I press to listen.

'Tan… Hi, it's me!'

Quelle surprise! Mary!

'I suppose you're on the net! Give me a call when you're finished.
Thanks!'

Yeah.

'Tan – me again. Just checking if you got my message… maybe not.
Erm… I'll try again a bit later.'

I bet you will.

'Tanya? It's Jean from work speaking. Look, I'm really sorry but I don't think I'll be in tomorrow. I've got terrible food poisoning. I'll stay off tomorrow but give you a call. Bye!'

Shit! I've told them not to ring me about work at home unless it's an emergency. Silly cow.

'Tanya? Red. Give me a call if you can. On my mobile before ten. Otherwise, don't bother. I'll catch up with you.'

Damn. Ten-fifteen. And what's that about, then?

'Tan... Hi-iii –' Mary again, petulant now '– I wish you'd give me a call... Can I come round tomorrow, please? Only there's this poem I found, I'd like you to show you... so... okay... bye then...' Her voice drifted off.

'Tan – Mary AGAIN! I'm going to bed now, but you can ring me on my mobile – doesn't matter what time. I'll be up.'

Okay – I'll try at 2am. Mind you, it wouldn't surprise me in the least if she was sitting there clutching her mobile, awake all night waiting for me to call.

I find that my need for real-time, off-line company is less and less these days. The people I need to be with – the people I need to see – are fewer and fewer. Even my need for Christiane seems less and less. I know she is there for me, as I am for her. But suddenly there seems no time to do anything. There are not enough hours in the day and I am wearing myself out with all my 'obligations' – real or imagined. I am 45, and maybe now it is time to slow down. How can I fit in all these time commitments? Mary, Christiane, Red? How can I fit in the other times, the other women, the other scenes in other towns? How can I fit in the time to go to work too? And the time to explore the internet – the sites, the opportunities – and the women I have met. And as for the everyday mundane things – when does a person have time to shop, clean, cook, wash, even? And how, after all this, is there time for me to relax, be at peace, have time to myself? Something has to give. Something has to go.

A typical weekend begins with me crashing into the house at about seven-thirty on a Friday, with Mary turning up shortly afterwards. Mary has said that she'd like to bring over a take-away, that Friday could be our 'Chinese' night. I hate routines and I despise the rituals that she is trying to impose on me – on us.

'I don't want Friday to be "Chinese" night!' I yelled.

'All right – Indian then?'

'No, idiot! That's not the point! I don't want these rules. I want to be spontaneous!'

'Okay, on Fridays we'll just wait and see what you fancy eating, then I can bring over whatever take-away you want.'

And then she wondered why I hit the roof.

Often I will just damn well go out on a Friday – or a Wednesday or a Sunday – or whatever day or night I damn well please. I won't be contained. I won't be dictated to. I won't be treated like a teenager. Like a child. And if I want to spend all night on the internet, then I will do so.

I haven't given Mary a key to my house, which is contentious with her, although she won't bring it up straightforwardly, outright. She wheedles and whines, bound with her unassertiveness, her indirection. I know where she's going but I won't help her to get there.

'It would be nice if I could have a meal ready for you when you come in from work, don't you think?'

'Not necessarily,' I say.

'Just once in a while – when you're tired from work? Don't you think it would be nice to get home and find that someone had a hot meal ready for you?'

'Not really.'

'I think it would be nice…' She trails off.

Or she'll try another tack, 'Do you think, since I'm over here quite a bit, that it would be okay to bring over a change of clothing and I could maybe leave, say, a pair of trousers in your wardrobe…?' She sees my sharp look and continues, less confidently. 'Or… bring a… a pair of pants and er… just leave them in a bag in the corner, till the morning…? Would that be okay, do you think?'

'I think if you give a woman a hanger, she'll take over your whole bloody wardrobe...'

'Oh, but no...'

'You know the joke? Except it's no bloody joke. It goes, "What does a lesbian bring on her second date? A removal van and her cat".'

'I haven't even got a cat!'

'Then you're not a lesbian.'

'But you haven't got a cat, either!'

'That's because I'd kill it. I'd forget to feed it or run over it or go away for four weeks in the Maldives and totally forget I even had a cat and come back to find a wizened bit of fur. Then I'd be wondering if it was a fur ball or something the cat had sicked up – and only then would I remember that I'd had a cat.'

'You're exaggerating.'

'Get away! Do you see a cat? No? What do you think happened to it then? I'm on an RSPCA blacklist, I am. Not allowed to keep a pet for the rest of my days. So that goes for you too, pet.'

In fact, the internet's my only escape. At least I can do what I want, speak to whomsoever I want. And not speak if I wish. The joys of anonymity. I remember my first time in a chat room. Not wishing to commit myself to words, not wanting them to appear – suddenly public – I would lurk there observing, eavesdropping. A voyeur. Then my first comment, my first statement in my first conversation – typed in slowly, too slow to be much use, too slow for my quick mind. Too slow to be a sharp, incisive witticism, well timed to be most effective. My typing skills have picked up considerably. I would not have myself be thought slow. I do not wish to be a wallflower in this virtual garden. And now I am eager for words, eager for the badinage of people I consider to be my friends. And my acquaintances. I write to some people. Who would have thought I would have pen-pals? E-mates! It seems ridiculous – adolescent – but the pen-pals I have are very special friends. My very special anonymous friends. Oh yes, some send photographs. Many, indeed. Many who are eager to show themselves, to be liked, to be understood, to be abased. I do not like to send photographs. I prefer to be faceless. I prefer to be anonymous.

I have adopted several personas. Personae. My screennames for all occasions. I find it easy to shift from character to character, from 'tanyahide' – the 'normal' me – the joke name that all my friends will recognise as mine. The name I use casually in the ordinary chatrooms and most often as my email address. The one they might think is the real me. In addition, I have the name I use for work: 'tehelliwell' – too tedious to dwell on. However, I am also 'MISS-TRESS', which came to me when one of the people who Instant-Messaged me told me that she assumed that I was a 'top'. I had not thought about it before. But there was no doubt in my mind. So to remove doubt in others, I created a new screenname. One which would make it quite clear and signal to any others who wanted to play. I thought that it would be an interesting experiment to try. A fascinating world to explore. I spend a considerable amount of my time online now as MISS-TRESS. I block out the complete psychos and the weirdos, who are mainly men. I travel around the women's rooms and I wait to see who bites. The name is all. I do not need to speak. They flock to me. You would be surprised at the women I meet. The quiet, reserved women. The women who are successful professional people – a barrister, a headmistress. The old, the ugly, the beautiful, the young. The ones who look like librarians! The ones who are suburban housewives. The ones who have cravings for more than their small sad lives permit them. More 'specialist' needs. I suppose you could say that I provide a service. But more than that – I enjoy myself. I get a kick out of it. I do not wish to analyse it. Anal-yse. To be anal about it. Suffice to say, you would be surprised. The more powerful a woman is in her daily work-a-day life, the more she wishes to be dominated in her private life or the virtual world. I am perhaps the exception to the rule. I have no desire to be subordinate in any aspect of my life. I am rigorous in this. It matters to me.

Before I met my 'special friends' – my subordinate associates – online, in the days before I became Miss-tress of all I surveyed, I was more vulnerable. Foolishly, I gave my telephone number to a lawyer from Washington DC. It seemed like almost innocent fun. We had hit it off and we had enjoyed a very intense series of emails. Very intense in time – perhaps five or six lengthy emails per day in seven days – and very intense in content. I was thrilled by the whole affair. But I had revealed myself – exposed myself – by telling her things that I had not told anyone else – things that I didn't even know myself, before this… relationship. Things that were true and things that were untrue. And the woman, Elizabeth, was not only a lawyer but a cellist and played in a string quartet. I know nothing of classical music but I had waxed lyrical about Bach and she would expound with such authority, such passion and such intelligence, that I was overwhelmed. She put me in mind of Christiane. I struggled to keep up with her intellectualising, her philosophising. It was a challenge to me. I bullshat. I used weasel words. I pretended that I knew what she was talking about. I used what tiny knowledge I had: 'Mozart – so light – he had not reached the depth and complexity he might have promised. Mahler! Such passion! Such anger! Too powerful. Too discordant with my own emotions!' We used a great many exclamation marks, I remember. She asked for my telephone number and with a recklessness that I do not act out in the real world, I gave it. We were intimates, after all. And it wasn't my telephone bill she was running up if she did call me. As she did one Saturday, within three hours of receiving my number. She telephoned me and we spoke at length. She just loved my accent. She wanted more.

'I feel so close to you!' she cried.

'Me, too – it's strange, isn't it? How intimate one can become in so short a time.'

'How would you feel if came over?'

My heart stopped. No! '… I don't know.' My mind raced.

'Well, I am saying I want to come over. I can just step on a plane to see you. You want me to come?'

'… Possibly. Probably…' I was struggling for words to express my horror politely, then I hit upon a Maryism: coyness. 'But we hardly know one another!'

'On the contrary, we know one another better than most... already. I have arrived at a stage in my life when I refuse to let opportunities pass me by. I take a risk. So – shall I come?' she persisted.

I panicked. I could not react coolly and hesitated from expressing anger, so I resorted to a Mary-like tentativeness. 'I think we should take the time to get to know one another better.' Yes, I was Mary. 'It's only been a week!'

'Sometimes, you just know. We could get to know one another better if I were to come over and see you. What if I said, in a couple of weeks I'll get on a plane and you could pick me up at the airport?' I was silent. 'Or I'll call a cab and meet you at your home... Say, why don't I book into a hotel if that's more comfortable for you? I'd like to walk Hadrian's Wall. Do you live near Hadrian's Wall?'

'No! Not really!' Grasping at straws. I recovered and remembered how Mary might be: kind but shy, 'Look, it would be great to see you, but not so fast. This is all too fast for me. Let's take it easy.'

'I have let so many things slip through my fingers – I don't want to let you go.'

I went cold. Hot. Easier to be Mary. 'Look I'm sorry, but I'm just not ready for... that.'

We exchanged a couple of half-hearted emails after that. We let the time between emails crawl to three, four days. Drift off. Let the distance come between us. Truth to say, I was terrified at the thought of her becoming real. A real live lawyer-cellist from Washington DC turning up in Saltburn, going to The Marine for a pint. Playing obscure twentieth-century cello concertos while I was trying to watch *Who Wants To Be A Millionaire?* Hiking off in the direction of Hadrian's Wall, with every expectation of my accompanying her. Terrifying. Too much. Almost out of my control. So now I am very careful. I am anonymous. I am cautious. I am distant. I am detached.

I make like my mother. I play a role. My mother had a role for every occasion. To teachers, a concerned parent: 'Such a bruise! My goodness! She does play roughly with her friends. We must be more ladylike, Tanya dear.' But largely she kept herself to herself. Or herself to me. To most of the outside world, my mother was unknown. She was a flickering curtain, a grey shade. Through a yard of seedy grasses, through a grimy windowpane, through a dusty nylon net in a darkened room. A grey shade. At sounds in the street, she rippled the curtain, a stiff breeze and on the glass she breathed her life's condensation in diminishing, vanishing rounds of mist. And to me inside, she was my mother. To me she was all too real.

I am afraid of people stealing my breath away. I am afraid of death. Afraid of being held too close. Afraid of the dark. Afraid of strange men. Afraid. But I have my bravado to protect me. I wear it like a shield and with it I am invincible.

8
Mary: A little pride

My mum had no problem with labels: 'That's not very feminine,' she'd say when I was a teenager ready for the school disco in my jeans and trainers. She would have loved me to have worn frothy dresses and stilettos. I'd have been more comfortable wielding a stiletto. She had a thing about my hair too. All my little kid photos show me with my hair curled or ringleted and trussed with big ribbon bows. I looked like Lily Savage's love child. My mum would have me sitting on her knee every night before bed while she put my hair in rags or rollers, ripping it out by the roots to accommodate her fiendish instruments of torture. When I got to be thirteen, one of her surprises to celebrate my teenagerhood was a home perm. Then, for the next five years, she insisted on this ritual humiliation every few months: an entire afternoon sitting on a hard dining-chair on an outspread newspaper in the middle of the living-room floor with my mum yanking and twining my poor stretched hair round her fingers with cigarette papers and soaking my flaming scalp with some noxious fluid that bleached my collars and stung my eyes. I had to sit for hours on end with a plastic bag on my head and a big snake of drenched cottonwool tucked behind my ears.

I don't know what was worse – the hours of pain and stiffness or putting up with my mum's incessant chatter:

'And she said, "Well!" So I said, "You know what that means," I said. "What?" she said. So I said, "Well," I said, "she is, you know." I said, "Haven't you seen her?" I said. "Seen her?" she said. "Yes," I said. I said, "Her!" "Really?" she said. So I said, "Yes!" I said... she said... I said... she said... I said...'

There can be no worse torture than a home perm with my mum as permanent waver. I was not waving but drowning.

And Vincent the darling child, the best-beloved, would spot me and start hooting with hysteria, rolling on the floor, crying with laughter as if he hadn't seen the same tedious routine month after month. He must have had the memory of a goldfish, because he always found it so bloody hysterically funny every time. He never tired of it. Sometimes he and his snotty-faced little mates outside would peer in through the window at me pulling faces and I would scream at my mum to close the curtains. Some privacy is necessary, surely? And when I 'humphed' and stretched and groaned and whined, my mum would always say, 'You have to suffer to be beautiful.' And Vincent would piss himself laughing all the more. Except when I was nearly nineteen and he was fifteen, when my mum was out of earshot and he muttered with honest, serious adult concern, 'Oh, Mary... You look fucking hideous.' I couldn't help but agree.

I wouldn't have cared if the hours of suffering under the home perm meant I didn't have to put up with the nightly rollers or rags. But no – she still insisted on those, along with a new adult instrument of torture: the hairpin. She would wind and wind strands of my hair up in her fingers, then jab the hairgrip into my skull. Every night. Till I left home. God forbid I should have straight hair. Or short hair. And I went away to college and carried on with the nightly ritual because she told me to and I was afraid what might happen. She had me petrified I would look like a dreadful beast, *au naturel*. Till one night I was too drunk to be arsed with all that rigmarole and discovered that the world didn't end if I didn't pin my hair up and people didn't gasp with shock when they saw me. And actually I looked a whole lot better – I didn't look such a prat as I did after my hair had been pinned every night like some war widow. *There were bluebirds over my head and shoulders*... But it took me another four years to get my hair cut short.

'Oooh, that's not very feminine!' she said, but she couldn't say I'd never get a boyfriend looking like that because I had one. What she could say however was, 'He'll never marry you looking like that!' And I'm grateful to say he didn't.

So I ended up a lesbian. Maybe it was the short hair that did it. But I went off to Pride on Tyne with a gang of mates and some other people from Lesbian Line, where Big Mandy was a volunteer. I still felt a tinge of disappointment because Tanya hadn't come. I rang her from my mobile in the minibus.

'I'm in the minibus!' I shouted above the rugby songs, with my finger in one ear.

'Good!' Tanya said.

'Where are you?'

'Not in the minibus!' she cried.

'Okay – don't rub it in! Up to much?'

'Not yet!'

'Okay... I'll ring you later, then?'

'No need! Have a good time!' She sounded quite brisk and cheery.

'You okay?' I said, puzzled.

'Oh, yes! Bye then!'

'Bye...' I said and looked at the mobile. It gave away nothing.

We got to the campus just before one o'clock and fifteen of us spilled out on to the tarmac. Kerry was already half cut from the Special Brew she'd been swigging all the way up the A19 and a handful of the others were too. I'd felt a bit queasy on the way, so I hadn't drunk any at all. I checked my mobile for texts. None.

'Raaah!' Kerry came running up behind me and swung her meaty arm around my waist. 'Where's the bar?'

She was wearing a rugby shirt (not very feminine, as my mum would say) and I'd decided she was possibly definitely butch. And drunk. The top half of her body swung from side to side as she walked and, with her attached to me, I was forced into her lolloping rhythm. I wondered if people would think I was butch too. I wasn't sure that I was. I tried to flick my hair back in a girly way like Tanya often did, but she was so petite and striking I didn't think I could carry it off like her. Clancy, fresh from a busride-long niggle with Clare, ran up and grabbed my other side, grinning maniacally. With her skipping on my left side and Kerry lolloping on my right, I felt like the hunchback of Notre Dame.

'The girls are here!' shouted Clancy. My girl wasn't, but I smiled bravely anyway.

A girl walking in front of us turned round to shout: 'I thought we'd have heard something before now… Have we come on the right day?' We were definitely the noisiest things around, but we spotted some pink balloons tied to the railings, which gave us hope. The next thing we heard was a voice over a tannoy and then we spotted a multi-coloured huddle of people crowding round a small stage outside the Union.

'Where's the bar?' Kerry swung off my waist to lurch over to the door leading into the union and everyone followed except me and Clancy.

I took in the straggle of people browsing the half-dozen stalls around the small square, desperate to see someone I knew. Clancy stood in front of me.

'Hey! You okay?' she said gently, squinting up at me.

'Yeah, you know… How 'bout you?'

'The same!' She pulled a wry face and then punched me in the arm. 'Let's go and get legless! Last one standing's a… poof!' An extremely camp guy with a thin moustache arched one eyebrow as Clancy dragged me into the building. We saw our crowd bustling at the bar. Kerry had already been served and turned round, her big face red and gleaming with sweat, saying, 'Raaaahh!' as she passed pints back to the others.

'Look at that beer monster!' Clancy ducked into the crowd to pop up at the front of the bar and somehow be next in line to be served. She always was – she put it down to natural charm and her ability to attract a barmaid at fifty paces.

I got my mobile out to text Tanya. I looked round the smoky bar at the loud people and Formica tables glistening with pools of beer, and at Kerry's wide eyes as she downed a pint in one with everyone roaring and clapping. And I keyed in a message: COOOEEE! AM HERE SAFE! MISS U! U WOULD LOVE IT! XXXXXX

Still, it wouldn't do any harm to lie. As Big Mandy said, it would do me good.

Clancy ducked out of the crowd again, three pints clutched to her chest. Clare was standing with her arms folded, sulky and wordless, but she deigned to take one pint from Clancy's hands. Then Clancy came to me, 'There ya go, Mare – sorry, but I had to drink the tops off the beer 'cause I didn't want it spillin' on my shirt.'

'Any excuse!' I took the pint and took a great swallow of it. I was thirsty now and, before I knew it, I'd finished my pint and was pushing through the press of people at the bar for more. Most of the others had gone out on to the paved area to see what was happening. I ordered more pints from a gorgeous-looking woman at the bar. I felt quite cocky. I suddenly realised that I was out on the town, surrounded by dykes but secure in the knowledge that I had a partner at home. Well, at her home. Well, I thought of her as my partner. Well, I was kind of secure – secure as I could be. I pushed out into the sunshine to hand out the round of drinks and felt for my mobile. No texts.

I stood and watched the crowd. Clancy and Clare, and Big Mandy further away, stood listening to a band on stage. They were the only people I knew. I saw Georgie nosing through a box of CDs on one stall. I wandered over to see what was on sale, clutching my plastic pint glass. I wasn't so thirsty now, which was reassuring since we had ten hours' drinking ahead of us. If I drank at the same rate as my first pint, I'd've had…120 pints by the end of the evening. Not even Kerry could drink that much.

I browsed the stalls: a nice one full of handmade jewellery. I stood for a while fingering some earrings which were dainty filigree and colourful enamel, thinking it was a shame Tanya didn't have her ears pierced. They had some lovely silver bracelets but they were quite expensive and I'd never seen Tanya wearing jewellery, so I thought I'd better not risk buying her anything. Georgie was still at the CD stall and I went and hung my chin over her shoulder. She smelt nice. Paco Rabanne, I suspected.

'Mmm, you smell gorgeous!' I sniffed her neck.

'That's because I am.' Georgie laughed and carried on flicking through the CDs. 'D'you like African music?'

'Humm… I know Ladysmith Black Momby-doo-dah, 'cause they did the soup advert.'

'Philistine!' She laughed and I stayed for a moment resting my chin on her shoulder. Then I got bored and wandered off, swigging my lager and stopping to peruse a stall selling incense and tealight holders. The table held small sacks of something, with little handwritten cards. I peered down at them.

'That's frankincense and myrrh, quite expensive but a relatively simple fragrance,' a southern accent began, quite well-spoken. I looked up to see a pale girl behind the stall, with long brown hair and a baggy cheesecloth blouse. She looked innocent and wholesome, like a vicar's daughter. She held up a wooden scoop of the small crystals and herbal flakes, took a pinch from it and placed it on an ashy burner. The substance immediately curled a grey smoke trail into the air. The vicar's daughter wafted it towards me with her hand.

I bent to sniff it but she said gently, 'There's no need – just hold back and let it engulf you.' She indicated another sack: 'A more complex fragrance is this one. This recipe is thousands of years old and was found in the pyramid of Cheops. It contains myrrh too, which gives it a depth, but it's far more subtle and complex. Here.' She took a pinch and dropped it on to the burning charcoal, where it gave a small hiss and the ribbon of white smoke curled up again. 'See, it has more character than the pure incense and is said to bring all your hopes and dreams to reality.' She wafted the smoke towards me, but I was already sold on it. 'It is very popular –' she smiled as I offered her my five-pound note '– and if the hopes and dreams of the pharaohs were realised by it, it must be potent…'

I looked forward to a quiet moment at home when I could meditate on Tanya and my hopes and dreams for her. Or, better still, make love with Tanya by candlelight while we became engulfed by the heady fragrance and made our hopes and dreams come true together.

9

Tanya: So many women, so little time

I was seeing Red maybe once, twice a week. The woman that is, although people would say I see red a lot. 'Tempestuous': thus have I been described – amongst other things, although tempestuous is one of the less offensive words used. A fucking psychopath. I've been referred to as that, too. Who can say how accurate that is? It is a matter of perception or impression. Perception suggests acuity: a degree of calculated sagacity. Impression is more two-dimensional. More... superficial, more shallow. There are many people who do not look beyond the surface. I prefer women who go deeper. I prefer women who are profound. I prefer women who go down...

Christiane. I saw her probably once a fortnight, although we spoke on the telephone most days, when she could reach me by telephone. These days I initiated most of the contact. I like to keep in touch and she is a busy woman. I most frequently arrange to meet her to dine out or at her home: a large old stone-built house in Marske, the next village to Saltburn, a walk along the sea's edge or a short drive down the A174 through the roads crossing arable land. Her house is solid, centuries old. I feel that we can be more private there.

Christiane opened the door and beamed. I held out my bouquet of flowers for her: lilies. I thought they would look particularly striking in her living room and had made a detour to a fine florist in Redcar especially for them. They cost twenty pounds, but only the best would do for Christiane. I handed them to her nonchalantly.

'Darling! White lilies! How funereal! Thank you!' she cried and cast me a sidelong look.

'Chosen for the design concept, not for their common associations,' I offered.

'Ugh! Never anything common! Perish the thought, darling!'

She threw the lilies carelessly into a vase, where they looked perfect. Christiane had an artist's eye for simplicity. Mary would have spent minutes trimming and crushing their stems, primping and arranging, worrying and testing.

She poured me a brandy, our small ritual which was the prelude to intense conversation then the inevitable promise of bed. She was indeed a handsome woman. Beautiful, you would say. I wondered at her slim figure as she stooped over the drinks, her greying hair pulled back in a French knot with tiny wisps escaping, backlit and shining against the lamplight, casual but elegant. I looked forward to releasing her hair from its pins, feeling its gentle weight on my skin as she leant over me. Taking handfuls of it in my fists, pulling her towards me, hungrily searching out her face, her lips. Passion.

I have been growing concerned by Mary's assumed 'ownership' of me. She lurks. She waits. She turns up on my doorstep as I open my front door. Considering that I was seeing Red a couple of times per week, Mary felt justified in wanting to claim the rest of my time. However, I often had other plans. I still liked to go over to Leeds once in a while or up to Newcastle, out on the scene where the living was easy and so were the women. However, I wouldn't go out with Mary there. That would totally blow my cover. I wouldn't go to Pride, either. I'm not into solidarity or public displays.

Weeks before Pride, I decided one Saturday night that I would drive up to Newcastle. I had not been out on the gay scene there for a while. I am my own woman, after all. A free woman, with free will. I called in at the newsagent's on my way, to pick up some cigarettes for the evening – my anticipation increasing. I even winked at the woman behind the counter. Then in the car I was unstoppable till I got to Newcastle city centre and found a place to park, before heading off to The Barking Dog. I liked to start there, because it was small and the intimacy made chatting to women easy. On the stairs I passed the familiar two transvestites who made the rounds of pubs and clubs: both approaching-elderly men in their complementary curly wigs and fur coats, heavy make-up creasing into their faces. The smaller rounder one with the golden brown wig said, 'Hello dear, nice night!'

I smiled at them and went into the fuggy bar. The place was fairly full and there were a number of women that I recognised, but none I knew sufficiently to approach. Mind you, that was not really my style. I didn't come out to get together with people I knew. Quite the reverse. I did not sit and chat to people. I am purposeful if nothing else and I cannot abide idle chatter. I like to scan the room, to make an assessment, to come to a conclusion and focus down on an individual. Preferably an individual who is alone, for they are the easiest, the most grateful; but I can also pick out someone in a crowd, someone who takes my eye, someone who is open to suggestion.

I smiled at the barmaid and took my usual alcohol-free lager, then lit up and browsed the bar area. Groups of women, seated. No one remotely interesting. Two fat women at the end of the bar, very butch. I'd seen them before and they nodded over in greeting. I preferred not to encourage them, so I gave them the briefest acknowledgement and started to engage the barmaid in conversation. Her name was Karen and she chatted easily enough, with a distant air. She wasn't interested in me and I was not interested in her, but we were grateful to save one another from worse fates. My mobile bleeped – a text: TANYA – RED. CAN U COME OVER? UNEXPECTED OPPORTUNITY! CALL ME X

It was ten to nine already – and it would take me at least an hour to get to Middlesbrough. Shit. Could I be bothered? I looked around the bar. Dammit. Nothing for me here. I decided to take an unexpected opportunity when it was offered. I drained my bottle of alcohol-free and left.

By midnight I was back at home, pleased with myself after all.

'I want to know where you *were*!' Mary's voice was getting shrill.

'It is none of your fucking business.' I managed to keep my voice down for once. But this seemed to make Mary more hysterical, so I had to hurl the lamp against the wall behind her, where it smashed spectacularly into tiny shards, pattering all over the floor. This shut her up.

Then I went up to bed, put the old bolt across my bedroom door, turned my CD player on really loudly and got into bed fully dressed. With any luck, Mary would piss off and leave me alone and I could get on with my night. I was desperately thirsty, gagging for a cup of coffee. Red hadn't offered any and time was tight anyway so I'd just got to it and left. The last thing I wanted was Mary on my back, on my doorstep, on my case. In my street, parked up, waiting for me to get back. Waiting to get hysterical. What kind of kicks did she get from this? It was sending me raving mad. I was too furious to sleep and still shaking with rage, so I swung the duvet off me and switched on my computer. I didn't really feel in the mood but I needed some distraction, so I signed on: MISS-TRESS. I would see who was available.

My buddy list showed that Amber69, Li'l Mo, Slave4U and Deelishus were online. I decided to go for Deelishus first. She couldn't spell her own name of course, but she was usually hot and game for anything.

I Instant-Messaged her: DEE.

I waited. A minute or two went by, so infuriated by the delay, I IM-ed Amber too. AMBER!

Then Dee's IM came through:

Deelishus: Mistress! What can I do for you this afternoon?
MISS-TRESS: It is night here, bitch.
Deelishus: Sorry, Mistress. I am but a humble Californian babe, awating your comand.

Then the IM box sprang up for Amber: 'Miss-tress! Your servant.'

Damn. I should have spoken to them one at a time. I liked to concentrate. I IM-ed Amber.

MISS-TRESS: Do not move from your seat. Do not speak to anyone. Await my IM and respond only to me. You will be punished.
Amber: Yes Miss-tress.

Then, my attention was free for Dee. 'Dee, what have you done today? Anything to please me?' I typed in.

Deelishus: Everything is done to please you Mistress.
MISS-TRESS: Good. Tell me.
Deelishus: I have worn my black panties only for you. I have looked at women lustfuly so that I am redy for you.
MISS-TRESS: You have looked at other women? Then you shall be punished, bitch. What else have you done?
Deelishus: I have scrubed my fingernails so clean that the skin is raw as you requestd…
MISS-TRESS: COMMANDED!
Deelishus: Appologies Mistress. At your comand of corse. And now I am clean and redy for your comand.
MISS-TRESS: Good. Touch yourself.
Deelishus: I am doing so Mistress. I am rubing my fingers gently over my pussy
MISS-TRESS: Lick your fingers.
Deelishus: Yes.
MISS-TRESS: Continue.
Deelishus: I am rubing ah ohh my fingers are slipery now and I am geting wet.

In spite of her spelling, so was I. 'Stop now. I am going to punish you now. They are my fingers. I want to hurt you. Tell me what you feel.'

And that was fun. I continued until Dee was all spent, then I turned to Amber, waiting obediently and I used her too. Then I had some words with Slave4U until I signed off, stiff in the neck and exhausted, three hours later. I ran downstairs for a drink and saw that Mary had gone, so it was safe for me to leave the bolt off my bedroom, slip into bed and sleep at last.

I woke at seven-thirty, annoyed that I was awake but unable to get back to sleep. Annoyed that I had only managed another three and a half hours of rest. Annoyed that Mary had turned up last night. Even more annoyed with myself for allowing her into the house. I should have known she was unbalanced. I should have known that was asking for trouble. I recognised that there was no chance of my getting back to sleep after winding myself into a tight ball of irritation, so I decided that I would get up and dressed. If I grew tired later I would go back to bed that afternoon.

Downstairs, I noticed that Mary must have swept up the broken lamp before she left, and that made me laugh. Same old Mary. Same old reliable Mary. My Housekeeper. My woman that does.

After my special Saturday breakfast, a cafetiere of coffee and two cigarettes, I decided to have a bath. A long hot bath, undisturbed. My special weekend treat to wash away the stress of the night before. I switched on the CD player in the bathroom and lit some lemongrass incense. With that burning and with fragrant oils in the bath, I luxuriated, lying back in a desultory mood, pleasing myself, pleasuring myself. I topped up the bath with hot water when it cooled and lay with my eyes closed, perspiration breaking out on my brow washed off with occasional scoops of bathwater. I had my blue bathroom ashtray on the small shelf within my reach and held my cigarette hand over the side. The phone started ringing. That irritated me and disturbed my solace, my safe place. I wasn't going to answer it, but it annoyed me nonetheless and spoilt the mood. It rang off, but I'd already decided to get out of the bath and was towelling myself down when its insistent ringing started again. I swore as I tied the cord on my dressing gown too tightly. I was still going to ignore the phone but its ringing was infuriating me. I vowed to re-set the answerphone to cut in sooner. Bloody hell – it was before nine on a Saturday morning! No prizes for guessing that it would be Mary.

'Tan?' she said querulously. I said nothing. She knew it was me anyway. A rhetorical question, unworthy of comment.

'Tan – are you okay?'

I frowned, 'Me, okay? Of course I am, stupid!'

'Erm, are you okay with me? I was worried...'

I blew out a noisy stream of air. 'Puuh!'

I heard Mary draw a long intake of breath. 'I was scared... last night.'

'Yeah. Right. I'm very scary.'

'Look, I know I shouldn't have gone on like that –'

'Too true,' I interrupted.

'Well, yes. I'm sorry, but I love you...'

'Yeah, yeah, well I'm sorry about that too.'

'Tan...' Mary's voice was starting to break with emotion again, but my throat was tightening in anger. 'Tan... I uh... I don't want to lose you!'

'Yeah, whatever...'

'I love you too much.'

'That's right – it's too much! And you're choking me!' I slammed down the receiver and switched off the phone.

I understood that Mary was hurt *again*, but I was losing my patience with her. It was a relief that she was going off to Pride with her mates. It was proving too much. The bitterness, the jealousy... re-curring like a nightmare, suffocating me.

Hanging on the chill air, the dirty laundry of our words, pegged out with her pain. Discord flutters grudges like unwashed sheets.

10
Mary: Incy wincy spider

Outside the Union, I drew my mobile out of my pocket. I frowned. Still nothing. I pressed for Tanya's number and the electronic voice cut in. Damn! She'd switched off her phone. I was just about to start a text when Clancy appeared, peering at my phone. I put it away hurriedly.

'Give it a rest eh, Mare? Enjoy the freedom! It's dyke heaven here! Loosen up and let's go women-spotting!' Clancy had told me that when she was single she'd collect women's phone numbers like a train-spotter collected numbers. I trusted she didn't mean to go that far today, but I smiled and went along with her.

'Look – what about her?' She indicated a tall woman with frizzy blonde hair, in a white vest.

'Too thin!' I downed the last of my pint.

'Nice arse, though… Well her, then!' She nodded towards a chunky butch dyke.

'Too butch!'

'Her?' A plump woman with auburn hair.

'Too fat!'

'Hark at you! Okay – what about her?' Clancy pointed to a slim woman with long brown hair.

'Too femme!'

'Goldilocks says, "and this woman is too-oo… lumpy!" Jeez! You're hard to please, Mare! Cilla Black never has this much trouble!'

'Thing is, Clance – I'm spoken for. Just not interested!'

'Hark at her!' Clancy said to a woman with spiky black hair who passed by and grinned. Then Clancy spun round and hissed, 'What about her?'

'Cla-ancy...' I warned, amused, 'I'm taken!'

'Bloody hell! You're not her possession!' she muttered into her glass. 'We're only doing a bit of window-shopping! Bet Tanya's not keeping herself to herself while the cat's away!'

My smile vanished and I gripped a tighter hold on the mobile in my pocket. I wandered off to stand by Clare. She glanced at me and managed half a smile. I nudged her. 'Having fun, Clare?'

She raised one eyebrow and said in a monotone, 'Absolute ball, Mary. Absolute ball.'

'Absolute bollocks!' Clancy was there again, waving a crushed leaflet in her hand, 'It's the gay barbershop quartet on next! They're called "Absolute Bollocks"! Is that great or what?' She bent over laughing, grabbing hold of Clare, who sidestepped away, hissing, 'Get off me!'

'I'll have to watch this!' Clancy wiped a tear from her eye.

The small fat guy compering was droning on about the afternoon ahead then announced, 'It's my pleasure to introduce the next act, who are – by their own admission – ABSOLUTE BOLLOCKS!'

The audience gave hoots of laughter and appreciative claps as the four men stepped up on to the stage, all wearing bright Hawaiian shirts. They were in various stages of receding hairline. They started up their four-part harmony. Clancy gripped on to me, crying with hilarity, then drew a few long intakes of breath, interrupted by howls of laughter, till she managed to get out her words: 'Sl... hee... Slapheads! They're... all... slapheads! Barbershop! That barber's got a lot to answer for! He he hee! Absolute Bollocks – my arse!'

The same camp guy with the thin moustache looked disapprovingly at us. Clancy's eyes were streaming with tears. I clapped my hand round her mouth and smiled apologetically at the guy. He sniffed haughtily and swung his head round to face the stage. Clancy wrestled away from my grip and whispered, 'It's okay – I'm okay now!' Then she gave a great whine... and howled, 'NO, I'm NOT!' and guffawed with laughter. She ran into the bar area and I followed her, having been entertained for long enough by Absolute Bollocks. I saw her at the front of the bar and shouted for her to get me a pint. Then I made my way over to Kerry and the others, who were sitting in a corner.

'No way!' Kerry was shouting, her big red face beaming. Two of the women, Hilary and Pat, were gesticulating a lot and the crowd burst out laughing. I dragged a couple of stools over to join them, feeling a bit sober and out of things with this gang. Hilary, a pretty black woman I'd never met before today, was obviously very drunk. She held up her pint glass, slopping beer all over Pat, who shrieked.

'Toast!' said Hilary, her voice thick and slurring, 'To gorgeous women! To us!'

'Toast? I'm starving!' shouted Kerry. 'I want toast! Do they do toast? CLANCY,' she roared, 'I'm hungry! Get me toast!'

The others fell about laughing, while some bloke who could have been the bar manager looked on warningly, trying to make eye contact with one of us. Since I was the only one whose eyes weren't wavering drunkenly or closed completely, he picked me, indicating for us to keep the noise down. I wasn't sure this was within my jurisdiction, but I hissed, 'The landlord says can we shut up a bit...?' to no avail. Then Clancy appeared with a tray full of drinks and packets of crisps, to great cheers.

Clancy sat down and grinned, took a swig of her lager, then showed the gang the leaflet and explained about Absolute Bollocks, continuing: 'Says here there's a women's band on later... Hope they're not Absolute Cunts!' A great roar came up and the bar manager looked daggers at me.

I got out my mobile for a sly peek. Nothing. I went to the toilet and sat in a cubicle to get rid of several pints, make room for more and try to ring Tanya. I called but the answerphone went straight on, so I left a whispered message: 'Hey Tan! Just called to see if you're okay! It's fun, but I miss you!' I wiped myself, then suddenly thought that she might not pick up her voicemail, so I texted her:

HI! AM ON TOILET. THINKIN BOUT U. LUVU. XXXX

And sent it. Then I realised what I'd said, so I had to text again:

OOPS! DIDN'T MEAN THAT HOW IT SOUNDED! I LOVU + MISS U, WISH U WER HERE 4 GOOD TIME. HAVIN FUN BUT NOT SAME WTHOUT U XXXX

I sent it and went to wash my hands. I looked in the mirror and sucked my teeth. God, I looked haggard and it was only ten to three. I wet my hair and tried to fluff it up a bit, give it some life. I looked at my mobile again. Nothing. I switched it off, then on again. Then Big Mandy came into the toilets.

'Hiya – Ah – I see what you're up to!' She laughed, and swung into a cubicle.

'Just checking my phone!' I said guiltily and went out. The crowd were still in the bar but I wanted some air, so I had a wander round the stalls again. I signed a petition against Section 28 and one against animal cruelty and I also registered for the mailing list of a women's bookshop. The entertainment was still Absolute Bollocks.

'All right, lads – give it a rest now!' someone sighed behind me. 'You *are* Absolute Bollocks – you don't need to convince us!'

I turned round to see a girl with purple hair tufted with multi-coloured butterfly clasps all over her head. But she was an adult – I don't think her mum had made her do it. She had a friendly, open face and a tiny diamond stud glittered on her nose. She rolled her eyes at me and grinned. 'There's only so much Bollocks a girl can take.'

'Too right!' I grinned back.

Her green eyes twinkled. 'Been inside?'

My hands went instinctively up to my face, 'cause I'd got blue felt-tip pen marks on it once, and they'd been mistaken for borstal tattoos. We'd been in a rough pub, and Clancy'd had to do some fast talking on my behalf, that time. So I was serious when I said, in shock, 'Oh! Do I look like I've been in prison?'

She laughed, more at my look of horror than my mistake, then shook her head: 'You don't look like a very Bad Girl to me! Hey, I'm Becky!' I introduced myself and she asked, 'Have you been inside the Union – seen the stalls and things?'

'No...' I frowned. I didn't know there was anything else.

'Well, come on then –' she grabbed my hand and dragged me off '– let's get away from these sad old baldies and find some women!'

Her hand was cool and dry, so I was worried mine felt clammy. As she sped off, with me attached, I was amused to see Georgie and Robbo looking quite impressed. I took a better look at her as she pulled me up the stairs. Nice arse, as Clancy would say. She was wearing a blue tie-dyed T-shirt and a short purple batik skirt over blue leggings and purple Doc Martens. Hmm.

We got to the top of the stairs and she stood panting, still holding my hand, her round face flushed with exertion. She gasped, 'Okay – where to?' I frowned. I didn't even know the choice so she carried on, 'There's Tai Chi for women...'

'Dyke Chi?'

She took a closer look at me, then laughed in surprise. 'Yeah! Or... well, there's a discussion on transsexuality...' I shook my head. 'Or there's the health market – loads of stalls on safe sex 'n' AIDS 'n' stuff- and some freebies – lube 'n' dental dams 'n' stuff...' I blushed, 'cause I'd never met anyone who'd got to this point so quickly. She must've seen my look of alarm because she laughed. 'I see you're not interested! So – there's salsa dancing later on – or a Wild Woman workshop in about half an hour! Up for that?' I probably still looked bewildered and could feel my hand getting clammier as she went on, 'Well, you're evidently a woman of few words, so what about getting in touch with your wild woman?'

'She's at home!' I said and felt for my mobile.

Becky roared with laughter, letting go of my sweaty palm to slap her thigh like a principal boy. 'Ha! I knew I'd like you!'

I took the opportunity to wipe the sweat off my hand on to my own thigh in case she held my hand again. She stood with her hands on her hips, looking like she was weighing me up. About thirteen and a half stone, I could've told her. Mind you, she looked young enough to be metric. In which case, I was way out of my depth.

11
Tanya: Childhood idylls

My remembrance of my grandmother is only of good things. Then I wonder if I have built a sort of idyll of her memory, an idol of her. I do remember peace there. But was it really always the start of summer at her house? Was the sun always warm on my skin when I was near her? Was there always the scent of blossom in the air? Was I always in the garden – her garden? Maybe there wasn't always the scent of baking and good home cooking aromas at her house. Maybe she didn't bake cakes. Maybe she didn't knit me soft wool jumpers. Maybe she didn't read me books and engender in me a love of words, a love of stories. Maybe she didn't sit me on her knee and cuddle me. Maybe she didn't sing me lullabies. Maybe she didn't exist. Maybe it's all a fantasy. Maybe I made it all up.

It is ironic that this angel – my much beloved grandmother – was the mother of my own mother. How could they have shared the same genetic make-up? How could my mother have learned such callous ways from such a loving mother as she had? So much for the nature versus nurture debate. What happened in that family? What happened there to my poor sick mother? What gave her that twisted view of maternity, that evil brand of child-rearing, that hatred of her first-born, her only-born? That relentless purpose: to make me suffer? Some liberal pseudo-psychological view might make allowances for her. Not me. I can vouch for her innate evil. Perhaps she was a changeling from my grandmother's fairy tales: a satanic malformed thing, swapped for my grandmother's own dear child. Left in my real mother's place as the clock struck midnight during a fierce and unearthly storm, whilst forked lightning cracked the livid sky and thunderous booms shook the house to its very foundations. Only that can explain it. My real mother was taken by some evil force and this... this thing was left in her place. That explained it. Changeling child. She was no kin of ours. But if she were... what does that make me? I despise even her memory. She was never one of my family. Not like the loving, idealised families I read about. An Enid Blyton mother making homemade lemonade and baking sticky buns with lashings of cream for all one's chums. Tucking one up in bed. In bed... Bed...

Of course, I hear that child-parent relationships change and evolve. We often feel alienated from our parents, especially during those introspective, brooding teenage years when we believe that nobody understands us. Dark moods assailed me then. Thoughts of death and murder. Thoughts of suicide and revenge. Teenagers are depressive and dismal creatures and parents are distant and alien forces. We can all imagine ourselves apart from them, not of their blood; we can believe that we have been adopted. Or wish that we had been adopted.

So when I ran away from home at the age of two, like Little Red Riding Hood it was to my grandmother's house I hurried with my basket. But I was no innocent, skipping blithely into danger. I knew the danger all too well and I was actively trying to escape it. Fleeing from the Big Bad Wolf. The same Big Bad Wolf that can huff and puff and blow your house down. Yes, I know that's a different story, but for me it wasn't. My grandmother introduced me to witches, wolves, trolls, nasty goblins, snow queens, wicked step-mothers. They held no fear for me. Mine was the grimmest fairy tale of all.

Granny was warm, home-baked; a caricature granny as stereo typical as any fairytale granny could be. If anything, Mary reminds me of my grandmother. Kind. Gentle. Always thinking of what I might like, bringing me gifts, always remembering my favourite sweets, my favourite flowers, my favourite bleeding washing powder, my favourite damn childhood memory. Her retention of information on me is phenomenal. Frightening. She could win quiz shows if her chosen subject were Tanya Helliwell.

'What is Tanya Helliwell's favourite colour?'

'Cobalt blue.'

'Correct. Name Tanya Helliwell's first cat.'

'Pusskin.'

'Correct. At the age of eight, Tanya Helliwell was punished in front of the whole school. For six points: name the crime, name the punishment, name the school, name the teacher who punished her, name the first person she spoke to afterwards and what she said.'

'Breaking a window. Five smacks with the school slipper. Armley Ridge Primary School. Mrs Sedgeley. Darren Boothwaite. "Look at me like that and I'll smack you."'

'Correct. How many pints of urine has Tanya Helliwell passed in her life?'

She'd get that right too, no doubt. She has gathered piece by piece an encyclopaedic knowledge of my life. She is an obsessive. There is nothing she doesn't want to know. She knows more about me than I do about myself. She would make a splendid spy: so comprehensively intrusive, so casually pervasive. There is nothing I could say without her committing it to memory and filing it away. I found it flattering at first. Now it is merely oppressive. She haunts me. She stalks me. She is really getting on my nerves. It is no longer flattering, it is plainly weird. But I do keep some things to myself. She cannot have all of me.

My mother also had a retentive memory when it suited her. Words would flash out and wound me: 'That packet of biscuits in the back of the cupboard! Where are they? You fat cow!'

Naturally I tried to keep out of her way, but until I was able to get away to college, until I was legally able to leave the so-called family home for good, I had to come back each night, eventually. Then it was a case of trying to sneak back into the house. She would sometimes wait up, but not because she worried about my safety and welfare so late at night. She waited up because she was counting down the minutes until she could fly at me, with every minute intensifying her fury until I returned to be faced with her, by which time she was spitting. On the other hand, sometimes she wasn't even up when I got back. You never knew. The delicious unexpectedness of it all...

If I wasn't back too late, I might just flounce in to be met by a barrage of questions and accusations.

'You said you'd be back at nine!' She would turn on me at ten past nine, her black eyes beady and shining with fury.

'Yes, but Alison's dad was going to give me a lift back and he was late.'

'Oh – late! I bet he was late! And what were you up to with him, you little slut? You whore! You bitch!' Slapping. Usually slapping when I was old enough to fight back. But I never did. The worst I would do was to grip hold of her wrists while she struggled to get a good hard hit on me. White-knuckled, I would grip on to her body's bucking roller-coaster – yank, bend, jerk, sway, thrash, kick, push, bite – until it came to a halt. Then she would suddenly swerve in mid-air and judder to butt me in the stomach, but there are only so many ways a woman can fight with her wrists held. There are only so many manoeuvres in unskilled hand-to-hand combat. And I had all hers in check. We would wrestle for a while, with her clawing and spitting at me. Although she was small, she was strong and wiry, but I could still restrain her till she tired of shouting and fighting, 'Bitch! Whore!' She invariably tired before I did, then I would let her drop gently to the floor and release her from my scratched hands. I'd wipe her phlegm or spittle from my face and, with as much dignity as I retained, I would go up to my room, lock the door and leave her snivelling and muttering to herself.

The locked door. My first step to independence. My first step to take control of my own life. There wasn't a lock on my door until I put one on, by myself. I know that I was in my early teens when I did it. I know it was neessary for me to stop her coming into my room at night. That I stop her trying to kill me in her usual way. Do you remember the eager anticipation of Christmas when you couldn't sleep because you knew that at some point Father Christmas was going to sneak into your room and leave a stocking full of presents? And how thrilling it was and how the excitement was all too much and you were half demented with wanting to stay awake and half asleep because you knew, even so excited, that nothing would happen until you did drift off, until you surrendered to sleep? Well, it wasn't quite like that. It wasn't Christmas Eve every night, but it was something like. Something more chilling. And it wasn't as if she did it every night. There was no rhythm to it, no ritual, no regularity. You never knew, until you had drifted off into an innocent sleep and found yourself struggling for breath, drowning in pillow, fighting to catch air in your lungs. I still have nightmares. It's strange that in your safest moments, years after your torment has stopped, there is still part of yourself that doesn't let you rest. That makes you wary. My mother has the last laugh, all right. I still am haunted by the memories. The smacking, the kicking, the biting, that is nothing. I have the scars, to be sure, but I could always take care of myself. I'm still here, aren't I? Physical abuse is nothing. Nothing like the panic in the black of night or the middle of some dream in which you can't catch your breath. You can't catch your own breath because someone else has taken it. Yes Mother, you may be dead and gone, but you still take my breath away. I cannot control and I cannot affect my nightmares and still I wake up gasping, crying, suffocating. In real life there are strategies to cope with anything. Secrecy is one. A lock on the door is another.

Naturally my mother was displeased with my lock. When she first discovered it, it was about one o'clock one morning and the first I knew was her hammering on the door with her fists and bawling and swearing.

'You fucking bitch! Open this door! Bitch!' Then the sound of something wooden against the wood. Smash! Bash! Crack! And other comic strip noises from that caricature of a woman they called my mother. I sat up in bed hugging my knees, rocking backwards and forwards, staring at the door and willing it to hold. And it did. I found her bedroom chair the next morning in a buckled heap outside my door, two gilt legs splintered and the pink velour seat ripped. She didn't get in and although I still didn't get any sleep that night I saw it as a victory. Even though she stopped hammering and shouting after half an hour, my mind would not let me rest. Victory! Yet an awareness that this was only one battle in a long war. Because she was not strong enough to shoulder the door down that night, she set about unscrewing the bolt the next day while I was at school. I had already made alternative arrangements for this eventuality, should it arise. I had another bolt which I studiously screwed in that evening. More hammering, more bawling. More bolts. I stole money out of her purse to buy bolts. I was waiting for her to tire of joinery. One day I came home to find that she had removed the entire bedroom door. She had made a terrible job of it, too. I painstakingly re-hung it, with a reinforced panel where her foot had cracked it. We were both extremely resourceful. I am not a strong, tall, broad-backed hefty figure like Mary, but it is possible to act with amazing strength should the need arise. Eventually my mother tired of this nightly siege upon my room and tired of the daily removal of the bolts. I outlasted her in that and I am proud of this fact. I outwitted her and I have outlived her, too. There is cause for celebration, after all.

What of the neighbours? All this row, even in the early hours of the morning? Surely someone must have done something? There's a lot to be said for secrecy. A lot to be said for the middle classes. Too polite to interfere. Mrs Shimmin, ill herself with Parkinson's disease, would never dream of confronting my mother. The neighbours in the house on the other side were so aloof that they pretended we did not exist. And one simply did not interfere. No police on our law-abiding terrace. No social workers in our bourgeois estate. Mrs Shimmin did her bit, by letting me stay and play at her house occasionally and by taking me to Sunday school... but you are never safe anywhere. You can only rely on yourself. You can rely only on yourself. You can rely on yourself only.

So I distance myself from Mary these days. She is becoming a liability. A danger to herself. A danger to me, moreover. And we can't have that. That will not do at all. Still, I have been foolish enough to entrust her with my secrets. Not all of them of course, but enough for her to use against me. Enough for her to tarnish me, to bandy about, to scandalize the neighbourhood. That is of no concern to me. But I am concerned for myself. She has enough of my small secrets to possess me a little. She has a piece of my soul and for all that I would want it back, I am uncertain how to go about it. I shall need to ponder on that. I need a cunning plan. To keep myself intact.

12
Mary: Wild, wild women

Becky narrowed her friendly green eyes: 'Hmmm, okay – if you don't want to do the health stalls, we've got time for a quick drink before going to the workshop and being wild women. How about I buy you a drink if you come with me – first to the bar, then to the workshop? Can you resist a free drink?'

'I guess not!' I grinned. 'But I warn you – all my mates are in the bar and they're pretty wild women!'

'The more the merrier! Sound like my kind of people!' She held out her hand, so I took it now that I'd wiped the sweat from mine and she dragged me all the way down the stairs again and into the bar.

'Okay! Where are your mates?' I nodded towards the noise and she raised an amused eyebrow. 'Ok-aaaaay. What d'you want to drink?'

I went to join the gang, who were suddenly twice as drunk as before. I hesitated, wondering if I should slip into a seat on the other side of the room. But too late – Hilary had spotted me and was shrieking. 'Oh! Thing! It's Thingy! Oooo-eeee! Thingy!' She was so loud, she almost woke Kerry up. Kerry just lifted her crease-marked face from the maroon velveteen bench, straggly hair across her eyes, smacked her lips together and settled back down to sleep. Big Mandy was stroking Kerry's hair and explaining that Kerry was 'operating from distress'.

Pat and Robbo were trying to remember all the words to "The

Womble Song", so every conversation was punctuated with, '*Overground, underground… NO!… Underground, overground, wombling FREE!*' Clancy was muttering something very seriously and intently to Clare, who sat with a thunderous face and her thin bluish arms folded tightly across her chest. A couple of the other women in our crowd were snogging passionately. I looked nervously across the room towards Becky, who was dangerously close to getting her change and coming over with the drinks. I decided to head her off and stood up, but Hilary caught my arm and beckoned me closer with a swooping finger. Her lovely coffee skin was flushed and her dark brown eyes were bloodshot, her focus wavering slowly from my eyes to my shoulder, to above my head, to behind my ear. 'Thingy! Don't go, darlin'! No! Tell 'er, Trish… Tell Thingy…'

'*Uncle BULGARIA! He … da-de-dah…da-de-dah… dah de dah-dah…be-hind the TIMES!*'

I was starting to panic – it was like bringing a vicar to a tea-party in hell. I was embarrassed and ashamed – I wished I'd never agreed to a drink. And what was I thinking, anyway? How had I got landed with this strange woman – Becky – when I had a girlfriend anyway? Oh, Tanya – will you forgive me?

'*Pick up – the pieces and make them into something NE-EW! Shh-s what we do…*'

Becky held out a pint glass to me. I grimaced apologetically and took it, thanking her. I had to shout above the singing and Clancy and Clare's now-raised voices: 'CHEERS! SORRY ABOUT THIS!'

Pat and Robbo's singing fell into sudden silence, so my voice rang clearly as I continued, 'MY MATES ARE IDIOTS!'

Pat and Robbo frowned, insulted. Hilary's head waggled precariously on her neck while she chuckled, 'Eejits… eejits.'

'You fuckin' whore!' Clancy shouted, drawing back her hand as if to slap Clare's face – then stopping herself. She ran off out of the bar.

'Oh, shit!' I said, 'Sorry Becky – can you hold this?' I thrust my pint at her. 'Best-mate emergency!' I pushed past the crowd and went off in Clancy's direction. She was speeding away and I had to run to reach her. I put my hand on her shoulder. 'Clancy!'

She swung round and for a moment I thought she was going to hit me. Her fists were clenched tight and she was rigid with fury.

She looked at me with wild eyes. 'Leave me alone!'

'Clancy? What is it?' I'd never seen her like this.

'Fuck off out of it, Mare. You don't wanna know!' Her small mouth was twisted and white, while the rest of her face was florid with rage. She glared at the ground, cocking her head taut.

I was at a loss: 'Clance – I'm your mate! What's happened?'

She sniffed hard, narrowing her nostrils, then rubbed her mouth and cheeks edgily. She tugged the skin beneath her nose thoughtfully. Her fingernails were bitten right down and little inflamed scabs had erupted from the raw skin around her cuticles.

'Hey… I can appreciate it if you wanna be alone, but I'm worried 'bout ya, Clance… Anything I can do?'

She laughed a cruel, dismissive laugh, then shook her head and said gently, 'No, Mare… no…' She took hold of my arm, as if to comfort me and she smiled unconvincingly. 'But thanks, pet. Look – I'll be okay…' I frowned at her. 'Mare, honest! Look – see me grin?' She bared her teeth in a semblance of cheerfulness. I looked back blankly, searching her eyes and seeing only her hurt.

She sighed a great, deep sigh, 'What can I say, Mare? Just a fight. Just another fight. Just something between me and… her. Not to worry!' She patted me on the arm. 'Look, you get off and do your thing, back in the bar. I'm fine. I'm not gonna do anything stupid, so don't worry. I'll see you later, yeah?'

'What time? Where?' I wanted reassurance she wouldn't try to run off back to Middlesbrough. I wanted to keep an eye on her. My stomach twisted in fear.

She smiled a more authentic smile. 'Synchronise watches? What are you like? Okay, let's say – couple of hours? Side of the stage? Get something to eat?'

'Okay – yeah – half six, then!'

'You bet! Now get off, back!'

'You mean get off your back!' I tried to make light.

'That's right! So long!' She dismissed me with a wave and walked off. I rocked on to the balls of my feet, ready to chase after her. But stopped myself. I watched her tiny, downcast figure hurry away. Then I headed back to the bar. I noticed Clare had disappeared, and everyone was a bit subdued, muttering amongst themselves.

Becky was now standing by the bar. She held my pint out again – 'Okay?' – and scrutinised my face for clues.

'Think so... just a domestic...' I took a great swig of lager.

'Worrying though,' said Becky. I liked her. Then I remembered Tanya and my mobile and took it out to see if there were any texts. Damn – one message. I pressed to read it:

STILL SOBER? DON'T DO ANYTHING I'D DO! T X

Only one kiss.

'Hmmm – I suspect I've lost my appeal!' Becky's voice cut through my thoughts of texting Tanya. I looked up, but Becky's face was still friendly and smiling.

'Oh, shit! Sorry – didn't mean to be ignorant. Just distracted.'

'You meant to be distracted?'

'Ohh... sorry, no...' I struggled, but she laughed.

'No worries! Just as long as your friend's okay...' She nodded towards my mobile, still in my hand.

'Oh! Different friend,' I explained. I blushed, shrugged and put the phone back in my pocket.

'Still up for being a wild woman?'

'Oh, God... er... yes!' I'd promised.

'I talked a couple of your pals into it, too.' She nodded towards the gang, who were still a bit subdued although Pat, Robbo and Hilary had started singing... 'Evergreen', I think, although you couldn't tell from the tune. If it was a tune.

'*...ONE! Love that is shared by two...*'

Becky whistled with two fingers: '*Phwe-eee-eep!*' I was impressed. Then she cupped her hand round her mouth to yell, 'Oy! Wild women! Follow me!'

I held my breath to see who was making a move. Really, if I was going to this workshop at all, I'd rather have made a fool of myself in front of strangers than in front of any mates. But by the looks of it, most of them would be too pissed to notice. Disturbingly, Big Mandy was pulling Kerry up by the arms. Kerry's head was still on the bench seat, but not for long as Hilary – still singing '*Every day, a beginning!*' – leant over and pulled Kerry's head up.

Actually, Hilary's voice was really quite good but I was still alarmed to see that Big Mandy and Hilary were trying to walk Kerry towards us.

Pat and Robbo, renewed in spirit, also stood up and joined in less tunefully.

'*Two hearts that be-ee-eat as one –*'

While Becky, a purple-haired pied piper, led this raggle-taggle staggering line of women up the stairs, we met Georgie halfway up. Sober and smart, she took one look at her partner Robbo – somewhat dishevelled and worse for wear, arm-in-arm with skinny Pat – and decided she'd better follow too.

'Do you think this is a good idea?' I hissed to Big Mandy, as the most sensible one of the crowd. She had Kerry's body slumped between her and Hilary. Kerry was barely conscious, her hair hanging like a mop in need of wringing out. Every few steps her half-attempts to walk would fail and they had to trail her legs behind them. Georgie took charge and picked Kerry up by the waistband of her jeans. It was now taking three people to carry her.

'I want to keep my eye on her.' Big Mandy puffed. 'Don't worry, we'll just fling her in a corner and she can sleep it off.'

'Do you think this is a good idea?' I hissed to Becky. She shrugged.

We burst into the room a little late for the Wild Woman workshop. Half a dozen people were walking round and round the room, saying hello to one another and shaking hands. The workshop leader was a small round woman with a halo of frizzy grey hair, who wore a loose patchwork shirt, dusty blue trousers, hairy socks with red sandals and a big name-badge. She stopped mid-sentence as we careered in dragging an unconscious woman with us.

Before the leader could speak to protest, Big Mandy held up her hand to stop her, saying, 'Awfully sorry!'

Kerry rolled out of her arms and sank to the floor with a soft moan. Hilary giggled.

'Sorry! She'll be okay... I just didn't want to leave her by herself...' Big Mandy explained.

'This is... okay...' The workshop leader came closer to inspect Kerry, with some alarm and distaste. She suggested that they leave Kerry in the recovery position. With some alarm of my own, I saw that the leader's name-badge labelled her HECATE WICCAWOMYN. I looked wildly around the room. Then I realised that looking wild was quite appropriate. Our gang was given big labels to write our names on, while the already-inducted members of the sect – Tabitha, Phyllida, Daz, Wilhelmina, Chandelier, and Debbie – were asked to hum loudly and monotonously, till we'd finished. I still looked around nervously, afraid that we'd walked into some Seventies time warp. Sixties, Seventies, Eighties – sometime decades past. Georgie dragged Kerry into a corner, where she was less likely to get trampled underfoot. She rolled her on to her side and arranged her arms and legs so she looked like a human swastika.

I stuck my name-badge on so my left nipple was now called Mary. I glanced sadly at the right one. I looked up to see where the others had put theirs. Disturbingly, according to their labels, Hilary seemed to be called AFRODEEZIA, Pat was called EVERGREEN and Robbo was called ADELAIDE, which *really* freaked me till I remembered that it actually *was* her first name. I suddenly wondered if I'd missed something. Had this Hecate-woman told us to write special names? My MARY looked so dull against all this AMANDA and GEORGINA business that my mates had got

into. Even Becky was REBECCA. I didn't recognise anyone. I felt in
adequate. Then I realised that Hecate-woman was talking and I'd
probably missed something else vitally important. They'd all moved
into the centre of the room.

'… And in your circle,' Hecate-woman went on, 'You will touch
hands with the person next to you… palm against palm…'

I hustled to get next to Becky. At least she didn't seem to mind my
sweaty palms. Hilary was laughing out loud, Pat and Robbo struggling
to overcome giggles. Big Mandy was looking threateningly at them. I
was crushed up between Becky and Phyllida, a girl with a huge mouth
and a pony-tail that made her look even more like a horse.

'Close your eyes and feel the heat between your palms…' I didn't
need to. I knew they were clammy already and I could also feel sweat
trickling down my spine. 'Then I want you to hum…' I ducked my
head suddenly to my armpit, afraid that I might be smelly. Becky
opened her eyes at the jerk of my hand and smiled. I remembered that
I hadn't returned Tanya's text. Oh, well…

'Softly at first… a single note… Your note… so you can barely hear
it…' All I could hear were Hilary's whimpers of restrained laughter.
'Then louder and louder…' The hum increased… 'Louder and
louder… Till humming is not enough and you need to make a louder
sound… Ahhh! … Then open your eyes… Ahhh! … Increase it… Loud
as you can!' A crescendo built up, till we were all shouting as loud as
we could. I was shouting till my throat felt like it would burst. 'And
stop!'

'Fuckin' hell!' A voice rang out from the corner. We turned to see
Kerry, up on one elbow, rubbing one eye with her fist and squinting
through her mussed-up hair. 'What the fuck's that?'

We all fell about laughing and chattering.

'Sorry!' Big Mandy said to Hecate-woman and bustled over to
Kerry. She squatted over her, talking urgently and low.

Hecate-woman tutted in irritation and said loudly, 'If you're not
taking it seriously, please leave! It is essential to concentrate…'

Tabitha, a pretty blonde teenager, nodded earnestly and scowled at Hilary and Pat, who were still smirking. Robbo was behaving herself, aware of Georgie's disapproval. Phyllida was still looking like a horse. I'd even heard her neigh at the end of the yelling: a sputtering kind of whinnying laugh. I gazed at her in wonder. Then I turned to Becky and gazed at her in wonder. She was good looking. My mobile weighed heavy in my hip pocket.

Hecate-woman was instructing us all to lie down on the floor, so we all clattered down and settled on the carpet. She told us to close our eyes and imagine that our bodies were really, really heavy. That didn't take much imagination. Thirteen and a half stone. I was really, really heavy. She told us to imagine we were becoming one with the earth. I could feel my buttocks leaving great craters in the carpet. Then Hecate-woman led us through fields – which I'm sure Phyllida enjoyed galloping through – and woods, describing things along the way. Someone – possibly Big Mandy – tiptoed across the room and settled down on the floor. Hecate-woman led us onwards, stopping to invite us to look around, and giving Phyllida a chance to crop some fresh grass. Her voice was soothing and even Hilary had stopped giggling. I thought about Clancy and wondered what time it was now. I felt as if we'd been here days. I wondered what Tanya was doing. Must ring her. I felt guilty. I could hear Becky's even breathing beside me and soft snorts from the horse on the other side. Becky was nice. She must fancy me… Or why would she grab me and want to spend time with me? Unless she felt sorry for me. Or someone had dared her, like the lads at school discos egging each other on to get off with the ugliest girl in the room. Nah – she was nice, she wouldn't do that. Did she feel sorry for me, though? Was I so pitiful? Or was someone testing me? Had she been paid to tempt me? A test of fidelity! If you're suspicious your partner's having an affair, you can pay a 'decoy' to try to seduce them and trap them! Would Tanya do that? Was it possible? Maybe! So far, had I done anything to encourage her? Sometimes it was just a matter of taking the decoy's phone number. That was enough proof. God! I must be careful.

I felt a foot poking my knee. I looked up to see Becky standing above me.

'Are you asleep too?' she asked, hands on hips.

'No!' I sat up and looked around. The room was empty except for our lot. Kerry lying in one corner snoring loudly, Big Mandy sitting beside her, chin in hands and Hilary and Pat both sound asleep on the floor in the middle of the room. Hilary had even curled up on her side, sucking her thumb. Pat lay sprawled on her back, like she'd been shot.

'What time is it?' I panicked. Had I been asleep? It was quarter past six. God! When was I meeting Clancy? Six-thirty. Plenty of time.

'Coming to the salsa?' Becky smiled.

'Oh, er... love to, but gotta see Clancy. You know... my friend who was upset.'

'Okay,' Becky's smile wavered. 'See you later then, at the disco?'

'Yeah... yeah...' I said distractedly and pulled out my mobile. I re-read Tanya's last text.

'Bye, then...' Becky moved off, uncertainly.

I stared at the phone: 'Yeah...'

DON'T DO ANYTHING I'D DO.

What did that mean, then?

13

Tanya: On my own

Want a piece of me? You want a piece of me? Everyone wants a piece of me. I get sick of other people's expectations. For fuck's sake! I have no obligations to anyone!

To be quite frank, okay – I like to have things to do. I like to be busy, but not to everyone else's agenda – not fulfilling everyone else's demands. I like to push myself to the point of exhaustion, but on my own terms. But so many demands! So many needy women! So many pulls on my time, for my attention!

I decided to take a break. Chill, for a day. Have a woman-free day to myself. And then the bloody texts every five minutes! I wished that I had never given my mobile phone number to Mary. It was sweet of her to keep in touch, nice that she texted me so frequently, but sweetness and niceness are traits too tiring to endure for long. Of that I was certain. She was annoying me now. Perhaps I was ungrateful and undeserving of the degree of love she gave me. But so much! So many texts! So intrusive – so possessive, so disruptive. Safer to leave my mobile switched off for lengthy periods of time. Which meant that no one could get hold of me. Not even Christiane.

So, what liberty! I took advantage of Mary's trip to Pride in Newcastle to wander around Saltburn, calling in to Sheila's delicatessen to pick up some fine cheese and some of Sheila's 'special recipe' stuffed peppers; wandering around the salesrooms, leaving bids on some small pieces of Clarice Cliff that took my eye. I stood chatting to the man in the Healthfood shop while I browsed through the spices, enjoying the heavy, heady scents and picked up my jar of tahina. Glorious to have no plans, no one to dash off to see or do. Yes: *sic*. No one to do! It was a crisp fresh day which cheered me mightily and I was even enjoying the dull weekly shopping at Somerfield supermarket, safe in the knowledge that I wasn't being tailed. I deliberately didn't switch on the computer, uninterested in cyber today. I got home and spread myself out on the sofa, switched my music up and indulged myself by reading most of the *Guardian*.

I also took advantage of Mary being out of the way when Red called me quite late in the afternoon, when I'd felt it safe to switch my phone on: 'Tanya – great news for you, I know. I'm unexpectedly free! So – fancy getting together? I've got hours to spare and the kids are at their grandmother's all night. I could even stay over!'

Now, I am not interested in domestic arrangements. I am not interested in kids. If Red tried to engage me in stories of her partner and her kids: the trauma, the delights – that was a complete turn-off to me. I did not wish to know anything of these matters. I did not care about the details of why or how Red came to be free that day. I did not care about her family. I barely cared about Red. It was simply enough that she was free – and willing. Obviously horny, which fact delighted me in a way I would not reveal. Suffice to say, I was glad to hear from her, having spent enough time in my own enjoyable company, but said coolly that it was also convenient for me. We were in the rare position of having two possible venues – both houses. Those days I rarely brought Red to my house. I was sick of Mary popping over at the drop of a hat (yeah – Mary Poppins, all right!) and, like players in a bedroom farce, Red and I had often hidden out of sight at the knocking of the door or the ringing of the bell. We had giggled in the bath or sniggered in the bed and I had taken to drawing the living-room curtains to give us some privacy from callers. Mary, most frequently. Still, situation comedy aside, it was beginning to infuriate me. I told Red only that I had a jealous ex who still bothered me, but I did not furnish her with a name and Red was not curious enough to enquire. I relied on Red's discretion and family situation to provide the safety we both needed for what she termed 'illicit' sex.

Sex is as nothing to me. A pastime. A diversion. An exercise. An amusement. A pleasantry. A service. A hunger. An itch to be scratched. Do not let us confuse sex and love, for God's sake. Incidentally, I do not believe in God, either.

So when Red, fired with the prospect of a clear evening ahead, suggested going out for a meal, maybe a drink, then coming back to my place – that felt too much like a date for my liking. Too much commitment. Besides, it was the coming back to my place I was more interested in. We had to make the most of these situations. It wasn't often that we got the chance to roll naked around anybody's bed without a strict one hour's evening or lunchtime slot to work in. It was quite safe for her to come over to my house, but I insisted that I went to hers. The kids were nearly always there when I sneaked around in the evening after bedtime, under cover of darkness. This seemed an ideal opportunity to give the neighbours something to talk about – to make her scream. I showered, changed, sprayed on some perfume (my concession to playing with fire: I like to leave my mark in another woman's bed) and drove off to Red's house in Middlesbrough.

'Oh, but can't we go out for a change, while the night is young?' Red said, with a petulant lip.

'The night is young but we are old,' I said, pushing her indoors.

'Time waits for no woman,' I said, pulling her on to the bed.

'Make hay while the cat's away,' I said, pulling off her G-string with my teeth.

Afterwards Red lay on her back, her hands tucked behind her head on the pillow, staring at the ceiling and twisting her lips to nibble at the skin in the corner of her mouth. I pretended to doze. She sighed heavily. I kept my eyes closed. She turned to look at me from time to time – I felt her shift in weight. Half an hour at least passed. Several more pointedly heavy sighs. Then she got up completely, put on her bathrobe and went out. I took the opportunity to get dressed swiftly, so that by the time she came upstairs with two mugs of tea, I was zipping up my leather jacket.

She looked furious, 'What? Where are you going? I've got all evening!'

'Maybe you have, darlin', but I haven't! Catch ya later!' I fondled her arse on my way out of the door and she shrieked and spilt the tea.

'TANYA!' she shouted down the stairwell, as I slammed the front door behind me.

'You motherfucker!' she screamed out of the window as I climbed into my car. There was something for the neighbours, after all.

I'd had sex. I didn't want to talk. I'd had quite enough, thank you – and conversation wasn't actually what I'd come for. The thought of more of Red's agenda appalled me. I felt sick. I now had an overwhelming urge just to please myself. A sudden burst of selfishness or self-preservation that was irresistible to me. An urge to get away, go home, do only what I wanted. Basic needs. I wanted to be in control. Get me out of here. Away from Red and all that she'd begun to say. Internet women were more malleable. I knew where I was with them. On top. And life was simple. There was no such thing as commitment for me there. I could flirt as much as I chose with whomsoever I chose. I was free. There was no one trying to control me. I was the one in control. There were no women there with family ties, with which they wanted to bind me. Strings attached. No mothers there. Well, there might be mothers but not in the worlds I inhabited. Or at least, none who made it an issue. Online, all was liberation. No one constricted me there. No one tried to pin me down. There was no one who wanted me to spend the rest of my life with them. No one who wanted me to become part of the family. No one who made demands. Motherfucker. My ears hummed. I could barely breathe. My chest was tight. A band of steel seemed to be tightening around my breasts, pressing in my breastbone, constricting me. Panic. I couldn't breathe properly. I needed to get to fresh air, far away. Escape.

So I sped off from Middlesbrough trying to catch my breath, driving madly through Daletown, regardless of CCTV and speed cameras but aware of the area's reputation for pollution, for asthma, for cancer, for killing, and for constricting your breath. Driving with my windows tight shut. My mouth tight shut. My heart tight shut. Then I hit the dual carriageway and the countryside. Doing the journey home while it was still light pleased me and I was able to recapture the satisfaction I had felt that morning by myself, out in the sun, out in Saltburn. The country air soothed me. I felt as if I hadn't wasted an entire evening. The sun was still shining and the light was soft: a painter's sky. I suddenly decided to drive down the Bank and park on the seafront, so I did. The pleasure of that! I sat outside The Ship Inn, breathing deeply of the sea air with the tide washing out softly before me. I sat quietly with my own thoughts for company, blocked out all that had happened and lived for the moment, soothed by the sound of the sea gently shushing the pebbles. The onomatopoeia of 'shore' and 'sea'. I sat smiling at myself for taking pleasure in the sea's whispering, like the rustle of leaves. But most of all, enjoying the dimming turquoise sky streaked with pink; breathing in the soft salt air and cradling a pint of shandy in both hands until the sun went down.

14

Mary: Pride comes before a fall

Clancy was standing outside the Union with her hands in her pockets and head down, scuffing the toes of her shoes against the outdoor stage when I ran up to speak to her.

'Oh, hi – God! Have you been here long? Sorry.' I panted and ruffled her hair gently.

'Nah! I was early.' She smiled and hugged me. 'Everything okay?'

'With me, yeah! But what about you?'

'Ah well, I've calmed down. Cooled off...'

'Ready to talk?' I didn't want to press her, but she was obviously preoccupied.

'Sorry, Mare. Don't think so, but it's nice of you to ask. Fancy something to eat?'

'Yeah!' I nodded and we set off into town, across the expanses of paving that made up the campus. Clancy was talking animatedly about Chinese, Indian, Italian, Vegetarian, Kebabs, Fish and Chips, Tapas... What did I want? She knew some good places and she was evidently-going-to-talk-about-food-or-anything-else-to-avoid-any-awkward-questions-about-Clare.

We settled on a good pizzeria Clancy knew and set about the garlic bread with a vengeance. Or at least, I did. Clancy set about it with a sad reluctance masked with smiles. When Clancy went to the toilet,

I sneaked a glance at my mobile. No text from Tanya of course, but I just managed to send a quick reply to her earlier message before Clancy got back:

HI! DOIN NOTHIN U'D DO! LUVU XX

Then I worried that she'd think I was being sarcastic. Hmm.

So, by the time Clancy got back, I was sipping my red wine like someone cool, nonchalant, casual, careless, unattached. Then our two steaming bowls of pasta arrived in the hands of a stunning waitress with black curly hair that reminded me of Tanya's, and I started to gabble about the Wild Woman workshop and everything that had happened since Clancy ran off.

Clancy wickedly arched one eyebrow and frowned with the other. 'Aha! So you have another woman!'

'What? No!' I said shocked, and felt myself turn red.

'Oh, no?' Clancy laughed and pointed accusingly at me with a forkful of linguine. 'You've only mentioned this "Becky" about eighty-seven times in the last five minutes! It's all "Becky said" and "Becky did this" and "Becky and me".' I pulled a face at her but she carried on: 'It's all right! Good on yer, girl! Get stuck in!' She pushed the fork-ful of linguine into her mouth and stabbed a mushroom, her mouth full as she went on, 'Will I be having to buy a new hat for the wedding?'

I was scowling so hard at her that my brows were swallowing up my eyes and I could barely see her cheeky grin. 'At least I've cheered you up,' I said with mock bitterness, still frowning.

'Yeah,' she sighed. 'I can do with all the cheering up I can get. Sorry, but as you've probably noticed, things aren't too good between Clare and me...' I nodded, poured more wine into her glass and listened. 'Well, Clare's been dead grumpy for months now and I've done everything I can... Tried everything, but I don't know...' she trailed off into sadness.

'What's it about, do you think?' I asked, gently.

'Well, first I was thinking, you know… Lesbian Bed Death…' She saw my puzzled look, so went on, 'Course, you haven't been a lesbian long enough to know about that… yet! But you know… me 'n' Clare have been together for ten years now. Well, the passion pales…'

'Aw,' I said, trying to be sympathetic but not quite sure what was a good thing to say.

'It's not that we don't love one another. I still love her so much! But I don't know… I think she's getting sick of me or something. She's picking up on everything I do… finding fault… And she was getting annoyed at me spending so much time with you…'

'Me?!' I cried, astounded.

'I know. Seems like she thought…' She glanced up at me guiltily. 'Well, she accused me of fancying you. Thought there was something going on. I told her she must be insane…!'

'Thanks! But how could she think…? We're more like sisters.'

'Yeah – incest! So I told her – you and me? Even the thought of it makes my piss boil…'

'Hey now! Watch it! I get the picture. No need to go overboard!' We both laughed.

Then Clancy stirred the remains of her pasta thoughtfully. 'There was some jealousy there, anyway. Then…' She sat for minutes, gazing into her dish. 'Then… I think… she's started seeing someone else.'

I tried to look blank. I didn't want to let my face show her that I wasn't surprised at all. I couldn't look shocked. It had been fairly obvious that Clare was out on the hunt. She'd even tried me! I didn't want to hurt Clancy, but I didn't want to lie to her either. I would say nothing.

Clancy went on. 'I'm pretty sure… but she denies it, so there's no way of discussing it rationally, sorting it out… working it through…' Her head was sinking lower. I hated to see her look so defeated.

'Clance… is that why you asked me if I was seeing Clare – when you came round, so upset? Before I told you about Tan? Ages ago?'

She nodded, 'You were both acting so strange and distant. Something was up. I was suspicious...'

'Oh... Clancy... I'm sorry.' I stroked her hand, 'But you know, you and Clare... you might be wrong... It might not be what you think...'

'Yeah... yeah...' she said softly and glanced up with a wry smile. 'Ah, Mary, you just want everything to be all right, don't you?'

She'd hit the nail on the head. I struggled to stop the tears brimming over. That's all I wanted. To know that everything was fine. That everyone was happy. I hate unpleasantness. I hate to see people hurt. Tanya's words came back to me: 'Everything is lovely in Mary-land. Get real.' My eyes stung.

'Hey Mare –' Clancy shook my hand to get my attention '– oy! You're supposed to be the one cheering me up! Like you say – I might be wrong. It's just – she's so negative lately, about us...She said... Oh, never mind. So – let's cross that bridge when we come to it, eh? Things'll work themselves out. To tell the truth, I feel better now I've told Clare what I think. Feel better now I've walked off my anger. Look, I'm sick of feeling down. I'm just gonna put all this aside for the time being.' I watched her carefully, her eyes were still troubled but she nodded firmly and tried to shake herself out of it. 'We're supposed to be having a good time! There's a whole night's discoing ahead of us... and hey! You've got a date! Your mascara will run if you don't get a grip of yourself!' I laughed and wiped my eyes. She grinned. 'See how brave I am. You too can have your world tumble round your ears and still come up smiling!'

I called for the bill. Clancy took my hand again, this time more seriously, more concerned, 'But hey, Mare – I need to know that you're okay, too. I can't talk you out of your... relationship – if that's what it is – with Tanya?'

I stiffened, 'What do you mean, "relationship – if that's what it is"? What else can it be?'

'Okay, okay,' she soothed. 'So it's a relationship. But what kind, Mare? It's not give and take, is it? It's not very healthy.'

'Fuck off, Clancy. You're a fine one to talk! Think you're a bloody marriage-guidance counsellor?'

Clancy burst out laughing and that made me laugh too, so we smiled while the gorgeous waitress took my credit card. And brought it back, of course. (Gorgeous as she was, I wouldn't let her get away with that.)

'I just love you and care about you,' Clancy whispered.

I whispered back, 'And I love you and care about you, too! ...But don't let Clare hear us saying that!'

Clancy winked. 'Remember – the very thought makes my piss boil...'

We walked across the town in silence. My heart was heavy with Clancy's hurt. I wanted to smack Clare for causing this. Slap her hard, friend as she was, for making my Clancy – my best bud – feel so bad. And I wanted to kill whoever it was that was threatening to break them up. But then, I'm always more defensive of my friends and family than I am of myself. I can take anything from anyone, put up with any shit for myself but, if anyone hurts the people I love, it's a whole new ball game. I'm like a thing possessed if anyone harms them. Even Vincent. For all that I 'hated' my snotty little brother, it didn't stop me flying to his defence when an older kid – Fiz – had deliberately burnt Vincent's hand with a cigarette. I blew into a violent rage. Vincent said I was like The Incredible Hulk, mutated and roaring with anger. I remember being blinded by a miasma of red fury, that's all. Apparently I flew at the kid's throat. When one of his friends had prised me off, my thumbs had left dark impressions on Fiz's neck. If I'd had the chance to press his windpipe harder I would have killed him. As it was, he hadn't even passed out. Just sat rasping for breath and coughing, with his wild eyes boggling at me in terror. He'd been scared enough not to pick on Vincent again. The bruises took a while to fade and Fiz had to wear them till they did: a marked man. Don't mess with me. Don't mess with a woman possessed.

When we wandered back to the Union bar, we caught up with our gang again. Becky had disappeared but Big Mandy came over to us with messages: 'Becky said she's gone home to get changed and she'll see you later.'

'Aha!' Clancy said meaningfully.

And Big Mandy reported to Clancy: 'Clare said she's gone back to her mum's and don't worry about the kids. She'll bring them back in the morning.' Clancy shrugged.

We went and sat down on the red plush bench next to the others. Kerry was upright for the first time in ages, but she still looked crumpled and woozy. Actually, that's how she usually looked, but this time, worse. She slowly swung her head towards us. 'All right?' She squinted as if we were shining a light in her eyes.

'Better than you!' Clancy said, 'Fancy a drink, Kez?'

'Bleeuurch,' said Kerry.

There was a quiz in the small hall before the disco began and a few of the gang wandered off there. Clancy and I stayed with Kerry, who sat with her mouth open till she wound up her strength to say, 'Where's Clare, like?'

I stiffened but Clancy answered brightly, 'She went home, Kez... Something came up.' Kerry's curiosity seemed satisfied with that, because she yawned ferociously and then her attention wandered to something else. Drink.

'What time's the bar open till, tonight?'

'Half-twelve I think, Kerry, so you've got plenty of time to get a few more in. Don't worry!' I laughed.

'No – I was just trying to work out...like –' we waited for Kerry's words of wisdom '– if I've got time to sober up before I start drinkin' again... or... should I just carry on right through...?'

We contemplated her dilemma for a few moments. Then Clancy pressed her lips together tightly and sighed. 'See your problem, Kez. That's a tough one, that.'

'Well, what do *you* think, like?' Kerry asked, earnestly.

'I think you're gonna have to phone a friend for that one, Kez. No good askin' the audience.'

I pressed my hand to my thigh to make sure my mobile was still in my pocket.

Kerry stood up, holding on to the table to steady herself and wavered there for a minute before she stood up as straight as she could manage under the circumstances and announced, 'Think I'll get a pint... of orange...' and lumbered to the bar.

When she came back I excused myself and went to ring Tanya. I was missing her like mad. Her phone was switched off. Shit. I pressed one of my 'saved' list messages to her – LUVU BABY & MISSU. WISH U WER HERE OR I WAS THER. ALL MY LOVE, UR MARY POPPINS XX – and I sent it. She'd know it was a saved message that I was re-sending to her, but at least it showed I was thinking about her.

An hour later we met up with the rest of our friends in the big disco hall and the place was rocking already. We meandered between the tables, peering through the darkness for people we recognised, before we spotted our crowd. The DJ's music was throbbing loudly and although I like to think I'm pretty funky, I didn't recognise it.

'Is this House or Garage?' I shouted twice into Clancy's ear.

'Garden Shed!' she shouted back. That'll teach me to ask someone ten years older than me.

Our crowd were sitting around three tables and if body language were anything to go by, they were really loud. Big Mandy waved at us. She was sitting next to Georgie who was immaculately turned out, as ever. They all seemed to have got changed. One woman even had a cocktail dress on, and her partner was in a tuxedo. I remembered that I'd left a clean T-shirt in the minibus and I'd meant to nip back and get it and have a quick wash, clean my teeth, spray on some deodorant. Too late now. I felt a bit uncomfortable and hoped I wasn't horribly sweaty. I looked for reassurance. I cupped my hand round Clancy's ear and hissed, 'Hey, Clance... they've all got changed. I've been wearing this shirt all day. Do I smell?'

'You stink, but I love you,' Clancy said with sincerity. I wasn't reassured and clamped my arms tightly to my sides.

Hilary and Pat were out on the dance floor and appeared to be pogo-ing. Showing their age. There was quite a crowd of people on the dance floor already. Robbo leant over and asked us if we fancied dancing. We didn't, but as soon as she'd stood up to get to the dance floor the music went down and the DJ's voice cut in: 'Thank you very much, lads and lasses! Now it's time for the real party to begin... with our major open-ing act of the evening... A huge Pride on Tyne welcome to... *Felicity Fellatio!'*

There was a round of applause and some cheers as 'There Is Nothing Like A Dame' piped up and a spangly gowned drag queen came flouncing across the stage in huge stilettos and a great train of sparkly pink tulle. We all groaned, apart from Robbo, who was strain-ing over the heads of people to get a better look.

'Oh, shit...' muttered Clancy. 'That's all I need to make my day perfect – some tranny in Barbara Cartland's cast-offs.'

'Aw he's all right, Clancy,' Robbo said. 'Give the guy a break!'

'I'd love to,' Clancy snapped a beer mat in two. 'Well, I'd have more respect for them if they actually sang the damn songs instead of miming the bastards! What's entertaining about that? Where's the skill in that?'

'It must be quite hard to synchronise your lips,' Robbo insisted.

'Maybe for you dear, but let me tell you – I have *no* problem with my lips. *Any* of them!' Clancy flounced off to the bar again.

Since the sound level was a bit lower, we had a chance to talk. Robbo had gone closer to the stage for a better look, explaining, 'I want to see if he's got his gear tucked away properly!' To which we all groaned and made general sounds of disgust, then we chattered and caught up with the latest news.

A great queen told us to: 'Shush! You dykes shouldn't be allowed in if you can't behave!'

We just sneered at him, although I had to hold Hilary back from threatening to punch him.

'For the love of... good women! Is he still on? Has he not been booed off yet?' Clancy came back. 'Shit! I think I'd rather watch Absolute Bollocks! In fact, I am watching absolute bollocks! Have they got no women performers? Who the hell's organised this anyway? Some misogynist? I'm going to complain!'

Felicity Fellatio had ripped off her sparkly skirt and was now prancing around miming extravagantly to 'Three Little Maids From School'. I thought Clancy was going to have an apoplectic fit. 'Jeeeee-sus CHRIST! For *fuck's* sake!'

'Just ignore it, Clancy,' I said between clenched teeth. A couple of big skinhead blokes were turning around, frowning at us. And some women at the next table were tutting.

Robbo came back impressed by absolute bollocks. 'I think they massage their balls into their bodies like sumo wrestlers do, then tuck their cocks under, between their legs.'

Clancy told her that was a cock and ball story if ever she'd heard one. Just as Clancy took another intake of breath for another complaint, her attention was caught. She nodded pointedly over my shoulder and muttered to me eagerly, 'Your luck's in!'

'Hi!'

I turned round to see Becky standing there grinning down at me. I caught her musky perfume – patchouli or something. I clamped my arms down and felt a trickle of sweat run down my back. She looked all clean and shiny in a little strappy top and combat trousers and her purple hair slicked back with gel. She looked... sexy. I fingered my mobile, guiltily.

'Hi! You look... clean!' I gulped.

'Oh well, thank you!' She gave a bemused grin. 'Can I join you... Or is it private?'

'Oh, no, no!' I pulled a stool towards her, 'Becky – this is Clancy.'

'Hi! Saw you earlier!' Becky shook hands with Clancy, bracelets jangling, and sat down. I noticed she had a little tattoo on her shoulder-blade. A Chinese symbol. 'Temptation', probably.

'I'll get you a drink. What would you like?' said Clancy and went off to get Becky the Bud she'd asked for, winking at me as she passed.

'Things okay?' Becky nodded towards Clancy.

'Oh, well... they are better now, but they'll be worse when she gets home, I guess...'

'Oh, dear... and you?'

'What? Oh... I'm fine.'

'That's good,' she looked at me, tipping her head to the side and giggled, looking at me through her eyelashes. 'I was worried I might not see you again.'

Shit. Even I realised she was flirting with me. I cleared my throat. 'Look... Becky. See... I've got a... friend, a girl...' I wasn't sure Tanya considered herself either of these things, 'Er... friend... who's a woman. A very close one. Very good one...'

'A very close woman? Very good woman? Not like *him*, then?' She nodded at the stage.

'No. Friend. Very close, very... intimate... friend!' I went red and cleared my throat.

Becky laughed. 'That's good, then! It's good to have friends!' I wasn't sure whether she was kidding me or not. Hmm.

'No, the thing is... The thing is... you're absolutely lovely.' Her eyes shone in the darkness and there was the glint of her nose stud, this time a tiny ruby. 'But... I'm really sorry, but I've got a... partner, and... I'd love to spend time with you... but – I have a... partner, and... well, you know...'

She looked momentarily crestfallen, then rallied. 'Hey, look – it's not like I was coming on to you, man... I like you, that's all. You seem nice – funny!' She grinned.

'You too –' I smiled '– but – I just want you to know – I can't get into anything... I'm faithful to my partner.'

She looked insulted. 'Hey! I wasn't asking you to sleep with me! You should be so lucky!' she muttered.

As Clancy came back, we were both sitting with our arms folded, backs slightly turned away from one another. The air prickled. Clancy handed Becky her drink and glared at me, shaking her head. I'd blown it, she thought. Well... yes, but that was my intention.

Love blossoms, and dies. Or it kills you first.

15
Tanya: A little of what you fancy

Black. Can't... breathe. Can't... Struggle. Hands are blind. Can't see... Can't feel. Black. Black... Soft black. Velvet black. Soft gentle humming. Black. No! Fight! Blood pumping through my ears. Black. One last... my hands! Swim in the air. Breathe... No... breath. Get nowhere. Black... Breath... Fight. Black... Can't breathe... Hands... Where are they? Breath... Catch... Breath. Take off... Mask! Can't. Black. Fingers... Breathe. Can't... Fight... Black.

I woke up whimpering again and struggling blindly. Mary held my head and stroked my brow, reassuring me with soft loving words. I fought with her until I realised that I was awake. Drenched in sweat and feverish. I burnt. My breath caught in my throat. I still struggled for air. I drank in air, greedy for it; my head bursting. And I cried. I cried. How I cried.

We do not talk about it. We have a tacit agreement. We don't go there.

I wouldn't tell her this, but I am happier when Mary is sleeping with me than when she is not. As safe as it is possible for me to feel, I feel safe with her. But of course, you can never trust anyone completely. Or anything. My imagination lets me down. My imagination can torture me with dreams made of reality, which are all the more frightening for that. I dream of sleep when I am awake, but I fear dreams when I sleep. Silly I know, but I like to delay sleep. Sex is a good ruse. Fucking long and hard into the early hours. Then sleep comes to me, and sleep is so heavy that there is little space or time for dreams. I am in control of my imagination most of the time. If I work my body to the point of exhaustion, my imagination is too weary and I am too tired to dream. Life can be exhausting enough, however, and the effort of sex isn't always as necessary as it seems. It's not just the sex but the supplementaries to sex. The preliminaries. The conversation. The drinks, the socialising, the travelling, the expense, the sheer bloody exertion of it all. The emotional eruptions. The time spent in these fripperies! So sometimes it is good to have Mary come over, with her dogged loyalty, her ease, her acquiescence. I can take out my frustrations on her and feel only her goodness, her love in return. It is to these thoughts that I cling when her emotional neediness drives me into a frenzy. She drains me at times with her pain, her anguish. I tell her she must keep them in check if she wants us to be together. And I simply cannot tolerate emotional outbursts every time I see her. After all, she suffers too and it may be kinder for us not to see one another if such grief pervades. Our time together must be good, otherwise there is no reason for it. Clearly she loves me more than anyone has ever loved me before. I am quite sure that she would die for me if need be. Sometimes the reality of that is overwhelming. It suffocates me, the strength and depth of her love for me. It is sometimes too cloying and too heady. Too much. At other times, unequivocal love is just what I need. To be loved without question. Love that is unconditional. That's the impression of her love that she wants to give me. Love that redeems all and love that is all-forgiving. I am to be assured that, whatever I do, she will love me. She will not leave me.

Red is getting on my nerves in different ways.

Of course, I still see Christiane. She stimulates me in every way and it is a tribute to her taste and selectivity that I can only take her to bed if I have intellectually stimulated her. There is a challenge! And who would not want to take up such a challenge? Christiane, so finely sculpted, slim and delicate, her blonde-grey hair still lush and silky, her body still taut after more than fifty years and two children. Her breasts still a pert palm-full; the harsh white scar of two Caesarean sections splitting her otherwise unblemished body. The nakedness of her pubic area, which thrilled me to kiss and to grip, growing damp with sweat and juices whether our lovemaking is gentle or rough. I always felt that I had worked to receive this reward, that I had courted Christiane and built up to this moment. We always went to bed but it was never assumed, never taken for granted. Never lust overcoming our intelligence. It was always a pleasing surprise. Possibly a miracle. It was a communion of souls, a meeting of mind and bodies, the apex of the triangle. But I always left Christiane in bed or left her waving dressing-gowned, from her front door. I always left her. I was never invited to stay and I never invited myself. I always said gently that I had better be going and she always smiled softly and said goodbye. And I would drive home through the dark roads between black fields, one hand on the steering-wheel, the other held up to my face to sniff the tips of my fingers. My skin humming from her touch, her warmth. I liked to remind myself of the scent of her. I refused to wash my hands until the next day and slept with my hand cupped to my cheek on the pillow just for the scent of her. Soothed by the scent of her.

I can while away an entire night online and work at the library the whole of the next day, unscathed. If anything, I am more energetic and more focused, as if all my senses are heightened. I am a little mad with lack of sleep at times. Overcompensating. I feel people looking at me oddly, but I would rather be actively out front, busy at the counter or at meetings; being hyperactive if you like, than sitting in my office going through budgets and other papers. Then, I feel sleepy and vulnerable; it does me no good to be by myself or quiet, when the mood is on me. I can always catch up with my sleep later. If it doesn't catch up with me first.

One Friday evening I had had a disturbing incident with one of our regulars, an old man called Marsh who came into the library every day. The incident had kept me back late from work, speaking with the police and I was worn to the bone. I wanted to forget about it, since I was really irritated with overwhelming fatigue and anger and I sought the solace of home. Frankly, people were the last things I wanted to see. I craved a warm bath and bed – alone. But when I got home, Mary was sitting on my doorstep. I felt my blood boil.

She sat with her chin in her hands and gave a weak smile. 'Hi!'

My heart sank. 'What are you doing here?'

'Oh, I brought you this!' She rummaged about in the leather bag at her feet while I nudged her out of the way so that I could open the door. She bustled into the hallway after me, but I was too weary even to protest. Completely knackered. I could barely speak. I went into the kitchen to make a coffee and Mary followed me in.

'Let me do that!' she said and took the kettle from me. I allowed her this and flung myself on the sofa, flicking the TV channels with the remote control. My head hummed.

She came through and handed me a red envelope. I looked at it.

'Open it – it's for you,' she nodded. I frowned and took it from her. I looked up at her hopeful rosy face and ripped open the envelope. A red card with hearts on it. I looked at her impassively and she nodded encouragement. I opened the card and read her bold handwriting. So surprising, her handwriting. It looked brash, confident, assured. Like her bulky frame. Deceptive. Who could tell the soft stuff from which she was really made? She had written: 'Tanya, you are my one and only true love and I will always be here for you...'

'Is that a threat?' I scoffed. Mary's smile slipped. '"You have the key to my heart!" Well, I've changed the locks!' I laughed.

Mary's face crumpled in disappointment and she went into the kitchen to finish making the coffee. I stood the card on top of the TV and returned to flicking TV channels. Complete crap, all of it. I left it on – switched to 'mute', but flicked on the stereo and turned up the music. Mary came back with two cups of coffee, looking sheepish. Mary-had-a-little-lamb crossed my mind, and I laughed.

'Ta!' I said as Mary handed me a coffee. Then she sat down and watched the silently flickering TV screen. She looked white and pinched and I could see a pulse throbbing in her neck.

'Hey, babe. Thanks for the card,' I offered. She shrugged and tried out a smile. My head was pounding with tiredness. I could barely be bothered but I said, 'Hey, fancy doing anything tonight?'

Mary turned in surprise. 'Oh, okay... What do you fancy?'

'How about *you*?' I said as charmingly as I could. 'Bed would be nice!' I smiled a winning smile and I won.

I used the last of my petering energy to give Mary a quick quiet fucking, then slipped into blissful unconsciousness with her arm wrapped around me. Next thing I knew it was morning and Mary was gone from the bed. Making breakfast downstairs, I guessed. I lay and looked up at the ceiling, flickering light and shadow from a breeze blowing the curtain. It was Saturday and I had taken the day off: no library. I therefore didn't care what time it was. Having said that, I had now reminded myself of the existence of time and immediately needed to know what time it was. Twelve-twenty. God! I must have slept for over fifteen hours. It was like being a student all over again. I was nocturnal. But where was my breakfast? I was starving. I hadn't eaten for twenty-four hours. My lips were dry and when I tried to summon up some lubrication, my mouth felt stale and parched. On cue, Mary came into the bedroom with a tray of food and drink. She was wearing my dressing gown, which was far too small for her. She looked comical, her huge breasts wobbling and bursting out of the thin silky gown. She held out the tray towards me. An offering from my very own geisha. My sumo geisha. I repressed the thought for once, dumbfounded by her usefulness.

'God! You are a mindreader!' I laughed, taking a plate offered to me. 'Hey, did I tell you about my mother once telling me that her uncle used to work on a mindsweeper – during the war? A *MIND*sweeper! Ha! I thought he must be a spy, gleaning important military information from the Germans. Turns out he was a bloody deck-swabber!

Mindsweeper, indeed. Bloody stupid cow. Bloody thick bitch.'

I took a huge bite of toast and wrenched off the crust with my teeth. Mary shuffled into bed with me and shrugged off my dressing-gown. I gave her buttery kisses all over her breasts, which made her giggle and then I pushed my hand between her legs until the coffee had cooled. All afternoon we rolled about in bed some more and drowsed, and even kissed and watched TV. All was simple and peaceful, good humoured and just what I needed.

16
Mary: Losing it

I'm getting sick of people thinking they can do what they like. Sick of people taking liberties.

When I was about 22, I had a disturbing experience. Although I'm tall, I've always had a baby face and maybe it was that and my youthful-looking clothes that made him mistake me for a child or a teenager. But if he did, then it's even more disturbing. Coming from town on the bus one evening, I swung myself out of my seat ready to get off. My eyes met the eyes of a man with a moustache, aged maybe in his thirties, standing at the door. He looked unaccountably angry and I knew it wasn't anything I'd done but, even so, it made me feel uncomfortable.

I jumped off and walked briskly up the hill into dusk. His footsteps. I walked more briskly. His footsteps quickened behind me. Him at my shoulder, his shadow on mine. I should've known. I should have been better prepared. He walked too fast. Kept pace beside me. Face turned into mine. I walked briskly. He overtook me, then turned. He grabbed me. Held my shoulders and caught my breath. Stopped every muscle, even the ones to scream or resist, with one look of hatred. I probably showed terror. My body yielded, probably. Possibly I gasped. He held my shoulders. Probably said, 'Look'. Paralysed, compliant, I did. The church railings were black. Car lights shone on the main road up ahead and I was held back by a man. A glance at his dick. He patted my cheek with a hot hand, said something wordless and swaggered off.

And in those two seconds of his striding off, I recalled my life as a woman: magazines, self-defence: How to Cope. What to do. Laughter. Laugh at them. They can't cope. *Cosmopolitan* said so. And now – now that he'd let me go, I was brave. Into the three metres of cold air between us I shouted words, the first words that came: 'You – *DICK-HEAD!* I've seen a bigger one on… a flea… You fuckin' wanker!' I followed him down the street. He walked briskly. Glancing back. I persecuted him. He quickened his pace but I jogged to keep up. Calling like a fishwife. I saw a man washing his car in the gloom and shouted, 'See him! Call the police! He's a flasher! A fuckin' pervert! Bastard!' The bastard passed the man and gestured dismissively. They spoke briefly and laughed, the men. We parted company. I wanted to get home.

At home, after calling the police, trembling with rage, I waited for an hour at the window, his handprint searing my cheek. I would wear it as a punishment. I'd dealt with the situation cack-handedly. I'd betrayed my sex. And what had he done? Stopped me. Shown me. Put his hand on my cheek and patted me.

My boyfriend at the time was angry for me, wanted to go out and look for the bastard. Kill him. I think that was maybe more to do with the bastard handling his, Steve's, property than handling me or any other woman. All I could do was think – he could easily have dragged me off and raped me. Or maybe he'd get a taste for it – enjoyed my look of terror – want to relive it. Want more. Do it again – this time to a real schoolgirl. This time worse. It was the fact that he'd physically stopped me. Held me by the arms. And to pat me on the cheek! That was the work of no ordinary flasher – a sick coward. That was something worse. Something more dangerous. And I kept re-running it. If I hadn't met his eye on the bus… if I hadn't taken the road up near the church… if I'd punched him in the face… if I'd followed him home… if I'd had a whistle… if I'd been a man…

The police took me out so I could try to find the man who'd been cleaning his car. I couldn't even remember which street it was on.

I was as much use as Billy Fuck-knows. And, as for my boyfriend, Steve, his macho posturing lasted well into the night when he moved from comforting me with cuddles to a hard-on he just couldn't handle alone. And sometimes, it's so much easier to comply.

I think there's something up. I think there's something wrong. I think there's something I don't know. Someone Tanya sees. Maybe Christiane. But how much does she see her and to what extent? Or is there someone else? I think I should find out. Last weekend I rang her up four times an hour, for four hours. I didn't leave any messages. I tired of that. I just stayed in and telephoned every fifteen minutes, between eight-thirty and twelve-thirty. I wanted to ring some more, but I knew I also needed to get some groceries before lunch. I had no bread or milk and the least I could do was pop into Somerfield in Saltburn. It's fifteen miles away and there are supermarkets nearer to me in Middlesbrough: Asda, Safeway, Kwik Save, Sainsbury's... a whole catalogue of supermarkets, but there were some irresistible special offers in Somerfield on something I simply had to have. Needed. I couldn't remember what it was, but I just knew that I had to go there. Besides, it was a fine day, a nice day to go to the seaside and I felt like the drive. And I could also drive by Tanya's house.

I cruised her house before I went to the supermarket. Her car was there. I tried her on the mobile: voicemail. I was now getting annoyed so I left a message – the first actual message in all the calls I'd made that day.

'Tanya – I know you're in there. I'm in Saltburn – not far from your house, so I'll knock when I've done my shopping. OKAY?'

This was really pissing me off. I hadn't been sleeping at all well and, as I pushed my trolley around Somerfield, I was feeling light-headed and faint. I'd cried myself to sleep again the night before. I just didn't know where I was with her and, when I'd confronted her the previous night, she'd been violent and abusive and flounced out. Although I felt for her and would forgive her, my own mental state was taking a downward tumble into depression. I wandered vaguely around the shop, not really certain what I'd come in for. I started to cry as I walked purposelessly past the bananas – which I found dreadfully sorrowful – and the cheese, which seemed unaccountably poignant. I leant heavily on the trolley. I *was* heavy. I felt loaded down with trouble and needed to rest all my weight on the shopping trolley to get myself around the place. With every step, I felt more and more stupid and sorry for myself. Tears were trickling down my face, the saltwater burning my sore eyes and cheeks. A great painful lump of sorrow stuck in my throat. I buried myself in the shelves when people came past, hiding my face in the produce. I was finding shampoo bottles an incredibly good read. I cursed my inflamed complexion and hoped I didn't see anyone I knew, because I'd got to know quite a few people in Saltburn since I'd started seeing Tanya and Somerfield was generally the place to see almost everyone on a Saturday. I was having a nervous breakdown in Somerfield on a mild Saturday morning. The bacon was mocking me.

I blew my nose and decided to brave the shoppers. I could pretend that my swollen eyes and puffy red face were proof of a cold. I have a bad cold, I'd say. I shrugged myself out of despair, stood upright and decided it was time to go shopping. I back-tracked to the entrance to start to fill my trolley.

I bought four apples, four tomatoes and four bread rolls. Four pints of milk and four yoghurts. Four cans of lager and four bottles of wine. Four tins of baked beans. Then I doubled back to the entrance again and picked up a bunch of freesias. I bought a pack of Lemsips, Vick chest-rub, some Olbas Oil and throat lozenges as evidence of my bad cold, which I'd decided was to be the flu. I stood with my mouth open so I could breathe. I was already snotted up with crying, so I didn't need to convince anyone. I turned the items around so that the bar code was facing upwards. I checked my mobile at the check-out. No messages, which was becoming typical. I was beginning to seethe.

'Ooooh, you suffering?' said the check-out girl as she ran the Olbas Oil through the scanner. 'Ooooh, hope it's not infectious…'

I could do without people being trained in friendliness. I read her name badge – Yvonne. I scowled at her beaming fresh face. Her eyes shone keenly, as if she really enjoyed her job. She must have been new.

'Bat code. Flu,' I said thickly, just to make sure she knew. I coughed spectacularly, snivelling into my hanky.

She looked sympathetic. 'Ooh, dear me, you do sound full of it!'

So do you, I thought, but I just paid anyway.

I stumbled through the crowds with my bursting carrier bags and concentrated on the pavement till I got to my car. A large, handsome Weimaraner stuck its nose in my crotch, to my embarrassment and to the owner's dismay. I loaded the shopping into the car and sat in it for a while to catch my breath and plan my arrival at Tanya's, then pulled the mobile out again. No bloody messages. So I drove round to her house and parked outside and watched. The curtains upstairs were still drawn closed, but downstairs they were open. She couldn't still be in bed, surely? It was getting on for two. Her car was still there. My heart was beating hard like fear, cracking my breast-bone. My mouth was dry and my lips felt parched and raw. I looked into my mirror, waited for my face to calm down and then combed my hair. Four times. I would go and ring the doorbell. I wouldn't run away.

Okay. Time.

I hammered on the door and waited, holding the bunch of freesias. I peered through the glazed panels, trying to make something out through the frosted glass. I hammered again. Then I cupped my hands round my eyes and looked through the front-room window.

Suddenly the front door was wrenched open and Tanya came hurtling out.

'YES?' she snarled, all hair and eyes. I stepped back into her flower-bed in fright.

'Ooh – I thought you weren't in...' I wavered, lifting my feet off the bedding plants I'd planted a month earlier and crushed a second ago.

'Oh, yeah? So why were you knocking then?' Tanya's forehead was knotted into a frown and her mouth twisted, making her ugly. Making me frightened.

'Can I come in?'

'What for?' Tanya sneered. I was aware of people passing by and the next-door neighbour had whisked her curtain aside to see what all the noise was about. She was a nosy cow and Tanya had once said that we must be sure to give her plenty of scandal. I really didn't feel strong enough to put up a good public show now.

'Shit – look... let's go in... please?' I thrust the freesias out at her. Somehow the stems had broken and they drooped sadly.

'Is that supposed to be symbolic? Get in!' Tanya flicked her head towards the front door and I sighed in relief.

If that was her idea of foreplay, suffice it to say we ended up in bed. I was careful not to upset her, not to aggravate her mood. Tanya was very rough, as if punishing me – and I, very soft as if deserving it. She never said where she'd been the previous night or previous days – and I, I was learning not to ask. I tried to act as if our lives together only existed when we were together. As if there were no life when we were apart. For me, that was quite true. I'd got it bad. And that ain't good.

17
Tanya: What men like

Yes, I do prefer to sleep with the light on. One of my little peccadilloes, you might say. I leave my bedside lamp on throughout the night at home. I do not like darkness as a rule and given the choice, I will always keep a light on through the dark. Sometimes I have no choice, of course, depending on where I am sleeping. Or with whom. I cannot really suggest to someone that they leave the light on all night – unless we are definitely not sleeping, which is easily arranged. I can recommend that the light is left on so that we can see one another: bodies, expressions. I can tell them that we should use all of our senses. I can make it an erotic experience altogether more preferable to having sex in the dark. Sleep is not on the agenda anyway.

I am usually very careful whom I allow into my bed. Yes, that may surprise you. But I am talking about real sleep, here. A quick shag – that is different. Then my bed is merely a venue. But to sleep! Then my bed is my sanctuary, my safe place and I do not like people to share it with me in general. In specific, Mary is permitted. I avoid settling down to sleep until I am exhausted. I do not like to lie awake in the dark with my imaginings, nor my memories and their reality. After I have stayed awake as long as I can, I prefer my own bed. I prefer to be alone. Or with Mary. My foolish heart. I do like Mary to be there. She knows me well enough, which means well enough not to laugh at my nightmares. She is my old retainer, my custodian. She knows not to be alarmed by me, not to humiliate me. She knows me well enough to reassure me that everything is safe now. I am safe now. I let her cradle me, rock me, hushabye-baby me, comfort me, safely.

And she does not hold me too tight, so that I know that I can always get away.

I have never liked men, really. That is not to say that I am a radical lesbian separatist, merely that I do not choose to spend my time with them. As a manager, as a librarian, I employ men on the strength of their experience, personalities, skills and sense of humour in the same way that I would select a female employee. I do not find men a threat in general. I do not hate them in general. But I prefer women. Particularly in my private life. Men – albeit not all men, *per se* – seem to have an unshakeable self-confidence that has been instilled by centuries of patriarchy. Or am I just a lesbian separatist, after all? Perhaps I am simply a woman who was brought up in the early sixties, un-politicised, then untouched by emancipation?

I remember playing in the street when I was four. Swinging from a lamp-post, quite probably. I imagine that I was in my little tartan kilt with its big, difficult nappy-pin fastening; my red complicated granny-knitted cardigan with hard leather buttons; my crisp white peter-pan-collared blouse; my liberty bodice's fiddly buttons done up to the neck. Out in the street, dressed to kill. I had dreamed of being able to whistle. I had seen a man do it in a film on television, putting his fingers in his mouth and giving a loud high-pitched siren alarm which commanded all attention. I had seen boys do it in the street. I had tried it with a fistful of fingers in my mouth, but it seemed impossible. I *even* tried blowing a blade of grass held between my thumbs like Auntie Moira had shown me. I tried blowing with soft lips like you do across the neck of a bottle of water to make musical notes. I had spent minutes of every hour patiently forming my lips and tongue into every conceivable configuration. Under the lamp-post I pursed my lips, sore from hours and days of trying. I suddenly just made the first tentative peeping sound like a frail bird. Eureka! I tried again. Success! I'd just taught myself to whistle. I was so proud!

At that moment a man in a hat stopped in shock and told me, 'Ladies don't whistle!'

I too was shocked. He must be right. He was wearing a hat, after all! An unshakeable confidence in his authority had led him to warn a little girl that she was stepping dangerously outside her feminine role and purpose – I had committed a breach of identity. And for me... A man had told me off! A man in a hat! A stranger! I was appalled: ashamed and humiliated. So I didn't try to whistle again for a dozen years after that. The bastard! I was four and I was happy I could whistle! I was whistling that I was happy! And him, the bastard in his fucking hat, he told me, when I was the age of four, I was a woman, so I couldn't.

My mother was what was called a 'looker' in her day. It was always her day. Frighteningly, these days I can sometimes look in the mirror and catch my mother looking back at me. Dark, deep eyes. Slim and fine-boned; brown, full, luxuriant hair – although mine is curly and hers was demi-waved. Slim and fine-boned. I don't know which characteristics my father contributed. Perhaps nothing. Perhaps he never existed at all. Perhaps she grew me all by herself like a tumour. Perhaps, evil changeling creature that she was, she stole me from a loving family. Father is a concept I do not understand. My mother did not speak of her past. Her men were always in the present. I believe that she must have had a lonely life until I became old enough to accompany her to adult places. I remember that we were out one evening in a pub when I was about fourteen. I would not have chosen to go anywhere, of course, with my mother. However, she had no friends; her sisters and mother were dead by that time; she didn't work or go to church and she needed to meet men somehow. She did not like to go to pubs alone. She wasn't 'that kind of woman'. This made me wonder what kind of woman she was. What kind of woman she wasn't. What kind of women there were, in the world. What kind of woman I would be.

The pubs we frequented were always a bus-ride away, since there weren't any pubs where we lived and she would rather operate outside the neighbourhood. She did not like the neighbours to know her business. She avoided saying hello to them if she could. So, in order to socialise, in order to meet her recurring need for men's company, she had to get out of the area. She liked to drag me on to the bus for several stops, into the city centre with her. She liked me to wear lots of make-up and she liked people to think that we were sisters. She dressed me like a doll in her old clothes, her high heels and she plastered me with make-up just the once. A cruel beauty lesson: dragging eye-pencil from the corners of my eyes, making them smart, so that I was glad to have to do it myself in future. Blue eye shadow. Eyebrow pencil. Black mascara. Face powder. Red lipstick. A spot of rouge. I was a parody of her own caricatured self. A hastily drawn impression of what was supposed to be real. She looked at me and appraised me as if she was looking in a mirror. My evil twin.

'Gloria! You're never her mother! You look just like sisters!' Wicked step-sister. Evil twin. Wicked step-mother. She liked people to be surprised that she had a daughter of my age. She took delight in the flattery of their amazement. She never denied that I was her daughter but she did love to see that people were shocked to discover it. Her! A mother? It would surprise me, after all, her motherhood. She hated that I grew pubescent. That people would comment that 'Tanya has grown into a very pretty young woman!' She hated that men would start to stare at me instead of at her. She hated that. She hated me. She would sit across the table, glowering at me, her mouth a scarlet gash.

Once we sat in my mother's usual corner of one bar and, as usual, she had bought me a vodka and orange. She hated to have to stand at the bar to buy the first drink, but she could make it last all night if a man didn't offer to buy us drinks thereafter. She flicked back her dark hair and snapped, 'Drink the thing, for God's sake. I'm not buying you lemonade here. You're hardly a little child!'

I was learning not to grimace as I drank it. I never touch vodka these days. Never touched it since the day I left. It makes me feel nauseous. Orange squash also makes me queasy, even at the thought. My mother drank gin and tonic, which I have since learned to drink with Christiane. Wrestling my demons. Laying my ghosts to rest.

Ron, a man who had sat with us on other occasions, came over. He always made me nervous. Something about the way he looked sidelong at my mother and me, his eyes' shifty swivelling, his gazing at my breasts. Small, dark, darting eyes that never looked at you directly. He was a thin, wiry man with a pencil-line moustache. In the lamp-lit pub gloom a patina of sweat glistened on his face and a stench of stale sweat hung over him, as it always did. Cloying. I had once protested to my mother that he 'stank'. She slapped me and told me I'd better get used to it. Testosterone. I never did.

'All right, darlin'?' He winked at my mother on this particular occasion. For all her middle-class airs, she delighted in the attention of the working class male. Her red shiny lips articulated a smile. She simpered. I seethed.

'An' you, little darlin'?' he asked my breasts. I said nothing, but my mother put her hand on his leathery arm, drawing him back to her.

She let me smoke in the pub. I smoked Ron's fags. Woodbines with a taste as thick as my own distaste. I sat and smoked one cigarette after another and watched the flickering lights of the one-armed bandit across the room, mesmerised by its garish chasing colours. I amused myself by discerning the pattern and rhythm of the sequence, watching it for deviation until it became a blur. Keeping my attention always on the slot-machine and its scintillating lights, waiting to be hypnotised. Waiting to be transported.

That night, to my mother's delight, Ron gave us a lift home in his new Ford Capri, patting my arse as I got into the back of it. I scurried upstairs and locked my door, but couldn't sleep for the violent sounds of sex downstairs and the rattling of my bedroom door-handle a short time later.

When I was small, the front garden was the edge of the world. I would swing on the wrought-iron garden gate, launching myself off from the pathway. The firm frame sang on its hinges, white-painted metal loops digging into the flesh of my arms as I hung over it. I remember the rush of air tugging my dress and hair back into the garden. The smell of privet blossom. Beside me, next door's sunflowers gave a dusty death-rattle. And I was a thin cry, snatched by the wind.

The last time I went to the house was to box everything up for the house clearance. When I took hold of the gate, crusty sores of rust bloodstained my hands. Bowed with age, smearing red on stone, the gate scraped the ground, shrieking.

18

Mary: Getting personal

Clancy says she's getting tired and bored with me. I didn't realise I was getting dull. Just when I thought life was more exciting than I'd ever imagined. Just when I felt as if my senses – and my sense – had woken up. Just when I thought I was invincible: I could achieve anything. Just when I really felt I was alive! Maybe Clancy's right. I've also started slowly to die. Little by little. Inside.

It's true, I'm the jealous type. I know that I should block out those thoughts, those painful thoughts that crucify me and send me into paroxysms of jealousy and paranoia, but I just can't switch them off. I just can't detach myself from Tanya even when she's not around. Most of all when she's not around! I want to know where she is. I want to know what she's doing. I want to know who she's with. I can't settle. Ideally, I'd be with her at all times. 'In her pocket.' That's a phrase she uses like it was the word 'abuse', but to me it sounds cosy and secure. I want to live in her pocket but I know that's just not practical – or possible.

I know she sees Christiane. But they don't sleep together. Or if they do, they don't have sex. And even if they did, it would be just sex. It wouldn't be love. But I don't want to think about it. My chest just gets tight and painful, like I know the meaning of a broken heart, and if I dwell on it too much I get such a headache that my head could explode. And I can easily cry myself so hard that I'm exhausted and bloated-faced: two red raw patches beneath my eyes that have swollen up and stay swollen into the next day. Oh, what misery! Suspecting that the woman you love doesn't love you. She says she puts up with me. I'm not as clever as Christiane. I'm not as sophisticated. But I love Tanya more than Christiane does! I'll show her! And one day she'll see, and realise that love doesn't mean pain. She'll realise that I love her and my love is limitless and everything will be all right. I'll have passed the test. I know she tests me. I know deep down she doesn't believe herself lovable. So all I have to do is be true to my feelings and show her what real love is. Teach her that you can be loved. Teach her to love.

I lie and stroke Tanya till she falls asleep, every night I'm with her. She'll turn over and I'll snuggle up behind her like a second skin. Her protector. And if the bad dreams come, which they have sometimes, I'm there to soothe her. I don't like to think of her on her own and distressed. I like her to know she's got me there for her, to let her know she's not alone. I match my breathing to hers and we breathe together: in... out... It's as if we're the same body, the same person. I want to be in her skin. I want to be that close. She is my life and I can't do without her. She can't do without me. She is amazing, and she's mine.

'Yeah, I was probably like that once, Mare,' Clancy says one day, tossing an apple across the room into the wastepaper basket. 'But hey, then reality kicks in! Then you'll come down!'

'Aw, I don't want to! It's what makes me alive!' I feel my eyes gleaming and Clancy looks at me strangely.

'But living like this'll kill you!' she warns, but she sees my face and breaks into a grin. She knows I won't listen. I'm determined and nothing will sway me from my purpose. Tanya is my purpose.

Clancy was more concerned about me than she was about her own relationship. I'd tried talking to her: 'Stop worrying 'bout *me*! Get your own love life sorted! That's taking close friendship too far and moving into denial!'

But selfishly, it was good to have her there for me. And I was about to be rescued by Clancy again.

'Chill out a bit, Mare. You ought to get out more, yourself, instead of getting all wound up about what Tanya's doing,' said Clancy. I rubbed her head thoughtfully as we lay on the sofa. I gazed out into nothing. Clancy wrestled her way up on to her elbows and looked hard into my eyes: 'Hey! Are you listening to a word I'm saying?'

'Mmmm.' I nodded and kissed her on the forehead.

'Bloody patronising cow.' Clancy grinned and we both burst out laughing. It was good to see her laugh. Things were still not resolved between her and Clare, but she seemed to be coping. At least they were being civil to one another, even having long talks, although they seemed to be drifting away doing separate things. It was obvious that they still loved one another. I was sure this would work itself out. Love like that never dies. I was starting to sound like a country and western singer. I pushed Clancy's head away off my chest. She rummaged about in her backpack by her feet and pulled out a magazine. 'Hey, let's have a look in the *The Pink Paper* for you!'

'I'm not in it,' I said.

She pulled a nasty face and flicked to the back pages. Classified ads.

'Here ya go!' she said, stabbing the page with her stubby little index finger.

'Clance, I don't need accommodation. Or a solicitor!'

She sucked in her breath. 'Oooooh, you! I'm looking for a woman for you!'

'I don't need a woman! I've got one!' My voice rose in a squeak.

Clancy looked at me askance: 'Come now... let's get you a nice woman... or maybe one that's not...! Let's see,' she ran her finger down the columns, 'here you go – a whole list under the heading, "You know what you want!" Hmm – that's no good for you, then! How about this...? *GWF*... What's that?'

'Great Wobbly Fright?'

'Goer With Friend? We could both be in there, girl! No – here's one for ya, Mare: '*Horny little devil looking for angel with dirty mind for hell-raising and hot sex.*''

'You're joking! Are they allowed to put that in there? Is it legal?'

Clancy looked at me from beneath her brows for a couple of seconds, then went back to reading: '''*Sexy bitch seeks some lovin'. London*''.'

'Yeah. Righty-ho.'

'Oh look now, if you're scared off by *them*, how about: "*Shy, quiet female seeks friendship or more. Countryside walks, cycling, swimming, squash…*"'

'Yeah, right. And I'm so sporty, Clance.'

'Well, squash, Mare. I was thinkin' you might like to squash her.' I punched her. She went on: 'Look! Here you go – "Women by Post"…'

'That's handy – they do home deliveries then?'

'Aye – fe-mail order! No, but listen… "*Female, 28, GSOH*"…'

'Er –' I interrupted '– Good Shag, On Heat…'

'Suits you!' Clancy went on. 'No-o… "Good Sense of Humour"– she'd need it, mind… So: "*Female, 28, sense of humour, many interests, seeks intelligent –*" that's you out, then "*– fun female to take it from there…*"'

'Take what from where?'

'Use your imagination! She's in the North East, Mare! Give her a go!'

'No! What have I told you, Clancy? I'm quite happy as I am!'

'Now we both *know* that isn't true, don't we?' Clancy looked serious. I took a second glance at her and she screwed up her little face and put out her tongue. And returned to reading: 'Look! This says North Yorkshire! That's close enough! Listen: "*Attractive, caring, loyal female seeks genuine woman –*" you're not a tranny, are you, Mare? … No, she sounds a bit dull. How about: "*North East: red wine lover, 30s, with wicked sense of humour seeks similar for fun and friendship*"? Hey! She sounds all right! Shall we give her a whirl?'

'No, we shan't, Clancy.'

'Awww, go on! Go on... go on... gwarn...' She nudged me. 'Just a teensy-weensy little phone call... You don't even have to leave a message. You can just listen to the voicemail message,' she wheedled, 'go on! Just for curiosity... Just for me... A tiny thing...'

'Mmmm – you are.'

'Aww, go on... Tell you what – I'll ring, you can listen and we don't have to do anything...'

She knew I was beginning to weaken. She knew I would do anything for her, but really! This was going too far! I shook my head. This was ridiculous! I simply was not interested. I looked at her. She was giving me her best shot at a puppy-dog look: all big sad eyes and little pout. She rested her head on my shoulder and gazed imploringly into my eyes. She made a little whimpering sound.

'Oh... Go on then,' I said. She ran for the phone.

Last week: I phoned Tanya up and as usual there was no answer. But I knew she'd driven home because I'd waited outside the library around closing time, saw her get in her car and then head towards home. She'd parked by the time I got there, so I pulled up in my usual spot just diagonally opposite her house in a side street where I could still see her door. I gave her a few minutes to get in and settle herself before I rang on my mobile. So her phone rang and, as usual, the answerphone cut in. I have an intimate relationship with her answerphone. '... after the tone...'

'Hi, Tanya? It's me. Are you in yet?' I paused. Sometimes she did pick up when she heard me. Or she might be upstairs on the loo. Any number of possibilities. 'Tan? Okay – well, I was thinking of popping round and I might be over in about... ten minutes. So if you hear a thump on the door, it's just me! See you soon.' I broke off and waited, watching my watch. I didn't want to look like I'd just been following her. I could just say I was in the area, but I'd give it ten minutes anyway. I drummed my fingers on the steering-wheel. Two minutes later, her front door opened and she came out, got into her car and started it up. Damn! She couldn't have picked up my message. Shit! What should I do now?

I set off in hot pursuit. Follow that car. I saw her indicating to go left, so I did too. I knew that if she turned right off the main road, she was probably heading towards Marske where Christiane lived. Damn these East Cleveland dykes, living so far from the towns. But no. She headed straight over the roundabout, heading towards Middlesbrough. Damn. I had no idea where she was going now. To my house? Shit! I didn't want to miss her. I couldn't overtake her because she'd see me. My only possibility was to head off towards Guisborough on an entirely different road and try to get there before her. My only choice. I put my foot down to the floor, wishing that the speed camera signs were dummies, and I swung down the rural roads, speeding through Guisborough and hoping Tanya was getting caught in as many traffic lights as I was. It seemed to take an eternity, with me glancing at my watch every few moments. Desperate – desperate to get there before her. I pulled up at home drenched in sweat. No sign of Tanya, so maybe I had beaten her to it. I ran into the house. No notes through the letterbox. I flung my keys on the table and sat down on the edge of my seat, ready to jump up when the doorbell rang. I waited for half an hour before I actually stopped to think that Tanya could have been going anywhere.

After I rang Tanya's mobile a few times, getting angrier and angrier, I telephoned Clancy. The phone rang for ages, then Clare picked up and sounded really irritable, like I'd woken the kids or something. No, Clancy was out, she said. She didn't ask if she could help and I didn't expect she could, anyway. She seemed really 'off' with me. Bloody nerve! I just didn't know what Clare's problem was these days and before I knew where I was I'd launched into the subject:

'Look, Clare – I know you were really pissed off with me for turning you down, even though it was a long time ago, and I guess you're afraid I might tell Clancy one of these days...' I could hear Clare choking, but I wanted to say my piece. 'But you *must* know that there's no way I would hurt Clancy. In fact, if *you* or anyone hurts Clancy…!'

Clare slammed the phone down. Bitch! Miserable cow!

I took some lager out of the fridge and cracked off the ring-pull. I'd taken four large swallows of it before I even drew breath. I wiped my mouth across the back of my hand, then took another four swigs. The can was nearly finished, so I took out another and cracked it open. There was a buzzing in my ears, like fury. I drank two more cans after that one. I forgot to eat. So when I caught up with Tanya at last, when I rang her home number at about eleven-twenty and she answered, I was a little pissed but otherwise really angry.

'Where have you *been*?' I snapped.

'I've been OUT!' she countered.

I thought fast. 'I was worried about you… I'd said I'd pop round, and then…'

'Oh, for FUCK's sake… I don't need this…'

'Sorry… No, no… I mean, I was just concerned that you were okay, that's all. And I've had Clare winding me up.'

'Clare?' Tanya spat.

'Yeah, I just rang her and she was being a bitch. Sorry. I shouldn't take it out on you.' Tanya was silent. A minute went past. I was puzzled. 'Tan?'

'You say you've spoken to Clare?'

'Yeah?'

'Just now?'

'Okay, it was a couple of hours ago now, but I'm still pissed off.'

'I didn't know you knew her that well.'

I furrowed my brow. I wasn't sure where this was going and my mind raced to keep up.

'Well, I wanted to speak to Clancy really, but… why?'

'Okay, so I'm here and I'm safe, so you can stop worrying now.'

'Okay…'

We let some more minutes pass in silence.

Then Tanya broke in. 'Do you want to come over?'

I looked at my watch: nearly twenty-five to midnight. 'Sure it's not too late?'

'Well, if it's too late for you...'

'I'll be right there.' I tore off my pyjamas, pulled on some clothes and sped the fifteen miles to Tanya's to spend the night with her. She needed me, after all.

19
Tanya: The Italian conception

Christiane. The extraordinary. She is my idea of a perfect woman, although I can see her faults too. She is by no means faultless, but reassuringly human. Still, sometimes I am filled with awe for her. Her intelligence, her skills and accomplishments. She also fills me with a certain pride, a self-satisfaction. I do, however, make every attempt to conceal the depth of my emotions towards her. My emotions feel juvenile, laughable. They make me vulnerable and that cannot be. Soon I shall be going on holiday with Christiane. It is to be a special time. It is our twentieth anniversary. It is also the first occasion we have been away together – in all our years together. The only time Christiane has ever devoted to our being together without her studies, her work, her colleagues, her own space, her own time, her other commitments getting in the way. Three whole weeks.

'This will be purely pleasure,' she says, arching one fair eyebrow, before sipping from a goblet of white wine. Only Christiane could still drink from a goblet.

'The pleasure is all mine.'

'I do hope not,' she warns, smiling. Then she stands up and fetches another bottle of Chardonnay from the fridge for me to open. She passes me the bottle, condensation beading its chill surface. I always open the wine. I do it so well, she tells me. And I do not even know whether it is her laziness, her incompetence, or her sense of chivalry that persuades me to do as she asks. She is not lazy. She is certainly not incompetent. Then it must be that she prefers to see me wrestle with the corkscrew. I try to do it as competently, as graciously, as possible. I do not grimace. I do not want her to witness any ugliness. I delight in pouring the wine into her goblet. I feel like a medieval knight, serving my lady. For she is certainly a lady. Courtly love. I stand and admire her as she sits back in the armchair, her long, delicate fingers clasping the glass. Her ash-grey hair pinned up and bound in a neat pleat, as ever. Wisps of it always gorgeously escape. I lean over to stroke a strand of it out of her eyes and she smiles up at me, the fine lines of her face deepening, furrowing her lovely skin. She is growing so old now, I realise. I smile back.

'I must buy you something from the jewellers on the Ponte Vecchio. A trinket. A memento of our time together,' Christiane says.

We have decided to go to Florence and will be staying in the hills just outside the city, in a villa owned by one of Christiane's work colleagues. It will be glorious. We have booked our flights, hired a car, researched the currency rates and Christiane is now entertaining me with tales of the Medici, travel guides, anecdotes, art history and exquisite coffee table books with lavishly glossy pages depicting the sights and scenes of the area.

'If you have not seen it, then we must visit the Palazzo Vecchio. Sumptuous in the extreme!' Christiane passes me a book, open at the page showing the Sala degli Elementi. Heavily gilded ceilings, brightly painted Renaissance allegories. She talks on about the Straw Market, the Palatine Gallery, Giotto's Bell Tower, the Uffizi, Piazza del Duomo, Santa Maria Novella, Ricasoli, San Marco, Viale dei Colli, Piazzale Michelangelo, Davizzi Davanzati. A litany of mysteries.

I am more interested in the passion in Christiane's voice; the shape of her mouth as she articulates unfamiliar words; the fire in her ice-blue eyes as she speaks. I am managing to control my excitement, but the romance of it all is unbearable. I am remaining nonchalant but I am devouring her animation, her enthusiasm, the atmospheric detail – and I am secretly too excited for words. It does not do to express excitement. To give people a power over you: the power to make your eager anticipation a mockery and the power to turn all your hopes into a crock of shit. I will remain impassive until proved otherwise. I cannot visibly look forward to things for fear that they will not live up to my expectations. Some may think me cynical, but I call it realistic. This holiday is imbued with such significance for me that it must be contained. For all the years I have known Christiane, ours has been a love beyond the pale: a love too deep to conform to the ordinary or the expected. We simply know that we are one another's partners: soulmates, but we do not require fidelity or domesticity to confirm our relationship. In fact fidelity and domesticity are impossible between us. That degree of separation and her aloofness are what have kept me in thrall for so long. We remain our own people. With Mary I fear merger, immersion, loss of self. It is fortuitous that this holiday – this celebration – comes now, when I am beginning to grow afraid that Mary and I are getting too close. That I am beginning to need her. What I really need is this time away from her. To recover.

I have not revealed this matter to Mary. Neither the holiday, nor the extent of my relationship with Christiane. I told Mary when we first met that there were important women in my life whom I would not give up. Principal of them all is Christiane. Mary understands that I will not surrender her and is aware that I see her occasionally. How occasionally and how frequently, she does not know. I try to dissuade her from jealous enquiry.

'Look Mary – the more you cling, the less I want to be with you. Face the fact,' I tell her gently, after my anger has subsided and her sobs have diminished. 'If you give me space – the more likely I am to want to be with you. That way we both get what we want.' She nods, her round sweet face red and tearful. I kiss her gently on the lips to confirm our agreement. Then I kiss her harder to reassure her that

I want her. Then I pull her off the chair, press her to the floor and make love to her until she cries again.

I have finished with Red. Call me old, or call me old-fashioned, but it was all getting too tiring for me. It was also getting out of control. Too risky. I prefer my dalliances to take place further afield and juggling two women on Teesside had already proved more than enough for me. The third – Red – had started out as casual fun, but I was afraid of it turning into a relationship rather than an arrangement. We had begun by being opportunistic in our sexual encounters: the en-suite bathroom at a party; during our lunch-breaks; while Red was out supposedly 'jogging'. Then whenever she was available – when the kids had a babysitter and she could get out. Or furtively, when all was quiet and safe at her house. I would spin over there whenever she gave the word. Heady days of pure sex. Like a hunger it ate away at us, and like starved souls we assuaged our appetites whenever possible. But that was not to last. Months went by. A year. More. She wanted to talk. She wanted me to meet her kids, wanted to tell her partner about us. That was not the point at all.

Yet she was a wonder of physicality: skinny and pale, her luminescent skin a traceable atlas of pale veins like the tributaries of a river system which I liked to follow back to the source with my tongue. She had a shock of ginger hair and luscious lips. Her lithe body: immensely erotic, terrifically energetic. I missed our regular rolls, but she was less available than Mary. She had too many ties and responsibilities. And sneaking into her house when her partner was out and her kids were in bed – once an exciting challenge – was getting far too risky. Like Mary, she was also assuming an expectation and displaying possessive behaviour. Too tiring. I enjoyed the months we had immensely and the greed of our coming together was exciting. However, if I should crave that again, I could get my thrills from my ventures into Leeds and Newcastle and from my online arrangements. Safer. Less intimate. No strings attached. Basically, I can get laid whenever I want to. Easy lay = Mary. Easy + thrilling = anyone online. Thrilling +

easier = anyone out on the scene. Thrilling + not easy = Christiane.

Christiane's enthusiasm is uncharacteristically childlike: 'I can't wait to see the churches again and the Madonna of the Long Neck, the Madonna of the Goldfinches, Madonna of the Chair...'

'Like A Virgin' comes to mind. But I resist the temptation to sing any of Madonna's hits. Crass and cheap. I would never make fun of Christiane when she is so passionate. I may tease her gently, but I would never dream of insulting her by making fun of her passion. She loves religious icons and has a couple of original gilt-framed Russian Orthodox icons of Madonna and Child on the wall of her dining room. Sixteenth century, she tells me. Shining with gold leaf and reds, blues, greens: their gaudiness appals me. The subject matter is questionable. Madonna and Child. The black-eyed Madonnas so grave, so two-dimensional and angular. The babies so freakishly knowing, bereft of innocence. I never can see what the fascination is. It means nothing to me. Mother.

The litany. The rosary. Veronese, da Vinci, Fra Angelico, Parmigianino, Pisano, Giotto, Michelangelo, Caravaggio, Donatello, Canaletto, Tintoretto, Titian, Rubens, Raphael, Sarti, Lippi, Gaddi, Daddi.

20

Mary: More personal

I'm quiet and peaceful when we're alone together. I try to give Tanya some soothing time outside her hectic world, to be the calm to her storm. I watch her to assess her mood, then make myself fluid to fit in with it: the oil to her machine, lubricant to enable her to function. You wouldn't think a librarian could be stressed out, but Tanya throws so much energy into everything! She's always at meetings, working late, away at conferences and things. Her life is frenzied, her emotions taut. People, people, all day long. And she pushes herself in social situations too. There's no such thing as a quiet drink if Tanya's in a crowd. She can't just sit back and let others entertain her, she has to be the centre of attention; she has to lead the conversation, be at the heart of the group. She has to be the heart*beat* of the group.

'Hey! Listen to this one!' She raises her hand and commands all attention. She is animated and enchanting; she talks to everyone but me, engages in conversations with everyone around the table, except for those she doesn't rate – like Kerry. And me. She charms everyone. She never mentions it, but I know she deliberately ignores me so as not to attract attention to us. She still doesn't want people to know how much we mean to one another and I understand and respect that, but it still hurts. If it weren't for the fact that I knew we'd be leaving together at the end of the night or I'd be meeting her at her house later, I would be distraught and jealous. But it's just her way. She never meets my eye in crowds. It hurts me desperately but I realise it's just her way.

I plucked up the courage after resentment had bubbled within me for months. 'Why do you ignore me when we're out?' I burst out as she opened the front door, when I'd been sitting on the step for ten minutes because we left the pub separately.

'I don't!' She frowned. 'Besides, you're here, aren't you? I'm letting you into my house – my bed. Surely that says something?'

She doesn't explain the detail, so I have to infer. She doesn't want her relationship with me made public, so she pretends she barely knows me. She keeps them all off the scent. It's her way and I've got used to it. It's what I agreed to, after all – under the terms discussed. And I do sit back with some pride to watch her in action. So clever. Such a performer. She could have had anyone. Straight or gay. And I am pleased she has chosen me, after all. I look around at the other women in the world, the woman she might have had. I can sit on the bus, secure in the knowledge that I am superior to all the other women around me. Tanya has chosen me, above all. Me, above the woman trailing two kids, spilling shopping bags and fury on the floor. Above the girl with wild and hennaed hair, dangling earrings and jangling chains, her portfolio clutched tightly to her chest. Tanya chose me above them all. She chose me, even above the lady Christiane. For all that Tanya says that Christiane is efficiently smart – immaculate – I'd say her passion's filed away with index cards. Tanya chose me above them all.

'Why do you like me?' I ask, playing with a strand of her curly hair, drawing its wispy tail across her nipple. She scratches it.

'Who says I like you?' she teases.

'Aww! That's not very nice!'

'Who says I have to be nice?'

I prop myself on my elbow and look at her. Her eyes are shut but I know she's nowhere near sleep, only a bit drowsy after lovemaking.

She isn't really sleepy at all. I blow on her face and she flickers a smile. I gently prise her eyes open, like I remember I used to do with my mum and dad when I was little and she bats me off, but she's gentle and joking too. Then I kiss her, full and softly on her lips and she is breathless.

'Do you love me?' I whisper.

She blinks in wonder: 'I think... I quite possibly... might do... When I come to think about it...'

It was me. She chose me to sit at home with in potent silence. To share her heat, thigh by thigh, filling my body with her body's warmth. Me to spend most nights with – locked in passion, locked in sleep. She's chosen me to share her secrets with. Things she would never tell anybody else. Her public sees her public face, hears her public voice, responds to her public thoughts. She puts all her energy into other people. She won't relax.

And then her childhood... I know such deep and dreadful things. Anyone would break after that – it's a surprise she's held herself together. When we're out, I watch her playing, working her audience. Georgie's laughing, wiping tears from her eyes, and already Tanya's launching into the next story, carefully orchestrated to draw in the stranger amongst us, Big Mandy's new partner, Mel. Mel's uncertain of herself, overwhelmed, but Tanya's turning on the charm, flattering her, working her little magic. She's remarkable.

It's no wonder she's distant, doesn't believe herself lovable – after all she's had to contend with. I know her mother was a bitch. But I don't really know the details. What little I do know chills me to the marrow.

Tanya says she can't form lasting relationships, she doesn't *do* relationships and I can fully understand that. But she's met me now. All I have to do is be patient and she'll realise what she's got now, with me, and she'll learn to express love with me. I like to offer her a contrast, to be the exception that proves the rule, but most of all I want to be a safe haven. I want her to feel secure, to settle, to root herself, to bed down. I know I can offer her the nurturing she yearns for, deep down. She likes to pretend she doesn't need love; doesn't crave it. But I'm the only one who sees her private face, when her guard is down, when the mask slips. Only I understand what she's been through. And I'm sworn to secrecy.

Sometimes she seems so ungrateful – she seems to take me for granted! I'm sure she doesn't realise how she comes across. She doesn't know that she hurts me a lot. But I am over-sensitive, after all. That's my problem, not Tanya's.

Although I don't tell her in detail, Clancy's assessed the situation: 'That's a load of crap.' She has other comments to make, too. In short they are: 'People never change. Especially when they don't want to. You have to move on.'

Sometimes though, Clancy can talk through her arse with the best of them.

I indulge her.

So anyway, there Clancy was in the living room that day, giggling and scurrying like a fieldmouse with the phone in her hand, clambering over me and crouching on my arm of the sofa, leaning over me and squinting down at *The Pink Paper* to read the phone numbers.

She sat, the tip of her tongue between her teeth, and dialled.

'Which one are you ringing?' I hissed. She waved away my question… hit the star button… punched in one number. Waited. I sat entranced and amused by her concentration and determination. Then she quickly punched in some more numbers and sank down on to my knee, to my 'Gerroff!' and held the receiver next to my ear, headbutting me to get close enough to it herself.

'Ow!' I yelped.

'Here you go! Here you go!' Clancy whispered in excitement. I found myself intrigued and strained to listen. A distant-sounding taped voice began. A monotone drone:

'Hi… I'm Alice. I'm twenty-eight. I'm a student. Mature, that is. I live in Darlington. I like… erm… comedy… pizza…um… God…

music. Some... I'm... er... honest and... faithful, and... quite interesting. Got lots of... interests. Oh, please leave a message, and... I dunno... maybe we could meet up... take it from there... Bye.'

Clancy and I both fell about laughing. 'She likes God! She sounds exciting!' Clancy said. 'Honest and faithful! Sounds like a one-, two-, three-, four-legged friend – a right dog! Still, she won't mind your spotty face. She likes pizza.'

I gave Clancy a casual punch. 'Awww, but it's so unfair! So embarrassing! What do you say on things like that?' I felt sorry for the poor girl.

'You say things that are going to get you laid!' exclaimed Clancy. 'You say things to sell yourself! God! Some people have no idea!'

'You seem to know a lot about it... Is there something you're not telling me?' I smiled.

'Tut! You know I'm all talk!' Clancy laughed and wriggled her bottom into my lap until I had to push her off.

'Next!' she said and peered at the paper.

'Oh, no Clance... Wasn't that enough?' I protested.

'No way!' Clancy dialled and held the receiver up between our heads.

A cheerier voice piped up. 'Hi! I'm Lindsay! Thanks for calling! I'm thirty-eight, a nurse, a single mother, and I like a good laugh. I like... red wine, white wine, lager –' she giggled '– God! I sound like an alcoholic! But I'm not! I also enjoy cinema, parties, reading, holidays, quiet nights in and wild nights out... or vice versa. Oh! Not that I'm into vice, of course –' laughs '– anyway. Must stop gabbling, because it's just too embarrassing! If you'd like to leave a message with your number so I can contact you, that would be great! Thanks for listening... and hope to hear from you soon. Bye!'

Clancy's eyes widened. 'Hey! Think we've struck gold here, Mare! She sounds a right laugh!'

I frowned at her. 'She's a single mother...'

'So? Are you casting nasturtiums? I'd be a single mother if it wasn't for Clare. In fact, I practically am a single mother. That's not very PC of you! Not very Police Constable at all! Don't you want to mix with mothers? God! If I'd known that! Are you racist too?' she squeaked.

'Hey, hey! Don't get carried away! I just don't know that I want to get involved with someone with kids, that's all.'

'Ah! So you're thinking you might want to get involved with her, then? I dunno, Mare – one phone call and you're anybody's! Planning the commitment ceremony already, and she doesn't even know you exist!'

I growled at her.

'Leave her your number,' Clancy said simply.

I bared my teeth and snarled gently.

'She's a nurse...' Her eyes twinkled and she rubbed her hands together lecherously. 'Think of the uniform! Ring again and leave a message. With your number.'

I snapped at her and grabbed her sleeve with my teeth.

'Just do it, Mare. It means nothing.'

I chewed and tugged at her sleeve, twisting my head from side to side and making growling sounds.

'Do it and I won't hassle you any more. Promise!'

I lifted my head and howled. 'Ow-ow-owwwwww!'

'You will, then! Great!' She passed me the phone.

21
Tanya: Home thoughts from a broad

The house was the same house as before. Grim. But shabbier. Dark stains mottling the rendering of the walls. The paintwork faded and peeling, the wood beneath it black with rot. A face: the same two blank unseeing eyes of the upstairs windows with cataracts of grey net curtains, the left one sagging on its rail like a wink; an eyelid paralysed after a stroke. The dark mouth of the door, snot-coloured and gaping. Mary was in there already but I stood at the gate, my hands holding on to the cold chalky frame that was blistered and pocked with rust.

'Look, the sooner you do it, the sooner it's all finished,' Mary had said earlier.

'Such a philosopher!' I muttered. 'Such words of wisdom!'

But regardless of my sarcasm, I knew that she was right. That it had to be done and the sooner the better, to get it over with. To get it finished. Over and done with. Forgotten. Was it possible to forget? I'd been putting it all out of my mind for years, yet it crept in like a mist, or like a slug or a leech. A small but all-pervasive thing, growing larger, taking over my thoughts, sucking the lifeblood out of me. Swelling, growing monstrous and putrescent. Not forgotten, not forgiven.

I had brought Mary along with me because she is such a good cleaner. She had driven my car and this time I didn't even care if she left the seat ratcheted back as far as it would go, the back-rest rigidly upright, the steering-wheel forced up, the mirrors giving me a view only of the roof and the sky. Things that generally infuriated me. All those changes. All those adjustments that had to be made. This time I didn't care.

We had pulled up at the tatty fence smothered in wild privet outside the house. Mary had turned to me and cried, 'Aww, jeez! We should have come before. It's a right mess.'

I lit up another cigarette and stayed where I was.

Mary was undoing her seatbelt. 'Are you stopping here, then?'

'I'll just finish this.' I gave a half-hearted wave of my cigarette hand.

'Well, don't leave me to do all the work, you lazy sod!' she said cheerily, but her smile was frozen and wary, checking that I could take the joke. I obliged with a chuckle. She laughed in relief, opened the boot and took out her big pink plastic stacking-box full of cleaning solutions. 'Guard the Hoover!' she said, swinging the heavy box through the screeching gateway and down the path.

My big girl. My big carthorse girl. My big practical good girl. Leave it to Mary. Mary will make it better. Mary will make it all right. You can rely on Mary. Trust Mary.

She lumbered back down the path towards me and leant in the window I'd opened. 'Give us the keys, then... Saves me having to break in.' She smiled. I opened the glove compartment and skittered my fingers around blindly until they closed on the cold tarnished keys.

'You okay?' she asked. I nodded. 'Come on, then. Otherwise I might think you'll switch seats, drive off and leave me!'

I smiled vaguely and clicked off my belt. Obedient child. Do as you are told. I flicked my ash out of the window. Mary went round to the boot, swooped out the vacuum cleaner with one hand and a mop, broom and full carrier bag with the other and plodded back up the path.

My strong girl. My steadfast girl. My big-boned, broad-shouldered, steady and sure girl. There's something about Mary. Mary Christmas. May your days be Mary and bright. And may all your Christmases…

Christmas meant no school. No shops. No friends. Nothing to do if the weather was poor. Nothing to do but sit in the house with the fire on. The radiogram on. Not too loud. Sometimes not on at all. Just the heaviness of the air, the brooding tension, the waiting for something to happen. Like the taste of a storm brewing, a heaviness fit to give you a headache, a burgeoning oppression that you dread but know that when it comes it will offer some kind of relief. The weather. The atmosphere. Charged. Safest to stay locked in my room. Reading my books. *Treasure Island*. *Little Women*. I wanted to be a pirate. I didn't want to sit and sew, surrounded by sweet sisters. *Pollyanna*! Pah! I threw that down in distaste. *Rebecca of Sunnybrook Farm*. The very title made me want to retch. I wanted to be Huckleberry Finn. I wanted to have adventures. Why were all the best characters boys? I wished I was a boy. Then you have power.

On Christmas Day I got books and clothes from my mother. I was not a deprived child. How quaint, how traditional that she thought enough of me to give me presents. That she bought into the old-fashioned Christmas spirit and she had Granny – her mother – and her simple younger sister Sylvia over for Christmas dinner. And I would be a kitchen slave for the day, chopping onions, making breadcrumbs, mixing stuffing; boiling giblets, stirring up gravy-powder and stock, stuffing the chicken; peeling potatoes, slicing carrots, topping and tailing Brussels sprouts; making custardy white sauce and steaming the Christmas pudding that Granny made us as a gift every year.

I had watched Granny do all of these things on very occasional Sunday dinners and the whole process seemed enjoyable to me, con-ducted with such openness, such chattering dexterity and joy, that it was no hardship to try them out myself at home. So, even at the age of six, I was an efficient cook and learned to tidy the mess away for fear of my mother's wrath. It was hard work on Christmas Day, but it gave my mother nothing to upset her and nothing to do but drink a glass of sherry or two in the morning, switch on the radiogram and sing loudly to carols, then have a glass of sherry or two in the afternoon and dance around the living room to the dance music on another radio station. My stout, cheery grandmother arriving all smiles and gifts, parcels wrapped in brown paper spilling from her arms. My silly, twittering, tragic Aunt Sylvia who talked of church and the handsome vicar and spoke of the flowers in their garden and how she couldn't wait to see them again. As if they were her only friends. Dear Clarissa Montague, Emma Hossler, Elsie Jury, Clara Butt, Dolly Mollinger, Madame Emile Mouilliere...and of course, the gentlemen: Lord Bute, Russell Prichard, Leonard Messel... I savoured the names ... so many grand and various floral friends. And of course... John Innes had bedded them all! Delphiniums, lobelias, aubretias, rhododendrons, hydrangeas, chrysanthemums, hollyhocks, cottage roses. A remembrance of summer. My granny's smiling, watchful eyes. Stories beside the coal fire, lolling on Granny's bosom, sleepy with food. A family Christmas. I think it was perhaps the closest thing to happiness in that house. Or perhaps I have imagined it all. It is possibly an elaborate fantasy. I did read a lot.

But beneath it all a simmering unease, a knowledge that as soon as they left my mother would either give me a walloping for some perceived misdemeanour – or else she would skip off or stump up to bed. This depended on her mood, the number of sherries and amount of food she had eaten and how irritated she had been by Sylvia's incessant chatter or how much notice they had taken of me: 'Tanya, love! You are an angel! Isn't she, Gloria? You must be so proud! Come here, my little love!'

I would lie awake as long as I could, preparing myself for whatever might or might not happen next.

Down the path, I heard Mary give a loud exclamation as she opened the front door. I looked at the cigarette smouldering between my fingers then took a long, deep pull at it, holding it in my mouth, breathing it into my lungs, trying to breathe it all in, to get the most out of it. A trickle of smoke meandered out of the car window. I watched it waver into the breeze and disappear. I sighed, opened the passenger door and got out.

The gate made a screeching sound on its hinges. One sagging end of it caught the ground beneath, chattering against the paving slab that buckled up to meet it. My hands were powdered with rust. The front door yawned like an open wound at the end of the mossy overgrown path. I hesitated before it. Then I took two steps and was in the garden. The grass was as high as my waist and each blade murmured, one to another, chafing against me. Whispering: *sussuration*. I like that word. Like resuscitation. I waded out regardless of the stinging nettles catching at my trousers and I stood in the highest central patch of grass, watching it wave a melancholy rhythm around me, whispering around my thighs. I sat down completely enclosed by tall feathery grasses and studied the variegated bands of green along the stems. The dry grey husks, the bright green new shoots, the dark green flat strong leaves.

We had stuck sticks in the ground. Sticks from out of the old Anderson shelter which was our shed by then. Auntie Moira helped me. She was quite young, younger than my mummy and younger than Sylvia, but she was still a grown-up. One day she said, 'Let's make a den', and so we did. We got some old sticks like the garden canes Mrs Shimmin used for her sunflowers and her sweetpeas. And some old table legs. Auntie Moira dug some soil up and then we stabbed the sticks into the hard ground and Auntie Moira screwed them in with all her might saying, 'Grrrr!' and patted the soil back in around them. I was worried that we didn't have enough sticks to make a real wall.

'It's a cage!' I sobbed. 'I don't want to live in a cage!'

'Don't worry,' said Auntie Moira and she got some old tarpaulin and tied it around the sticks with hairy string and pegged it up with dolly pegs. Some of the sticks wobbled, so she had to get a brick and bash them in. 'Now – do you want a roof?' She flapped some of the tarpaulin over the top. 'Only, if you do, it'll be very dark.'

'No! No roof!' I said quickly.

I lived there for the whole summer, cross-legged with rose-petal plates, privet saucers and acorn cups. Teddy and me at home. Auntie Moira often came visiting, although she didn't fit inside my house and had to sit outside. I remember her smiley freckled face, her straight white teeth. She made me giggle with tickles and funny words, funny stories. My face felt strange, unused to smiles.

'I wish you were my mummy,' I once said after she had made me laugh so hard that my sides ached and I was lying in her arms, blinking at the sky, feeling the sun on my upturned face.

'I wish you were my sister!' Auntie Moira said and gazed away towards the kitchen door.

Next time she visited, Auntie Moira said, 'Shhh!' and put her pointy finger in front of her mouth so that I knew it was a secret. Then she brought her other hand from behind her back and gave me a tiny china tea-pot with little pink and blue flowers on it that she said my mummy and my aunties had used when they were my age. Only I wasn't to let Mummy or Auntie Sylvia know that she'd given it to me. They might be cross. I looked at her solemnly and gave her my most serious promise. One that David Nobbins had told me at school where you have to lick your finger, hold it in the air then mark a big cross over your chest and say very, very seriously – because it will come true and you have to mean it – '*Cross my heart and hope to die!*'

I didn't die of course, but Auntie Moira did. That worried me greatly, because I was even more afraid of my mother's witch powers. Auntie Moira died of pneumonia, her breath smelling like wet leaves. I saw her lying in her bed, her chest rattling with every desperate inhalation, struggling and fighting for breath like I did in the night. But for her it was every living moment. As if someone was slowly and steadily suffocating her; holding her breath. Taking it away. Every breath she took. She was seventeen.

22
Mary: What women want

So under duress I'd left a message on this Lindsay's voicemail but I hadn't heard anything. Which is what I told Clancy every day she asked and today was no exception. She stood grinning at the doorway but looked crestfallen as I rubbed her newly-shaven head and chirped, 'Nope! No news on the nursing front!'

'Aw! Bummer! Ring her again, Mare – she might not have picked up your message,' she said as I followed her up the hall. 'Got a coffee for an old mate?' Clancy threw herself into the chair and swung her leg over the arm.

'Sure, yeah... entertain yourself while I make it.'

'Okay then, I'll masturbate but I'll try not to come all over your loose covers...' She grinned at me.

I tutted disapprovingly. 'Please see that you don't.'

'Okay.'

Clancy is full of herself today, I thought, as I gushed water into the kettle. Still, it was good to see her happy. She'd been a bit low over the last week or so. Not like her at all – she'd been staying in and keeping herself to herself. Masturbating? I sniggered. I could hear her singing in the living room, while I stood in the kitchen as the kettle boiled, and it made me smile.

'Here, you old wanker!' I handed her a mug of coffee.

'I hope there's frigging sugar in it!'

'Of course, sweetie.'

'Have to keep my energy up.' She winked. 'And that was a wink with an "I".' Then she dissolved into laughter at her own joke, so I knew she'd even surprised herself with her pun. Hmmm. That puzzled me. For good measure I peered over the rim of my cup, frowning at her.

'What?' She grinned.

'What's up?'

'Who says anything's up?'

'You do – by your very self-satisfied, smug expression!' I exclaimed.

'That's an awful lot of "S"s for such a little girl…' she teased.

I scowled at her. 'Puh! Okay – so don't tell me then, you cow! I'll have my coffee back then, thank you!'

Clancy made puerile retching noises and giggled. She was positively twinkling at me, her sharp little eyes daring me to press her for information. She sat cross-legged on the armchair going 'Hee-hee-hee!' over her coffee cup, then narrowed her eyes against the steam to take a sip and put it down on the table beside her with a 'Tut!'

'Come on, you're starting to get on my nerves now,' I warned her. After all, I was her mate and I hardly kept any secrets from her these days. None that mattered.

She still sat with her little freckled smirk, taunting me.

'Bitch,' I snarled, only half joking. I could see that she was bursting with something and it was starting to infuriate me. She was obviously going to tell me what it was, but in her own sweet time. 'You're just toying with me, you smart-arse.'

'Reeling you in.' She winked, making reeling-in motions with her hands and clicked her teeth. 'You're so easy to wind up these days, Mare. Chill! There's a dear. All in good time. I shall reveal all.' She lifted her T-shirt and flashed me her vest. I grumbled into my coffee.

She sipped and smirked for all of a few seconds before bursting out, 'Oh, you're hardly any fun at all! Okay! You've forced it out of me! I'm in love!'

I spat out a mouthful of coffee, coughing and catching my breath. Clancy sprang up and bashed me on the back. She laughed while I turned puce and boggle-eyed, holding my throat and gargling the coffee I'd inhaled. Clancy was enjoying hitting me on the back, I noticed. She did it rather too vigorously for my liking and I struggled away, flailing at her to stop. She collapsed giggling on the floor, waving her arms and legs in the air.

I managed to catch my breath back. 'What? What d'you mean?'

This amused Clancy even more. 'In love! In love! In lo-ove!' she sang, still lying on her back waggling her limbs like a stranded beetle.

'Who with?' I frowned in disbelief.

Clancy was exhausted with laughter, hee-hee-heeing and breathless now herself. 'Who do you think?' she managed to gasp and struggled on to one elbow to look at my face.

I was bewildered. Or – God! Had she been meeting people from *The Pink Paper*?

'Is it... Have you been ringin' up *Pink Paper* people?'

Clancy started to piss herself laughing: 'Hee hee! No, you div! Someone you know!'

Jeez, I couldn't imagine. No one I knew, surely? I racked my brains: Kerry? Big Mandy? Georgie? Robbo? Anyone we'd gone to Pride with? Oh, God – not Becky from Pride, surely? I'd always half-regretted that. Clancy still lay on one elbow, one querulous eyebrow raised to taunt me.

'I... haven't a fuckin' clue!' I cried and Clancy hissed a last laugh as I kicked her gently. 'Tell me, you cow!'

Shit! It wasn't me she was in love with, was it? She didn't mean me, surely? 'It's... you don't mean me...?' I went white.

'You daft bat! I've told you – the thought makes my flesh crawl!' Clancy said in disbelief. 'It's Clare!'

'*Clare*? What... *Your* Clare?' I didn't understand.

Clancy opened her eyes so wide that her eyebrows shot up to her close-cropped hairline: 'Yes, *my* Clare! Why? Are you *so* surprised?'

'Yes,' I said in all honesty. 'Well, you haven't exactly been hitting it off for a while!'

Clancy tapped the side of her nose and winked. 'All sorted! And it's fuckin' wonderful – and vice-versa, let me tell YOU!' She took an enormous swig of coffee and held up the cup, victorious.

I had to marvel as Clancy gave me an animated replay of her love life so far, her eyes twinkling mischievously like they used to.

'Aw jeez, Mare – I'm tellin' you – it's like I'm flyin'! Phwoar! I can't remember when things felt so right between us. When we've been so happy!'

All this from a woman who'd been in the depths of despair, on the point of breaking up with Clare a couple of months before. She must have been thinking the same thing, because her face clouded with past hurt. 'But we've put all that behind us now. If anything, it's only made us realize what we've got together. What we could have lost!'

I couldn't imagine a life without Clancy and Clare as a couple. They had kids and they'd had them together, which is no easy thing and that kind of commitment isn't easily shaken. And I'd been so caught up in my own traumas that I'd really not thought about Clancy's. No woman is an island. Waves of guilt lapped gently on my shores.

Because I sat there gaping in wonder, my coffee went quite cold. She said they'd been suffering from Lesbian Bed Death for years and hadn't had sex since before Jamie was born – over four *years* ago! I was horrified. But now it was all discovered again. It was all new and satisfying, and… supreme.

'It's even better than before! Better than it's ever been!' Her eyes shone and she took a mouthful of coffee to punctuate the end. She'd shocked me and my idealistic picture of couples. I was so hung up on their past lack of sex as a loving couple that I struggled now. *Four years?* How could any couple not make love in four years?

'You can be pleased for me, you know!' Clancy laughed as I sat with my mouth open and my brain whirring. Clancy was so matter-of-fact about something that sounded so final. 'It was just a bit of

Lesbian Bed Death,' she said, shrugging. Just a bit of *death*? I choked. Was this what was to come to us all? I knew that as people got old like my parents, they weren't much interested. All passion spent, if there ever had been any. But Clancy and Clare! Even before things had got bad! I'd presumed they had loads of sex. I'd assumed all lesbians had loads of sex. I'd presumed... everyone was like I was with Tanya.

God! I was shocked.

'What?' Clancy grinned. 'Are you surprised that me and Clare have got it together again? You thought we were past it? Too old to shag?'

'God!' My mouth was dry. 'No – I'm surprised you ever lost it – that's all!'

I think I must be so naïve. But then, what did I have to go by? My mum and dad in their separate beds in their flannelette nightwear. I never saw them kiss. Never saw any affection, actually. And come to think of it, never had any affection from them. Victorian values and all. I craved affection now. I vowed I'd never be like them. Never be like my mother, scared of intimacy, afraid to get close, petrified of sex. In fact, I'd gone out of my way to be quite the opposite. I've always snuggled close, I've always offered sex, I've always pushed the limits. It's like casting a spell against coldness and whipping up a sexual ritual to ward off the evil: loneliness. But there's always a bit that gets to you in the end. That tiny fear that you will – after all – turn into your own mum. Would I take up take up crocheting instead of sex? The lost art.

But being a lesbian had freed me up somehow. Who needs men? And the sex... there was always the sex! Fantastic! Soft skin against soft skin. A delirium of intimacy. It's like Clancy said – better to be a practising lesbian. Practice makes perfect. And I aimed to be perfect. So yes, sex was important to me. Then I felt loved. I knew Tanya loved me when she made love to me. On the rare occasions when we had slept together without making love I felt afraid, bereft. I needed to snuggle close, wrap myself around Tanya's back if it was turned away from me, cup my hand around her breast. Know that she wasn't rejecting me. Then Tanya would almost invariably stir, turn around and start to caress me, chew at my nipple, rub between my legs until I got wet and then fuck me. Yes, love and sex go together better than a horse and carriage, for me. Sex. Had to have it. I was shocked to hear that Clancy and Clare had lived so lovingly without it. How could that be? They'd touched, hugged, stroked, in public – and yet, for so many years, not had sex! Unthinkable to me. But anyway, things had turned out sour for them recently – accusations, deception, possession, huge words heavy with emotion. High passion. High drama. But through all that they'd reached some kind of nirvana. All's well that ends well and here was Clancy with her face splitting with smiles, all in love again as if it was the first time.

'Your face'll crack!' I warned her, 'how can you fit all those teeth in one mouth?'

'I feel like my heart is bursting with love!' She smiled.

'Oh, shit...' I muttered.

The first time I had sex with anyone was with my fiancé. I'd just about forgotten I'd ever had a fiancé. The thought that I nearly married a man! Another life entirely. My mum told me, 'Never sleep with a man until you marry him.' And she also said, 'You'll never get a man to marry you if you sleep with him.' Well, that was almost true. But it was I who didn't want to marry him afterwards. So the first time was with Steve. After the first time, the momentous occasion of my first sexual encounter I said: 'Was that it?' I couldn't believe *that* was what all the fuss was about! A bit of resistance, a bit of prodding, and some groaning (his, not mine). We must have been doing it wrong, I thought. For goodness sake – there had been wars over sex! People had been killed for sex! Multi-millions of pounds changed hands every day, for sex! *That* couldn't be all there was to it, surely? I spent hundreds of pounds on *Cosmopolitan* and sex manuals trying to discover '101 foolproof ways to the multiple orgasm'. *One* would have been nice! I was desperately researching every source to find out how to do it to my satisfaction. So much money – so many years – so few orgasms. And all I had to do in the end was sleep with a woman! Why didn't *Cosmopolitan* and all those sex guides say that? It was a male plot! For ultimate and multiple orgasms – sleep with a woman! *That* was to my satisfaction. So yes, I thought 'Bed Death' – if it existed at all – was a heterosexual affair born out of boredom and old age. I was horrified to think that people as vital and young as Clancy and Clare with their affectionate, passionate ways could have fallen into some kind of sexual vacuum. That their nights were filled with winceyette pyjamas and the reading of good books. It horrified me. Shook me to my very roots. It made me question my identity, my existence. My God, would this come to me? Would I ever find that I wouldn't want to be with Tanya? I wanted to spend the rest of my nights locked in volcanic passion, skin to skin, skin inside skin with Tanya. Surely it wouldn't end? I couldn't imagine anything different! Clancy and Clare must be exceptions to the lesbian rule. Or maybe Tanya and I were the exceptions... It was different for us.

23

Tanya: Spring cleaning

'Oy! Are you out there?' Mary's voice broke my reverie. I stood up and dusted myself down. 'Oh! There you are! Couldn't see you above the grass, you're such a tiny thing!' Mary was trying her best to be jolly, to cut through the tension, to chase away the bad things. I smiled.

'Come and look,' she said, 'Cause I don't know if you want to check these things out, or just chuck them. Check –' she held up a maroon-bound book '– or chuck?' In her other hand: a faded straw donkey holding an empty brandy bottle, thick with dust.

'Okay.' I sighed heavily and walked towards the house.

'I've opened all the windows and chucked out the bins, because there was a bit of a stink. We should have come over before...'

I sighed again. I stood in the doorway, one hand on either side of the frame. The hallway was still dim, musty curtains hanging at the window and door. The carpet was even browner and more raggedly threadbare than I remembered. Depressing.

'I've chucked out the obvious rubbish: junk mail, old food packets and that kind of thing. But I wonder whether you want to sort through any of... her things.' I looked steadily at her. 'Or not...' she trailed off.

'Whatever you think...' I lit up another cigarette and appraised the hallway. Pictures still on the walls. Mary had swept up a pile of mail into one corner and a couple of bulging binbags sat in the kitchen doorway.

'Right!' Mary clapped her hands breezily, 'How about... we go into the living room, you sit down and I'll sort out the cupboards. You can tell me what you want to keep, sell or throw.'

Keep, sell, throw. Check or chuck. Check. Chuck. Check. Chuck. Check. Chuck. *Tempus Fugit*. Check, chuck, check, chuck, check, chuck. Time flies when you're having fun.

'Whatever,' is what I said. I followed her into the *parlour*. Not the living room. The parlour. Mary called it the living room, but that wasn't right. Nobody lived here. Ever. I was too tired to argue. What the hell did it matter, anyway? Parlour. Living room. One room. Another room. Come into my parlour, said the spider to the fly.

'I've battered the dust off that chair for you,' Mary said. I sat down. The red velveteen armchair. I was honoured. Was it Sunday? Was I the queen?

The same pink floral wallpaper discoloured by sunlight. Cheap framed prints of faded cottages in the countryside. The glass lampshades fuzzy with a thick layer of dust overhead. I hadn't been in this room for years. Perhaps no one had. The ceiling corners were heavy with fluffy-stranded cobwebs. Some of the slack threads swung in the draught from the open window. But one web strung from the centre of the bay window to the wall looked sparkling and new, strong and resilient.

'Now, Tan... the pictures. The ornaments. What do you think?'
'Chuck.'

Check. Chuck. Check. Chuck. Time and tide wait for no man. No woman. No one. Check. Chuck.

'Are you sure, Tan? You could sell them.'
'Okay.'
'Or is there anything you want to keep?'
Silence.
'A memento?'
Silence.
'Okay... can I use my discretion, then? Chuck the kitsch and keep the cash?'

Check. Chuck. Chuck. Kitsch. Keep. Cash. 'Okay.'

I breathed in the scent of my cigarette. Familiar. Soothing.

'Who's this?'

I swivelled my head and focused hazily on the frame Mary was holding towards me, focused into: black and white photo of a stout and smiling woman. 'My granny. Keep that!'

'Oh, good!' Mary grinned in surprise and encouragement and placed it in a cardboard box on the floor where she was kneeling.

'And this?' She held up another photograph. I frowned to make out the figures. Three girls and a boy, squinting against the sun. The tallest was my mother, looking willowy and serious against the smaller children. John – a year younger than my mum, Sylvia had once told me, who died when he was sixteen. And Sylvia. Poor, highly strung Sylvia who committed suicide when she was thirty. And then Moira – carefree Moira, the fairest one of all. Lovely Moira, dead for want of breath. Her lungs stopped their agonized working and her heart stopped dead too. Seventeen. My mother survived them all. My mother, the imposter. The changeling. The evil one who deserved to die. She outlived them all. All dead.

'My mum, my Auntie Sylvia, my Auntie Moira and the boy is my uncle... John.'

'Wow! I didn't know you had such a lot of family!'

'I don't.'

'Keep?' she queried.

'Chuck.'

'Are you sure?'

'Are you going to question me every time?'

She dropped the photo into the bin bag. Dead people. I didn't want to see dead people. I would be dead myself soon enough.

Several items later I was bored and pissed off and the air felt too thick for me in the parlour. Too hung with cobwebs and dust and memories. I could hardly breathe. Had to... do something. 'Can we make coffee here?' I snapped.

'Well, there's water, but I didn't see any coffee and we'd have to get some milk...'

'So – no, then!'

'Well, I didn't think to bring any. There's Coke and crisps in the car, but I could easily...'

'Great! No fuckin' coffee!' I stood up and prepared to flounce out of the door. Mary, quicker than a flash, was up before me and in the doorway blocking my way.

She touched my arm. 'Look, I'll do it... you sit down. There must be...'

'No, no!' I said wildly, then realized that if she didn't see me calm down I would get nowhere. So I calmed down. 'Look, I would just like to get out. Fresh air. Trauma...'

'I'll come with you.' Mary wiped her hands on her jeans, frowning.

'No! No... look, I'm not much good, am I? Would you mind very much if I just went into town for an hour...'

'We can both do that!'

'No...' I said, steadying my voice. 'Fact is... I need a bit of time to myself... away from here...' Mary's eyes hardened. 'And, like you said, the sooner this place is cleaned up the better. You're doing a great job and I'm more of a hindrance than a help... I'm as much use as a chocolate fire-guard...'

'Oh, you're *not*...' Mary softened.

'Not even as much use as a chocolate fire-guard, then!' I grinned but still looked anxious. 'Look, you'd get on better if I weren't here – you're too busy being concerned about me, attentive to me...' She started to protest but I cut her off: 'It'll do us both good if I take my-self off for an hour or two...'

'Two? You said an hour, before!'

'For God's sake! Don't begrudge me time to myself!' I hissed. 'This is bloody hard for me, you know!'

'Sorry,' Mary's eyes were clouded and sorrowful, 'I just want to make sure you're okay.'

'I am. I will be. But you have to let me do what I need to do. I'll be back later to help.'

'Okay.' Mary's lip wobbled.

I pulled at her shoulder and she bent her head so that I could kiss her on the mouth, a brief dry brush of the lips like the stroke of a grass in the wind.

'I do love you, you know,' I whispered. Her eyes shone and she let me go. She even helped me to get away by adjusting the mirrors, the seat, the steering-wheel. I rewarded her with the bag of Coke and crisps she'd packed.

I drove into the centre of Leeds, my head fuzzy with dust, my skin crawling with imagined spiders. I panted for air, especially the city air. I parked and dashed into Harvey Nick's to use the washroom, where I pumped out great handfuls of their perfumed liquid soap and rubbed hard at my face, hands and arms until I saw a plump middle-aged woman, camel-coated and dripping in gold, looking at me in the mirror, aghast.

'Out, damn spot!' I shouted, meeting her eye in my mirror. 'Here's the smell of the blood still!' I held my hands up theatrically, slick with suds. She bustled out while I shouted after her, 'All the perfumes of Arabia will not sweeten this little hand!'

I laughed and scooped up great handfuls of water to rinse my face and hair. I rubbed my hair on a towel, still convinced that I was dusty. Then I went down to the perfume department to spray myself with anything – perfumes of Arabia or anywhere – that would freshen my hair and skin. I smiled indulgently at the over-made-up assistants who looked politely on. Then I hit the High Street with confidence. I found a coffee shop and patisserie in Victoria Arcade. I ordered a big, squishy, fresh cream gateau and a cafetiere of strong Java coffee and sat at a bistro table outside, waiting for my heart rate to soar or my arteries to harden.

Wired by the caffeine boost, I felt a need to be with gay people – if only to stand at a bar surrounded by gay people. I didn't want to go to a straight pub, with men trying to chat me up. Having to look miserable to put them off and still encountering 'Cheer up, it might never happen' and worse from rebuffed men. I just wanted to be able to get a drink and sit easy without stress or unpleasantness, and admire the women. I wasn't sure of the clientele in Leeds gay bars during the day, but I made my way to the nearest, feeling thirstier for the scene than for a drink.

I found a great wine bar with a minty green painted décor, cool frosted glass tables and curved beech and aluminium chairs. While I ordered my drink I stroked the lilac curved marble bar and its chill refreshed my warm palms. There weren't many people in there apart from a couple of gay boys either side of the bar and a foursome of baby dykes, none of whom particularly interested me, but it felt comfortable for me to sit and read the papers. I'd picked up a *Pink* and a *Diva* magazine and, for the first time in ages, I felt relaxed enough to sit and sip a spritzer, beginning to melt into a holiday mood. I could get a taste for it. This was a trial run for me. Only a couple of weeks to go before I flew off with Christiane. Once today was over, I could leave things in other people's hands. Clear things, get my mother's house on the market, forget about it. I had another couple of white wine spritzers, read some features and flicked through the personal ads. Interesting.

Back at my mother's house later that evening, Mary was not particularly happy to find me turning up a bit drunk in a taxi. I'd abandoned the car in the city centre four miles away, so we had to go back and pick it up. She didn't complain about paying for the taxi, though. I'd blown all my money. She appreciated that I was emotionally distraught.

Mary's big moon face was flushed to a dark ruddiness with exertion. The faint lines across her forehead and at the side of her nose were ingrained with grime, despite her attempts to splash away the worst of the all-pervasive dust. A dirty watermark blotched her jawline.

'Oh, babe, you are an untouchable! Your hair can't decide whether to be damp with sweat or stiff with dirt.' I smiled.

She ran her fingers through her hair and made an exaggerated pretence of getting her hand trapped in a knot of it, grimacing. 'Ow!'

She had been working really hard since lunchtime and had made astounding progress in the house, clearing every room of everything but the furniture, sweeping, hoovering, and sorting the rubbish from the valuables to box tidily away. I walked from room to room feeling only emptiness. The kitchen. The so-called heart of the home. The living room and its saggy old sofa stained with memories, I avoided. Emptiness and relief. My bedroom was a smaller cell than I remembered – but even then the room had hung over my shoulders like a protective cloak – a suit of armour, growing smaller and tighter as I grew. I swung back the door and ran my hand over the bolt and the lock I had screwed on myself. I fingered the over-painted screw holes from past failed and torn off bolts, locks and latches. The yellowish painted patch of wood I had nailed, glued and crudely bolted over the gaping wound my mother had kicked into the door. I stood at the murky window where I had stood for hours, years, overlooking the back garden.

Its dark greenness lured me now. I trailed my hand down the banister and, bless her, Mary had even polished that, so that it squeaked cleanly where I touched. Growing dusk as it was, I walked into the garden. My refuge. My safe place. The grass and the soil and the tumble of weeds and wild flowers. The lupins and red-hot pokers and wild rosebushes ran rampant. Where years ago I lived quietly with the caterpillars, the butterflies, the scurrying beetles and armoured woodlice, watching slow-inching earthworms undulate through the grass. My fingernail ends were always tight crescents of black dried mud, compacted dirt. I stood where Moira had built my den – and thought of her laughing in the sunshine, with her dazzling smile dismissing all my fears. Now I brushed the palm of my hand across the wavering fronds of tall grass, feeling their soft feathery heads against my skin and I cried. Silently. Mary, ever watchful, came out and put her arms around me. I tensed and tried to gain control, feeling silly and embarrassed.

'Just… sentiment. Stupid…' I said, wiping my nose across the back of my hand.

'No… no…' whispered Mary and I allowed her to hold me close but not too close, so that I knew I could get away.

We went home with the car full of boxes of things Mary thought I might want to keep or that might be heirlooms. I told her I didn't want to keep anything. I told her that the house clearance people were welcome to take it all.

'I told you – I don't care about any of it! It's just you, droning on! You wasted your time sorting it!'

Mary went quiet and concentrated on driving.

I looked sullenly out of the window, seeing nothing. Pondering.

'I really do appreciate what you've done today, my love,' I said ten minutes later as she drove us up the A1. 'In fact I'd like to take you out for a meal to thank you… But as it is, you're a bit too filthy and sweaty for a restaurant and we're both exhausted. What say we get a takeaway, go back to my house and we can have a lovely bath… eh? But since you're so dusty, I'll get in first and I'll leave you the water…? Lovely, special, perfumed water. Some of that nice stuff I bought you for Christmas –' I rested my hand on her thigh '– and when you're all clean and fragrant in bed, I'll thank you properly. I'll give you your special reward… How does that sound? Mmm?'

Mary's face broke into a wry smile. 'Actually, that sounds lovely!' She brightened up and didn't even mind paying for the curry.

24
Mary: A close call

I was surprised, if not shocked, to pick up the phone, expecting Tanya but hearing a strange voice gabbling away as if she'd known me for ages: 'Mary! Hi! This is great! So lovely to speak to you at last! Thanks very much for getting in touch! It's Lindsay.'

My mind was blank. Lindsay who?

'You left a message on my voicemail... *Pink*... *Paper*? I had an ad in there.'

Blood rushed to my face. 'Shit! I mean, yes! God! That was ages ago! I'd forgotten! It must have been a couple of weeks!'

'Oooh – that's funny – they usually only keep the messages on for two days – it's a ruse to get you to keep ringing up and running up your phone bill! I only picked up your message last night, but you sounded like such a great laugh that I just had to call you! That thing about the bungee-jumping! What a hoot!'

I frowned. My brain was flickering wildly. Bungee? That wasn't me! She must have mistaken me for someone else. And I'd definitely not called in the last week. She must be mistaken... But how did she get my phone number? Nothing made sense.

'Erm,' I said.

'So – let me tell you a little bit more about myself... I'm a nurse, as I said, but I work in a GP surgery, so as for your suggestions about bedbaths... well! You cheeky thing!'

I was stunned. Completely bemused. She rattled on regardless.

'... Erm, I've got two kids but they're pretty grown up now... Have to be, with me as a mother! They're sixteen and fourteen... Oh, did I say I was thirty-eight? Well, I'm thirty-nine now. It's not that I lie about my age, just that I had a birthday last week! Oh, listen to me wittering on! So tell me, how is the shoe shop? God, I'd love to work in a shoe shop! My favourite things!'

Weird. I hadn't said I worked in a shoe shop. I hardly told anyone. It was only a tiny shop. Only part-time. Hardly worth mentioning. In fact, I hadn't mentioned it.

'Oh, fine. Great. But I'm only there three days a week –' I was struggling to connect. 'Well, actually, it's a bit dull most of the time...'

'But you make it sound such fun! That bit you said in the message about your boss telling you to keep your eye out for shoplifters, 'cause he was expecting some and you were practically strip-searching everyone who went in or out! Hilarious! And then it turned out to be SHOPFITTERS your boss was expecting! Oh, I was creased up!'

I was scouring my mind. This was weird. I hadn't said that. It was definitely a little anecdote of mine, but I certainly wouldn't have left that on a stranger's voicemail. It had been embarrassing enough leaving any kind of message. I think I'd just given my name, age and serial number. And Clancy had been disappointed when I made the stilted call: 'Aw, jeez, Mare! That's no good at all! You'll never get a woman that way! Aw! Make an effort!'

Clancy. ... Clancy! Hassling me to leave another message! The cow!

Lindsay's voice cut through my realisation and horror. 'Anyway, I did enjoy your message and you sounded so bright and cheery – a woman after my own heart. I know it's weird talking to a stranger on the phone –' she must have sensed my wariness '– but I wondered if you would like to meet up for a drink – a coffee sometime? Just for a chat?'

'Oh... er... okay. I'll give you a call,' was all I could think to say. She'd caught me off-guard and also I'm crap at saying no. I even took down her phone number.

We said goodbye. I seethed. Apparently I had a doppelganger, a Mary impersonator. Wait till I got hold of her! If Clancy liked pretending to be me, then she could damn well go on a date with this Lindsay woman! I'd swop with Clancy – I've always fancied being small and slim.

'You're getting fat,' my mum had told me. Often. These days I thanked her for her consideration and observations, generally taking her for the silly old interfering bat that she was. But when I was eleven, twelve, thirteen, fourteen, fifteen, sixteen, seventeen, eighteen... I was secretly – if not visibly – shaken and wounded. My formative years. The times that I was looking for reassurance, for support; when I was finding out about myself, unsure of myself, worried that I was fat, spotty and probably ugly.

'You want to get rid of those spots!' my mum would say. 'You want a good wash! I never had spots when I was your age. I had a lovely clear complexion. You want to steam those blackheads out. Get rid of those vile germs! Every one of those blackheads is going to grow and fill up to be a big, matter-filled boil you know, seeping germs and pus. That's not very appealing, now, is it? No boy's going to look at you with those horrible spots. Big, fat ugly-looking girl with spots... *Acne*, is it? I've never heard the like! I never had acne. You want to squeeze them out. I don't know what's wrong with you! You want to sit over a bowl of boiling water with a towel on your head.'

My mother made me want to walk around the streets with a towel over my head. I wish I'd had the nerve to tell her to boil her *own* head.

My mother's philosophy was similar to St Ignatius Loyola's: 'Give me a boy until he is seven and I will give you a man'. But hers was: 'Give me a girl until she is eighteen and I will give you a snivelling, fat, insecure incompetent'.

I came from a slim, petite family with slim, petite minds. Only my brother Vincent approaches me in height, but he is spindly rather than solid like me. I am twice the width of any of them. As wide as the whole family standing in a line. As big as a crowd. But I do know I'm not really that fat. I know I'm not. It's just that I felt that big when I was younger, since I believed my mum's publicity. And for all my heftiness, my mum treated me like a fragile thing. Fragile in everything, except my feelings. They were up for grabs, fair game for being thrown around the room, smashed against the walls, belted with a baseball bat and crushed under foot.

And yet she wouldn't let me out of her sight. I was too precious, too delicate, for the dangers of the wicked world outside. When I was young, I couldn't go round to friends' houses because she didn't know them. I couldn't have friends round because she didn't know them. She'd worry about me if she didn't know what I was doing. When school friends called for me she said, 'Not today, thank you!' She said that every day. Every day was not today. Yet Vincent was allowed to roam the streets and rampage round with his snot-faced gang of little urchin cronies, 'cause he was a boy. And when he came back into the house my mum would bow down before him as if he were a prince, scurrying backwards as he walked, swathing his path with sheets of newspaper. Every step he took, she bobbed down and placed a piece of newspaper on the carpet underfoot. Then she would put a carefully unfolded newspaper down on one chair and tell him to perch on there and not move until she'd run him a bath and prodded him upstairs along the newspaper trail to the bathroom. If she ran out of newspaper, I swear she'd have prostrated herself and let him walk all over her.

So that was then, but I was free now. I could read library books and even go to the toilet without washing my hands if I wanted to. I didn't have spots, I'd lost some weight and I knew I wasn't ugly, just fairly average to pleasant looking. But on bad days when I felt awkward and low, I was plain. I couldn't see what anyone could find attractive in me. I was lucky to have Tanya at all.

These days, I'm sure Tanya is growing gentler with me, more patient. Her wild unprovoked tantrums are fewer than they were when we first met. I really think we might've turned the corner. She's like a wild thoroughbred horse: proud, powerful and deceptively strong, but wary of humans and frightened inside, lashing out to protect herself. I know that with my love she'll eventually come round to the idea that she *can* love in return, without fear. That there's a future for us. I read a book about a horse-whisperer (not that I think handling Tanya is like breaking in a horse – she'd kill me!), and she does need to know that I am strong for her, good for her and I'll do her no harm.

She even gave me a present the other day. Me! It was steeped with significance, a little piece of our history from a beautiful, romantic evening down on the beach. Precious. While we were walking arm-in-arm along the shore in Saltburn, just as the sun was dipping into the sea, she gave me a piece of coloured glass she'd picked up from the sand. Precious to me for the moment it represented.

'Look at this,' she said, her voice so quiet that I could barely hear it, so that I had to lean down to catch her soft words. She held the blue pebble of glass up to the sunset. 'See how it has been tumbled smooth by the tide, all of its sharp edges soft now. So fragile, yet so strong.'

'Like you!' I whispered in wonder. A warm, tingling feeling washed over me.

Tanya smiled. 'Oh, *you*...' Then she laughed. 'Take it. It's yours.'

I rubbed the glass pebble with my thumb. It felt warm with the heat from Tanya's hand and comforting, as if imbued with power like a talisman. Opaque and chalky blue. I stared at Tanya, feeling open and emotional but still worried that she might be winding me up, searching her face to see how much of a joke it was to her. Her eyes softened as she held my gaze, then she took a deep breath and looked out to sea, murmuring, 'If we stood side by side... here, by the sea... You would see the tide, but I'd see opportunity.' I stared at her, amazed. 'I would breathe the waves, gull-cold, chilled by wings and hear their whispered warnings.' She swallowed. 'And you would draw me to the shore.'

I wasn't sure how to take it. Was she talking to me, about us, or was she just thinking aloud to herself? I stood behind her, clasping my arms around her.

'That sounds like poetry. Is it?' I wondered, feeling stupid and dull. Unworthy.

'If you like.' She paused and we both listened to the soft rush of the tide before she went on, clutching my hands around her body in front of her, holding me to her: 'Love isn't about staring into one another's eyes... but looking out in the same direction.'

We watched the sun melt slowly into the horizon, leaving pools of coral light on the distant water. The warm feeling made my skin hum and the tiny hairs on my arms stand on end, charged with electricity. I bent down and nuzzled my lips into her neck at the sensitive spot I knew she had. She nestled into my shoulder. In the distance, the sea was shimmering and shifting like molten metal. Closer, it was a metallic silk moiré, dark turquoise and more fluid. The tide went out whispering, leaving rippled impressions swept by the next wave, smoothed by the sea's shape. It was spellbinding: the sort of evening that changes your life, filled with possibility and promise. Then there was a sudden turn in the weather, a sharpening change in the wind. The stiff grass on the cliff wavered in alarm as dry-blown sand showered us. I winced at the salt sting and the lashing from strands of her windswept hair.

'It's getting cold now. Let's go home.' Tanya pulled away from me but reached out to take my hand. In my pocket I turned the smooth blue pebble of glass over and over in my palm. Smooth. Precious. One. Two. Three. Four times for luck.

'But you should be grateful!' Clancy gaped, swinging Jamie the four-year-old over her hip, as I marched into the kitchen demanding coffee and explanations with menaces.

'I should be...? Hell, Clancy!'

'Ooh! Mare! Children about! Cover your ears, Jamie!' Jamie obliged, good-naturedly.

'Well, just what do you think you're doing, Clancy? Pretending you're me! Leaving messages on strange women's... answerphone things!' I hissed.

'Just helping out a poor misguided friend!' Clancy said, the picture of innocence.

'Then you should have just kept out of it! You have no right!'

Jamie was struggling to slither down from Clancy's hip. 'No darling, you can't go yet,' she said to him, 'you're Clancy's only protection from a vicious beating...' He looked blankly at her, his pouty wet lips open in innocent wonder.

'Clancy!' I warned.

'Oh, go on then, Jamie – save yourself!' She let him slide down her leg and he ran off, disappearing through the kitchen door as she cried, 'You're free! Run! Run like the wind, Jamie...!' She clasped her hands together in a melodramatic pose, calling after him: 'Remember me... won't you?'

'You crazy woman...' I couldn't help but laugh.

Clancy came over all Latin-American: 'Me, crrrazy? You crrrazy! You crrrrrrazy, crrrazy lady! Tut!' She clicked her teeth loudly for emphasis.

'I really am annoyed at you. Seriously... stop making me laugh,' I said, giggling.

'Aw, come on, Mare. It's the chance of a date, isn't it?'

'No way!' I squeaked.

'Okay. Where's the harm? You could just go for a coffee. The worst you can do is waste an hour of your life going to meet her. At best... Wa-hey! I should be charging you for this service!'

I frowned. 'What about Tanya?' I said gravely.

'What about her? She has plenty of other women!'

'She does *not*!' My voice went very shrill and high-pitched.

'Oof! Mare! You're piercing my eardrums... It's my *tongue* I wanted doing, next!'

'She has women friends, but she isn't unfaithful. No.'

'Yeah...' Clancy raised her eyebrows.

'Well, I don't know how you can say that. We're together. Tanya loves me,' I said indignantly.

'It's love... but not as we know it!'

25
Tanya: Trust

I rolled off Christiane and lay on my back looking at the ornate white ceiling rose, the edges of which were picked out in gold leaf so that they glowed in the subdued light from the candles beside the bed. I rested there for some time, entranced by the flickering shadows rippling the ceiling, then I turned towards Christiane. She lay with her eyes closed, with the candlelight's dramatic cast on the fine lines of her face, the traces of her ageing, the dark hollows of her eye sockets. Her neck was more wrinkled, with shades of the organ pipes beginning. Characterful and distinguished, I felt. Not old. Suddenly I thought of my mother in the hospital viewing room, of her face yellowing, smooth and waxy. The tip of her ear tinged pale russet. They told me she was at peace. I hoped that I would be too. Here, I was at peace, with Christiane. I leant on one elbow and watched her, calmed by her peacefulness, the steadiness of her breathing echoed by mine until completely attuned with hers. I watched her chest rising and falling, the sheet covering her breast lifting gently and rhythmically, until she opened her eyes and laughed. 'Is this what they call neighbourhood watch?'

'Yes. I'm on guard!'

'On guard?' She roared with laughter.

'Protecting you!' I grinned and slipped my hand beneath her waist.

Her skin was warm. I wanted to climb in it.

'It's you I need protecting against.' She smiled.

The holiday was nearing and I was feeling good about being with Christiane. However, I was right to cut my losses, to prioritise my time and my women. I had already taken Red out of the equation and these days I seemed to have less energy for going on the internet too. Real life was getting to be all I could cope with, after all. I was tense enough with the strain of showing merely casual enthusiasm to Christiane whilst erupting with elation inside. Added to that was the stress of maintaining an ordinary love with Mary in the knowledge that I would shortly disappear for three weeks with another woman. As I said before, I was getting old and these heights of emotion were exhausting. Dizzying. Still, I've always been very good at keeping my own counsel. Keeping secrets. It's always been a way of life to me. Family secrets.

For although I knew that my mother's treatment of me was unlawful, as was her men's oppression of me, I did not say a word. Strangely, it was not through a sense of loyalty towards my mother. Neither did I keep quiet for fear of her fury or Ron's revenge.

'Tanya?' Mrs Patterson – the games teacher – had called me over to her after a netball match. She had been my favourite teacher, a strapping woman with short curly dark hair who had always worn an Aertex blouse and whose nipples were forever erect. It hadn't been just admiration of her physique, though. I had respected her and her no-nonsense attitude and had no doubt been a little in love with her. 'You don't seem to be very happy. Is there anything wrong?'

The week before she had asked me about a big bruise on my leg. Now she looked at me kindly and reached a hand sympathetically to my shoulder. She was becoming dangerous.

'No.' I frowned at her.

'Well,' she said doubtfully, 'just remember that I'm here to talk if you ever want to. You *will* just come and talk to me if... you're worried about anything?' Her concerned brown eyes narrowed.

I said, equally doubtfully: 'Of course, Miss. Thank you.'

I ran off to get changed, cursing her and my carelessness under my breath. I could avoid getting undressed in public. I could avoid the unnecessary advances of teachers. I could choose not to do any netball and hockey practices after school. I could take myself out of this danger. But I enjoyed sport. I liked running around, pushing myself hard, stretching myself to my physical limits, attacking goals and nets, tackling and defying people. I liked the aggression of it. And it kept me out of the house. So I still went to practices and played for teams. I wore a tracksuit whenever possible. I avoided the showers and turned up already changed into full kit. I took more care to smile a lot and not to let the mask slip. Otherwise people think you are vulnerable. They can take your power from you.

I told no one. My silence was from a sense of my own shame and humiliation, from fear of repercussions from the intervention of do-gooders. I did not want sympathy and intervention; I did not want to be a poor victim saved by social services or the community; I did not wish anyone to know. In my own wordless attempts to take myself out of the situation – by packing a bag as a toddler to run away to Granny's; by spending time with Mrs Shimmin next door or Auntie Moira; by playing in the park – at least I was taking control of my own destiny. At least I was taking some action. I did not have to rely on anyone else. I still do not have to – nor do I wish to – rely on anyone else. Mary would have me depend completely on her. Her need is palpable and she sucks me dry at times with her neediness to be needed. A terrifying thing. She suffocates me with her love. She would even breathe for me. I need to escape. Yet there are times when it is a blessed relief to surrender to the watery bubble of her care, to relax into the dense salt lake of her love, to be lapped by warm nurturing water. However heavy your heart, it's possible to float effortlessly and trust that you will be held steady, so that you do not drown or flail in fear. Safe in the knowledge that you'll be held secure, that the water will never be allowed to lap across your face so that you can't breathe… Can't… catch your breath. Sometimes it feels as if it might be good to relinquish myself… to someone trustworthy. Although I cannot trust anyone entirely. Not even Mary.

'Hairy Mary.' I looked up from between her thighs and grinned. She was red-faced from her coming; a mottled red flush emblazoned her neck and trickles of sweat ran from beneath her breasts. Her eyes rolled into a semblance of consciousness and she smiled drowsily.

I pursed my lips and blew her wiry black public hair and she murmured, 'Cold. You spoil the moment.'

'Oh, was there a moment to spoil? I thought I just spoilt you!'

'Oh, you… cow…' she said tentatively, then lifted her head to ask, 'but do you love me, really?' Her frank baby-blue eyes looked at me, all honest and good.

'Now – that would be telling…'

I am good at secrets. A lifetime of practice. Deception comes easy to me. There are no lies that I would not tell to protect myself or my integrity. I look after myself alone; I am crap at looking after other things. I once won a goldfish at the fair and it committed suicide. I hadn't actually wanted a goldfish, but I had at least made the effort and put it in a bowl of water. However, by the time I came back from work the following day it had leapt out of the bowl and was lying drily on the carpet like a scaly, wizened carrot paring. Only I could have a suicidal goldfish. I am like that. People give me plants and animals and I kill them. It's a gift.

Whereas Mary, she is something else. She doesn't have a garden of her own, so she has adopted mine, in her indirect, tentative way.

'Tanya – would you mind if I cut your grass?'

Why should I? Go ahead.

'If I just trim down those shrubs and weed out the borders, there would be room for some lovely bedding plants. If I buy some, would you let me plant them up for you?'

Your time, your money – do what you like!

She had spent two weekends working solidly in the garden while I sat connected on the internet talking to the Americans with whom I had developed very mutually satisfying relationships. Tired of being hunched over the computer, I came down and took her a glass of lager and sat on the clipped lawn. I suddenly looked around at what she had done. The garden was transformed. I'd had no time for it myself and the most I had done was to cut the grass once or twice in the summer. Although I'd been pleased with the result, I couldn't manage the regular upkeep. I also convinced myself that it was better to let nature take its course. I quite liked the idea of wildflowers and weeds bursting through. I was all for a low-maintenance, no-maintenance garden. I had even thought of paving it over for ease. After all, I didn't need to hide in the grass any more. My den was my house. My bed was my safe place. Until sleep overtook me.

I had been sitting all Sunday morning talking to Slave4U and Li'l Mo and the others. My eyes were streaming with the concentration of reading the screen and I was hot with the words and the images that had been flashing before me for the last seven hours.

Slave4U: Miss – I am tugging on my chain as you have asked me and with your permission, I would like to elaborate on the scenario you have laid out before me.
MISS-TRESS: Then do so.
Slave4U: Miss – I am lying stark naked at your feet, on my belly with my wrists bound with chain above my head. My butt is red and raw from the sound whipping you gave me <WHIMPER> but you have asked me to turn over… I part my thighs slowly…

Yes, Slavey has a way with words. I leave the rest to your imagination. Mine had certainly had a surfeit. And there was more. Each of my women has their own individual charms and specialisms and idiosyncrasies. Yet reality kicks in. I succumb to the usual necessities in life: I need to visit the toilet; I get hungry and thirsty. Unlike some people, the quirks of my virtual life do not flood out into my own life. I do not frequent fetish bars or kit out my bedroom as a dungeon. I am not a real-time sadist nor a masochist, since I wince at the concept of self-inflicted or consensual pain in reality. I haven't even had my ears pierced. Neither would I actively physically hurt another person. I am aware that for my internet friends, the boundaries are more blurred. I have seen their photos: the shaven heads, the holistic piercings, the extreme tattoos; the scratchings, the scars, the burns. I know from their casual talk, out of role, that reality and virtual reality slide seamlessly into one another. I know that for some of them their fantasy is their reality. Their descriptions are more graphic than I could imagine. For me it is entirely fantasy, a game: pure and simple and harmless within its own context. I cannot deny that I derive great pleasure from having a host of women who make themselves available to my whims, who will prostrate themselves at my feet and do whatever I wish, endure whatever extreme and exquisite cruelty I can devise. But, I reiterate, the fantasy is divorced entirely from my real life. And it is not a fantasy I wish to enact in the real world.

So this is the condition in which I went down to the garden, eyes red-rimmed and mind racing, armed with a gesture of lager.

Mary was kneeling at one of the borders, her trowel chivvying some recalcitrant weeds from beneath the hedge.

Mary, Mary quite contrary. How does your garden grow? With silver bells and cockle shells and pretty maids all in a row.

I sat down in the shade of my tree, on the grass that Mary had cut for the second time in a fortnight. I called her over for a lager. She came and sat down heavily beside me and grinned, her face sweaty with exertion. 'Get plenty of work done? You've been up there for ages!'

'Ohhhh, yes.' I grinned back. 'Time for a break! You must need one, too!'

'I don't know... I think I'm on a roll now. I feel as if I've made a difference!' She sat back against the apple tree and took a long drink of lager, then appraised the garden. 'What do you think?'

The place was looking damn fine. 'Mmmm... you certainly *have* made a difference,' I had to admit. 'It's brilliant. Well done, old girl!'

She smiled, wiped the back of her hand across her brow and continued to survey her estate. My estate.

'I hope you don't think this means that you're getting your feet under the table, though. Don't let it give you any ideas!' I warned, only half-joking. 'Cancel that order for the white picket fence...'

She tutted. 'Ta-an! I told you, I just like doing it!'

'Me too!' I growled and reached for the crotch of her jeans. 'Fancy going to bed... now?'

'Oh, but I'm all dirty.'

'I know!' I said with enthusiasm.

26

Mary: Not everything in the garden is rosy

One. Two. Three. Four. I rearranged the pens in my pen pot near the phone four times. I touched each one four times with my index finger, just to be safe. Oh, I'm so stupid. So gullible. Things had been lovely. Ecstatic! Then turned so quickly to ugliness and pain. I felt punch-drunk and disorientated.

That morning Tanya and I had planned to go out – twenty-five miles away – to Whitby for the day. We'd decided to scare ourselves silly in the Dracula Experience, race one another up the steps to the Abbey, have fish and chips and ice cream, wander round the antique shops and bookshops and hold hands like we always did when we were out of town. I always waited for Tanya to slip her small hand in mine as her silent consent that we were far enough away from our public to be ourselves. A couple. We'd been lying in bed the night before, chattering like schoolgirls, giggling and deciding on all the things we'd do. I was so looking forward to it!

We had got up early, Tanya waking me up with a cup of coffee and a croissant. 'Aw! Sweet!' I'd said, genuinely touched.

'Isn't it just! Don't get too used to it, though.' She'd given her usual throwaway comment to take the sentimental edge off anything nice she said or did. I was getting used to it. 'I'm just a bit soft in the head this morning.'

'Aww! It suits you, though.' I had smiled and hugged her. She'd kissed my cheek. I'd ruffled her hair, kissing her gently on the lips.

'I love you,' I had said, looking deeply into her eyes. She had returned my gaze just as lovingly and that proved that she only needed reassurance that I loved her, and everything would be normal. This would be normal.

We had got up and dressed and had just been leaving when it all happened. We had nearly been out of the door and on our way. Tanya had already been wearing her mirror sunglasses, the ones that always disconcerted me because I couldn't read her eyes, but she had stood relaxed, dangling her car keys from the end of her index finger and smiling. She had looked really cute in a little black vest and white cropped trousers, with her lush springy curls tied loosely back. Cute and sexy. I'd just wanted to enfold her in my arms. We had been so happy. I'd hugged her and buried my face in her clean soft hair, breathing in the sun lotion that she'd rubbed into her shoulders.

'This is so great! We're going on holiday!' I'd said, chuckling. Her whole body had suddenly tensed and she'd broken away. Roughly pushed me away, her fingers biting into my arms. 'What's the matter?' I'd asked, worried that I'd squeezed her too hard, hurt her somehow.

'Get *lost*! That's it! We're not going!' she'd snapped, whipping off her glasses and glaring at me cruelly.

'What? Why?' I'd taken a step towards her, but her bark had stopped me in my tracks.

'FUCK OFF OUT!' she'd yelled, smashing her fist down on the hall table.

But I'd been bewildered and had wanted to know what I'd done wrong. Couldn't just let it lie.

Hours later, at home by myself, I was still none the wiser, still trying to rationalise it. So I'd been crying on the phone to Clancy again.

'Oh, for God's sake, Mare. Take some control of your life, will you?'

It hurt me that even Clancy sounded exasperated with me. I was being pathetic. I stabbed the pen I was holding into the pot.

'Look, you were telling me only yesterday that everything was wonderful and all your dreams were coming true. So – was that fantasy again?'

It was true. I'd only just been saying – feeling – that things were getting better. I felt closer to Tanya and I'm sure she felt the same. Then, I don't know… maybe Tanya had realized that things were going too comfortably. So the situation had got nasty. Words. Mugs. Fists. All flew. Words hurt worst of all.

'Clance – you don't know her like I do!' I talked over Clancy's snort. 'She sabotages herself. If things are going really well, she panics that it won't last, so she deliberately tries to destroy it all. Sabotage!'

'Oh, fuck! You've been listening to too much of Big Mandy's psychobabble shite again!'

'Clancy! You don't understand!' I rattled the pens furiously in their pot.

'You deserve better! Face it, Mare – she's an evil bitch who's never going to make you happy! And you're a fuckin' idiot if you can't see that!'

'Clancy! Oh, it's no good talking to you!' I slammed down the phone. Seconds later it rang again.

'Excuse *me*!" Clancy exclaimed. 'But you never even said *goodbye*!'

I was so cross I couldn't speak.

'Okay, listen then, if you can't bear to talk to me. See, all I care about is a great friend of mine: a smashing, funny, kind and lovely friend who's being crucified by… well, by her missionary zeal –' I snuffled as she went on '– her single-handed crusade to make the world a better place and to make one woman a better person. And you can't do it, Mare.'

'I *can*!' I squeaked. 'It just takes time… and reassurance…'

'Yeah, Mare – and how long has this been going on? Two years and more? Getting nowhere? It's like the Forth Bridge. You patch up one bit and by the time you've done that, another bit needs fixing. You're never done. And that's her pattern, Mare. She's distant and she's nasty.

So you go, "Come, come, come!" and gather her up... She gets close, close, close, then she panics and pushes you away...'

'But I just need to reassure her –'

'Crap! She needs reassuring about nothing!' Clancy cut in, sternly. 'The more you get close, the further she'll push you away. Recognise it? Face it. Nothing is gonna change. You can't change anything. You can only change yourself!'

My head was fuzzy with distress. What she was saying probably made sense, theoretically. But Clancy didn't know the things I knew. The damage Tanya had suffered. It would take years to repair and I was probably the only person who truly cared enough about her to help her through it. I really loved Tanya and she needed me because I was going to help her along the road to recovery. And there was no gain without pain. Clancy didn't understand.

'You need to move on, Mare. For yourself.'

I wasn't interested. I counted the pens. One. Two. Three. Four.

27

Tanya: We are going on holiday

Naturally it came out in the end. The truth will out, as they say. I suppose I could have just disappeared for three weeks without a word and come back tanned. But perhaps I owed Mary some kind of explanation if the subject arose. So in the end, one evening Mary said, as she often did, 'Are you doing anything tomorrow night?'

I took a drag of my cigarette and said, 'Actually, I'll be in Italy!'

'Yeah –' she laughed '– so do you fancy coming over to mine?'

'No.' I stared hard at her so that she wouldn't misunderstand. 'I will be in Italy. Really.'

She looked blank. I saw her glancing from my left eye to my right eye and back and forth, flickering from pupil to pupil, looking for a trace of humour, a trace of lies. Her face was covered in confusion.

'You're joking?' she said querulously.

'Nope.' I switched on the television and tried to look interested in the news. Bored now. Let us move on. And so to the latest war zone. Our overseas correspondent.

'What do you mean, you'll be in Italy?'

'I just will be.'

'Why?'

'Because it's hot.' I stubbed out my cigarette.

'What... is it a holiday? But... why haven't you mentioned it?'

'To retain my mystique,' I muttered, staring at the screen.

Mary sat up in silence for a few moments. I could almost hear her mind whirring. She swallowed, and licked her lips. 'Are you...? Who are you going with?'

'Christiane.'

She was quiet for a number of seconds. I still looked at the television screen, but out of the corner of my eye I saw her white face crumpling, struggling to understand. I switched up the sound.

Mary's voice wavered: 'Tanya... but why? ... Christiane?'

'Because she asked me!' I spat, growing irritated.

Mary sat rigid beside me. 'Why didn't you tell me?' she started, her voice beginning to rise to a wail.

'Because I knew you'd react like this!'

Her face contorted. 'Do you think so little of me?'

'Yeah – if you like! Yeah, in fact – I think nothing of you!' Mary looked at me, tears welling up in her eyes and her lip quivering. 'Oh, for *fuck*'s sake!' I shouted. Mary dissolved into sobs, holding her face in her hands. Great racking, theatrical sobs. 'Jesus fuckin' *Christ*!'

I slammed the television remote down on the floor and went off into the kitchen for a can of lager. After cracking off the ring-pull and taking a hefty swallow from the gassy can, I grabbed hold of a double packet of kitchen rolls, swung down the hallway back into the living room and threw the kitchen roll at Mary. Considerately, I thought. It glanced off her shoulder and hit the wall, but at least she stopped sobbing enough to look up in surprise. I sat down in the armchair furthest from her and concentrated on the images on the television. I couldn't see them. Mary snuffled into the tissue for a few minutes, then blew her nose loudly.

'Watch you don't blow your brains out,' I said.

She looked at me for a moment, then said through gritted teeth, 'And will you be sleeping with her?'

'No – we'll be too busy fucking.'

28

Mary: Plenty more fish

One, two, three, four.

One. Two. Three. Four.

Earlier. The day before. Days before – I forgot – I was... I could hardly say it. Not believe it.

One. Two. Three. Four. I was cleaning my shoes. Rubs. Counting the... one... two... three... four... rubs. Rubbing them clean. Rubbing them black. Rubbing them. Rubbing them till my white, clenched knuckles were scraped and sore and ingrained with black polish. One. Two. Three. Four.

From far away I heard long, terrible howls. Starting at my heart, anguish ripped through me. My mouth was a wide 'O' and I was that 'O'. A cipher for pain. I was pain itself. My face cracked with grief. My mouth and cheeks ran with thick, snivelly tears and saliva.

I tossed the shoes, cloth and polish aside and I curled up on my knees, rocking myself backwards and forwards with great dreadful sobs that wrenched me, whole; that were my whole body. The day before. A night ago. Days ago... How Tanya... left me... I did everything she... could want... Off with that... Christiane woman! Was I so awful... such a bad...?

I counted my breaths. One. Two. Three. Four. Long shuddering jerks of my whole body. Long shivering breaths. One. Two. Three.

Four. And I had been sitting there. Days and nights. Four days and four nights. Trying to make sense. And the pain was too much to bear. I sat with my hot, sore face in my wet hands. I wished I were dead. Pills. I could drown in a bath. Slash my wrists. Electrocute myself. One, two, three, four. Pills. Bath. Slash. Fry. One. Two. Three. Four.

I clambered up from the floor and ran upstairs. I pushed the plug in the plughole of the bath and turned the hot tap on full. My hands were trembling and so weak I could barely turn the tap. I was humming a tuneless, sad song without any words, without any meaning, just a wavering hum which broke now and then into a whine or a sob. It was the saddest song. The most dismal song I've ever heard and it was coming from me, from my heart. It was my heart's song, and it was rending my very soul into pitiful shreds. Tiny tattered shreds, so I could feel nothing any more. I was numb. I was sore and fragile and wrapped in cottonwool. My world was muffled. I couldn't hear and couldn't see. Couldn't smell. Couldn't feel. My senses, all gone. Hear no evil, see no evil, speak no evil, smell no evil, feel no evil. Hear no. See no. Speak no. Smell no. Feel no. Five is not good. Three is not good. Five minus three is two. Two and two is four. Four is good. The water was rushing. But I heard nothing. One. Two. Three. Four. Just counting. In my head. Still room in my bursting head to count.

I did everything. Anything to please her. Still no good! Still wrong! Lap-sang-sou-chong. Perhaps it was the tea. I would brew the best for her, drumming water into the kettle. Fresh. While she beat the retreat. I would watch it boil, rolling it hot. And her, cool. I would warm the pot, cupping my hands like an offering. I would hold a teaspoon between two fingers to lift dunes of the stuff, measured for two like a sand clock. One... two. One... two. My alchemy would steam, then seeth and rumble to a stop. I'd put a lid on it fast, then count time flowing so painfully. One... two... three... four. I would strain the sediment. Carefully. Such a delicate gold in her white china cup, and then her telling me she couldn't stand this scented stuff.

I smeared the condensation from the mirror with the back of my hand and looked at my face, bloated like a drowned one. Like a corpse, swollen and purpled, my eyes almost healed over from hours of hard crying. Tiny pinpricks of eyes. Piss holes in the snow. But not snow. Bulbous, inflamed flesh. Piss holes in volcanic lava. I was unrecognisable. I didn't exist; it wasn't me. My features were distorted, distended, ugly. No wonder. No wonder she didn't want me. I looked like shit. I was shit. I was calm now. It was all right. All cried out. I sighed. Once. Twice. Three times. Four.

I stepped into the bath and I knew it was far too hot, but that didn't seem to matter. Physical pain was nothing. My feet, my legs felt tight, bursting like rotten fruit bubbling from a skin that's been slit. I looked down indifferently. I flinched as my bottom hit the scalding water and sucked my breath in... oooh... But it was okay. My skin burned. And beneath my skin, my flesh boiled. At least I felt something. There was a vermilion tidemark across my arms, my stomach, as the water swung back and forth as I moved. There was sweat all over my face. It even ran through my eyebrows into my eyes. That was not supposed to happen. The water was lapping my shoulders. I lay back and thought of Italy.

Two hours later I was still scrubbing myself clean. One, two, three, four. Round rubbing rings. Then I'd move on to another patch of skin. One, two, three, four. Quicker and quicker. Scrubbing myself with the rough side of the bath cleaning sponge. The scouring side. And my skin was already red anyway. And I'd used up all the hot water and the soap was a thin sliver. I was shivering now and knew I had to get out soon. My fingers were white and spongy, white and wrinkled as prunes. White and spongy as a drowned corpse.

My mother bathed me until I was twelve. Until I could shut the door pleading modesty and pubescence. Till sharing a bath with my eight-year-old brother was unseemly, even to my mum. Until then, twice a week, I had to endure my mother scrubbing at my neck; a cold, clammy flannel being rubbed into my ears, my bottom, every orifice. But Vincent didn't get off lightly either. My enduring impression of him is of a tight-faced ball of misery, his hair a black tuft, sitting in grey waters, wailing that soap was in his eyes, knuckling it into them even more, a red-faced squall.

He's an accountant now. One, two, three, four. He's very particular, very precise. He's got a tiny blonde wife who looks down her nose at me from her three-inch heels, despite me being a foot taller than her. I'm more or less the same height as Vincent – six feet tall. I imagine their sex life is a wonder. They probably do it on towels. And have a shower – separately – afterwards. She possibly douches. So, probably, would he. Or take an enema. He's the type. Before and after.

These thoughts made me real again. I got out of the bath and towelled myself down. My fingers were not my own: there seemed to be a good half inch of flaccid dead skin bubbling off my fingertips and the soles of my feet. I was surprised to see that my skin still prickled with goose flesh. I thought I'd worn it away.

I was tired, but I thought the storm had passed. It was time to return the calls and return to the real world. Clancy had taken to hammering on the door and shouting through the letterbox until I let her in. The neighbours. To save the neighbours. But other than Clancy, I'd seen no one. Spoken to no one. Clancy had held her tongue and held me and listened and made me tea and poured generous amounts of scotch into glasses for me and been everything a friend could wish for.

And a few days later, she capped it all by saying 'I told you so' with excellent timing, just when she knew I could take it without wailing like a banshee. After that, I thought she took friendship too far. She moved on to persuading me to get out and about and make new friends. And she'd started by fishing out the old personal-ad person again, this Lindsay woman.

'So what are you going to do?' she asked.

I looked at her dumbly. I hadn't even thought that far. Do? What was there to do?

'You know... with your life? Now? Plans?' I frowned, so she went on: 'E.g. love life: what about Lindsay?'

'Cugh! What about her?'

'You like her, don't you? Has she been in touch?'

I nodded. She'd left a message on my answerphone, but I hadn't really listened. Just something like, 'Call me – let's go out for a few drinks or something.' Or something.

'Well then, ask her out!' Clancy said simply, her little face gleaming, beaming.

'Tut! Clance... I'm not in the mood... I'm grieving...'

'Oh, for the love of God! How long are you going to feel sorry for yourself? Shit! She's not dead! She's just a bitch! Don't break your heart over *that*!'

Too late. Too late.

Clancy put me under pressure to move on and I buckled under it. So, after another day of getting my emotions in order, I rang Lindsay up quietly, explained I hadn't been well and asked her to meet. Just for a coffee. Not a date. I felt weak and weary, but wanted to please Clancy, feel better and exact my own quiet revenge on Tanya.

'What do you do when you've fallen off your bike? Get up in the saddle again and ride!' Clancy had grinned.

But I wasn't sure you were supposed to swap your bike for a different model. I struggled to get my voice and my emotions on an even keel, to move the conversation on. My dull, addled brain was really too sore and tired for any more arguments and nausea was rising from the pit of my stomach that I was trying to swallow down. I tried to divert Clancy: 'Okay. Okay. Leave it, now, please... Clance? Look, I'm even going to meet this Lindsay, aren't I?'

'Good girl. Have fun. Remember, what's sauce for the goose... is sauce for the goose...' Clancy started her list of wise old adages: 'A Rolling Stone gathers no Kate Moss. Leap before you look. There's many a slip, 'twixt lip and clit...' I'd heard them all before. Clancy's Old Dykes' Tales. 'And moreover,' she went on, 'plenty more fish in the sea. You just need baited breath...'

And now I was set up for a blind date. No. A coffee. Not a date.

I looked in the mirror at my impassive, slightly downturned mouth. My eyes looked big and sad and my hair needed cutting. Whatever would this Lindsay think of me? Hang on! What was I thinking? What would Tanya think? But it was only an arrangement. A date. A coffee, I meant. I had a sick oppressive feeling in my chest, the more I thought of it. I felt treacherous and wicked. I couldn't tell Tanya. I wouldn't tell Tanya. But I must forget Tanya. And anyway I'd betrayed her already.

Town. Saturday afternoon. I opened the front door of Annie's bar, my heart pounding with anticipation and fear. I still shivered with the hurt of the past week. What was I setting myself up for this time? And worse... what if Lindsay didn't turn up? What if Lindsay didn't even exist? What if a twenty-four stone, seven-foot homophobic sadistic trucker guy had put an ad in to lure some poor sucker to her fate? I'd been reading too much crime fiction. I started the slow walk upstairs to the bar. The stairway was mirrored on both sides with flickering fairy lights and my reflections accompanied me side by side. I was wearing a black jacket and black jeans. So were my other selves in the mirrors. We looked like Reservoir Bitches. On heat, Clancy would say. We all went upstairs. At least I wasn't alone.

I took a deep breath at the top of the stairs and looked at my watch. I was a few minutes early, as I usually am. I hate to be late for anything, because I get anxious and nervous. Sometimes I arrive so early for appointments that I end up being late: I arrive at places three-quarters of an hour too early and worry about that. Taking up space, taking up time, or sitting outside suspiciously like a burglar casing the joint. If I am too rudely early, then I go off to find something to do in the meantime. I go to the shops or for a drive around and end up in a queue to pay for something I didn't even need. Or I get stuck in a traffic jam or lost and end up late for whatever it was that I was too early for in the first place.

Still, at least if I was here too early I could be sitting nonchalantly with my pint at the table of my choice, at a relaxed advantage by the time she arrived. If she arrived. I looked around the bar. No one I knew and no women sitting alone. No huge truckers either. There was a foursome of straight-looking people sitting round one table. Two middle aged couples, men and women – the women round and brassy-blonde, with throaty laughs. Annie's had a mixed clientele during the day but I never usually went in then, so it was a whole new experience for me. A couple of gay guys were standing at the bar with the barmaid. That was all.

My head still felt thick and woozy from spending part of the night before in tears. I stood at the bar and asked for my usual pint of lager. As the girl was pulling the pint, I suddenly realised that I'd forgotten I was just out for the afternoon – I'd asked for my usual when I'm out for the night. Here I was, meeting a woman for the first time. And here I was, drinking a pint of lager at three in the afternoon, when Lindsay had only suggested a coffee! What a dope! What would she think? She'd think I was an alcoholic! God! How embarrassing! Did I have time to knock it back quickly before she came in so I could order a coffee instead? Yes, a coffee would be far more appropriate. Far more sedate, far more sensible. Far less like an old drunk. So I took myself up on my own challenge, swung the pint glass up to my mouth and swallowed and swallowed down in one, with my eyes shut till my ears pounded with the gassiness and the strain and I drained the glass. I belched.

'Thirsty?' I turned round to see – to my horror – a strange woman with a wry smile on her face. 'Hi! I'm Lindsay! I'm guessing you're Mary?' She held out her hand.

I looked at her, appalled. Then I looked at her hand, aghast: 'Oh... shit!'

'Pleased to meet you, too!' She laughed, shaking my trembling hand.

'Oh, sorry – I, oh...' I recovered. 'Hi! Would you like a drink?'

'Yes, I think I have some catching up to do! Gin and tonic, please!'

I was grateful she was drinking alcohol, although I paced myself by ordering a Diet Coke. I still wasn't sure if she thought I was some old lush. Lindsay stood with me at the bar, obviously highly amused. Evidently at my expense. We went and found a seat in a quiet corner. Although *we* were the noisiest people around the place.

Lindsay was bubbly: 'Hey, I don't blame you for being nervous! *Course* you could do with a drink to settle your nerves! I was nearly shitting myself too! Silly, isn't it? It's not like it's a date!'

'No!' I cried.

She chattered on and I watched her lips moving, her whole face animated by cheeriness. She was like Clancy, with her cheeky grin and joyful outlook, but bigger, blowsier, you might say. She had short, shiny brown hair with red streaks in it and a plump, pretty face. And startling pale brown eyes. As a rule, I didn't like brown eyes. But hers were something else. They were not only remarkably attractive but had such a warmth and friendliness in them. I found myself staring into them, getting lost in them but feeling totally at ease. Not like Tanya's dark, deep eyes – which penetrated you, but gave away nothing. I felt relaxed, at home.

Tanya made me uneasy. You always had to be on the alert, ready for her twists and turns of intelligence. That was part of the challenge. Whereas Lindsay seemed genuinely nice: the kind of woman you could take home to meet your mum. Not Doris Day, though. No way, Doris Day. She was sexier than that. I liked her style: smart jacket, white shirt unbuttoned to show just a hint of cleavage. Ample bosoms, you might say, too. I found myself sitting back admiring her. I didn't hear half the things she said but I liked the way she said them. Her nose crinkled up when she laughed. She looked me in the eye when she talked and seemed interested and honest. She drew me out, asking me questions easily and comfortably and made me laugh. I felt myself visibly chill out. She even noticed when I'd nearly finished my Coke and sprang up to buy me another drink. I felt appreciated and looked after. This time I asked for a gin and tonic like hers. She had a bit of banter with the barmaid, then turned back to me and gave me the most beautiful smile. I felt a wave of warmth wash over me. She was lovely. Although I still felt tender and heart-sore, I was enjoying myself. If I was honest, I was having a great time.

She came back with the drinks and continued her story about her last girlfriend. I sat and watched her hands playing with the glass.

'… And then, well… We both knew it wasn't going anywhere. Sad, but it was for the best…' She smiled and took a sip of her drink. 'What about you?'

God! She was asking me questions. What could I tell her, when all I knew was that she had a cute smile, dimples and wonderful eyes?

'Oh, er… well, I've only really had one long-term relationship… with a woman, that is… And well, that hasn't… didn't… really… work out…' God! What was I doing? I talked to the tabletop, embarrassed to meet her gaze. But somehow I didn't want to tell her what I'd been telling Clancy and myself for years: that Tanya was the only one for me; that Tanya and I were together for ever. Those felt like desperate half-truths. I didn't even know what would happen when Tanya got back. What I was telling Lindsay suddenly sounded like the truth. 'I really loved her, but… like you say… when it's going nowhere… it's time…'

'To get out. Yeah.' Lindsay nodded.

'Mmmm.' I cleared my throat nervously and stole a quick glance at her.

'You're obviously still quite cut up about it,' Lindsay went on, smiling sympathetically, coaxing me to intimacy. 'Has it been quite recent, the break up?'

'Yes, quite recent.' But then, maybe it had been over for years. Maybe it had never got started. Or maybe I was telling myself lies to make me feel better. Tanya still was my partner. Wasn't she? She was, really. We hadn't actually broken up. My soulmate. I think. I thought. Despite… Hmmmm. Clancy's threatening words flitted through my mind. We'd see how it went.

Lindsay brightened again. 'Hey, we should go out on the town sometime – we can go have some laughs!'

I looked at her square in the face and said as frank as I've ever been, 'You know? That sounds like a really good idea!'

It would do me good to get out more. Take Tanya's example by having my own time and my own friends. I'd see how it went. I felt naughty. Wicked. Playing with fire.

'You're on, then!' She laughed and held up her glass. I chinked mine against hers to clinch the deal. I barely thought of Tanya.

Don't forget Tanya. Mustn't forget Tanya. Lest we forget...

29

Tanya: The Italian experience

Heat. A great shimmering heat haze rippled the runway. As soon as we set foot off the aeroplane and hit the hot Italian air, my headache alleviated and I was able to relax.

Christiane looked at me and smiled. 'Who would have thought you would be an anxious flyer? Is this better?'

'Much.' I grinned. If she wanted to believe that I was nervous of flying, that was acceptable to me. But I had actually been tense with fury: furious with Mary, furious with myself. I'd had no sleep at all and was completely stressed out by the time I picked up Christiane from her house where she stood immaculate and cool in a white linen suit. Only she could wear white. Ordinary human beings spill things down their front as soon as they wear white. It is a law. At the very least, ordinary human beings would get dusty whilst travelling. But then again, Christiane is extraordinary.

I was emotionally and physically desperate by the time we got to the airport. I needed to get away. I needed a holiday. It was years since I'd managed to get away. I'd snatched some weekends from time to time, but the last time I'd been abroad at all was four years ago with my girlfriend of the time and a couple of other friends. It was disastrous. I hate groups of people. I hate the expectation of doing everything together: 'Shall we go to the beach today? Tomorrow we'll go to the city!'

I hate plans made by committee. I hate people vying for leadership. I hate plans made by leaders. And I hate having to spend each day as a compromise. I lasted two days before snarling bitter recriminations, then I moved rooms and did my own thing amidst hysterical resentment and the need for evasion. Holidays: I hadn't prioritised the time since. It seemed like too much effort for myself and too indicative of togetherness for Mary and me. It might have given her ideas.

So I was really looking forward to this holiday with Christiane. Which was against all my principles. You do not look forward to anything. If you look forward to something, it all comes crashing down around your ears, so it's best not to look forward to anything. If I had learned anything from my time living with my mother, I had learned that.

At the hospital when close to death, she was more manageable. Quiet and docile. The demons had left her perhaps. Nearer my God to thee. You might even have imagined her to be thoughtful. From the stitched seam of her mattress ticking a curl of feathers wisped away; soft and brown, like baby sparrows. She scratched and picked at the paint on the wall – eggshell blue, cracked and flaked. Milky eyes, weaving thoughts, threading straws to clutch, her mind was bound by twigs and shreds of grasses. Her hands were speckled as a thrush, pecking at the walls; worms of veins on her dappled hands. The rumble of the wheels of the trolley bearing meals down the corridor was the roucoulement of pigeons, she imagined. From time to time she stirred and shrugged herself painfully from her bed. There she stood, window-stunned. Her skin in the mirror was yellowed and pimpled, her hair sparse and matted as if newborn from the egg. And from her small high window, she could see a little sky and sometimes birds flying.

Coo... coo. Carrroooo. Little pigeon woman. Little shrunken pigeon woman. How quaint, how cute. She was quite the darling of the nurses on the ward. But then, she always liked to be the centre of attention. She sang music hall songs:

The boy I love is up in the gallery...

The boy I love is looking down at me...
There he is... Can't you see? A waving of his handkerchief...

And the nurses would lap them up, taken in by her turn-of-the-century repertoire. They were misled, mistaking social history for old age. When someone is old, their years and their history mean nothing to the young. What's past is past. The nurses in their twenties and the care assistants in their teens thought she was Victorian, not a small child in the Second World War. Deceitful as ever... She should have been singing rock 'n' roll. That was her era.

They would coax her, smiling indulgently: 'Sing us a song from the Good Old Days, Mrs Helliwell!' That was ironic. The Old Days were never Good. She was never married – never Mrs Helliwell. But my mother was harmless at this late time in her life. Even I realised that, but it didn't stop the memories. The knowledge of how she had been and what she had done. What she had not done.

I didn't send Mary a postcard. Somehow I didn't think she would appreciate it. Having a lovely time. Wish you were here. I did think about her, of course. I spent quite a lot of time in contemplation, sitting on the veranda in the sun, reading magazines with a glass of wine in my hand, waiting for Christiane to get back from her meanders around Florence. I had seen enough. I'd had enough culture for myself, whereas Christiane was eager to spend every available moment drinking in the sights again and committing them to memory. She wanted to pore over every church and every painting; every sculpture in every piazza, palace and place of worship. She was a devotee of the Cult of the Virgin Mary. The Madonna and Child fascinate her. I do not share that fascination. Perhaps it is something to do with being a mother. And I have never wanted to be a mother...

Christiane and I had a splendid time, although we amused ourselves rather than each other. For me, my entertainment was relaxing in the sun, looking out over the olive groves towards the village; reading, drinking wine and eating good food, with only an occasional foray into the city with Christiane.

For Christiane it was galleries, the opera, the ballet. It was a time for us to explore our own interests, yet come together occasionally each day and most evenings. Being together and yet remaining apart. I'm not possessive and demanding, not the clingy type that Mary is. Mary. She would have gone on holiday with me with every expectation of being married by the time we returned. Her expectation would be that by now she should have really got inside my head, really got to understand me. That we two would be 'as one'. Maths isn't her strong point, poor deluded Mary. Still. I missed her, for all her irritating ways. Her affection, her loving. Her suffocation. However… I had needed a break.

My favourite holiday memory was one of our sitting one evening with the doors open on to the verandah, eating the simplest of meals: red ripe tomatoes, freshly torn basil, crushed garlic, thick green olive oil and hunks of crusty bread.

'Darling!' Christiane exclaimed. 'This is quite possibly the best meal I have had in my life!'

'Me too.' I raised my glass of red wine to toast her. My love. She was radiant. She had let down her long hair from its usual coil. Her long, soft, salt and peppery blonde hair. She had let it down like Rapunzel and I knew that I would climb it to reach her, to release her, to spend glorious moments of happy-ever-afterness with her. And I knew after all that she would never be mine.

30
Mary: Fishing

Clancy hung over the back of my chair squealing into my ear, 'Well, come out with all of us, then! Ask Lindsay to come out round Middlesbrough with a crowd of us. Less pressure. If you're not up to sparkling conversation yourself, I know some people who are! Go on... who knows? You might even enjoy yourself!'

I half smiled. She was right, but I just wasn't sure I was ready yet. If I was honest, I knew it was time I got things into perspective. Moved on.

So I rang and asked did Lindsay fancy coming out on the town with some of my mates? Did she ever! So that was that. But at the back of my mind, Tanya was still there. She'd never go away.

I hadn't been out with my pals for a long time, because Tanya had been spending quite a lot of Saturday nights with me before she went away. I'd better get used to doing without it. Her. But it wasn't over, was it? We'd said harsh words, but hadn't definitely finished – hadn't discussed things. I had doubt that we ever would. Maybe best to drift away...

We met upstairs at Annie's bar where it was hot and crowded. I found myself straining to look out for Lindsay and couldn't settle till I saw her peering through the swarming bodies looking for us. Looking for me. The whole gang was out: Big Mandy, Mel, Robbo,

Georgie, Kerry. I had such a great time! I couldn't recall the last time I'd laughed so much. Lindsay turned to me, her eyes sparkling and said, 'Your friends – they're great! This is the *best* time!'

Big Mandy caught me by the shoulder in the toilets and said, 'Keep hold of this one, Mary. She's lovely, and she obviously cares a lot about you.'

'She's a nurse,' I said lightly. 'They're paid to care.'

'Not off duty,' she pointed out.

Clare was out, talking to me for the first time in ages, even being friendly. 'Your new woman seems nice!' she said, nodding.

'Oh, she's not my new woman!'

'Well, she's not your old woman!' Clancy piped in, clasping Clare to her waist, 'though you're working on it, ain't ya, Mare?'

I couldn't help but feel warm and fuzzy. I had been feeling fuzzy before we came out, cottonwool fuzzy: numb. My head still wasn't straight (but for a lesbian, that's okay… I reminded myself). I felt as if I needed gentle treatment. And Lindsay was so sensitive to my moods, cheering me up, making me laugh, taking me out of myself. Yet she kept quiet when she sensed I was thoughtful. *There* for me. I wasn't really used to attentiveness.

I'd had a few lagers and by that time I was in Strings, the local nightclub. She asked me if I wanted to dance.

'Oh, I don't know if I've got the energy…' I said shyly.

'Then don't use any!' She led me to the floor, put her arms around me and that was it.

Her lovemaking. Our lovemaking. Made me cry. I cried softly in Lindsay's arms and she held me without a second's thought, without question. Just held me until my sobs had subsided, knowing that I'd tell her when I was ready. If I wanted to tell her at all. And I hardly knew why I was crying: confusion; sadness; grief for something lost. Grief for what I'd been missing, until now. Or relief. And oh, the difference between women! The softness. The heartbreaking, silky softness of it all. She touched me in some deep part of myself that no one had ever touched. And I felt so full of love. So vulnerable. So scared.

As far as happiness or fulfilment was concerned, Lindsay seemed to feel just as bowled over as me. Although it was early days, heady with lust, I was realistic too. But for the time being, I would enjoy the moments. We spent every available minute together, touching. Kissing. We saw one another the next day, the next night, the night after that. Her teenagers were great; the boys and I got on like a house on fire. And I was so full of her and of love for her. So filled with her love, too. It was a dreamlike state and I was aware of its time limitations. There was unfinished business, nagging at the back of my mind like the reality of consciousness at the edge of a dream. A bad taste in my mouth, a gall rising in my throat like a bitter aftertaste after a beautiful meal, cutting through the sensuous delight of it. Nothing to do with Lindsay. But away from Lindsay, in the parts of my mind that weren't taken up by thoughts of Lindsay. In those dark corners. In the scary parts: Tanya.

31
Tanya: Back home

I got back from Italy pleased and sated. I had achieved what I set out to achieve and felt healthy, tanned and energized.

I looked at the telephone. The message light was flashing. Nine messages. Now we'd see what was what.

Mary. Calmer than when I'd left her: 'Tan. I just wanted to say... you really hurt me. Uh... I don't know... I don't think I can forgive you. Bye... um... It's Mary.'

Clever girl! I laughed.

One message from some stupid bastard from work about something trivial; one from my bank; another from Mary: 'Tan. I've been thinking... and... um, I think... I can forgive you.'

Oh! How very big of her! I was honoured!

'I've thought about it and I just want to... understand...'

Jesus! Save me from people who just want to understand!

'Ring me when you get back, please.'

One from Stella, a woman I hadn't seen in months. One from a woman I was at college with: Nic. It was as if my past life were flashing before my eyes. Then two calls with no messages, not so much as heavy breathing. Two hang-ups: I have no hang-ups! I hate it when that happens. Probably Mary, although she wasn't usually backwards in coming forwards.

Another from Mary: 'Tan. I think we need... There's... things have been happening since you... went away. Please ring me. Soon as you get back. Please.'

How intriguing! I went upstairs to dump my bags, found my bed completely irresistible and slept undisturbed for fourteen hours.

Opening my eyes, I realized that it was Saturday afternoon. Glorious decadence. I stretched like a cat, reaching out far from the musky warmth of my little nest to the cool, crisp sheets of the rest of my bed. I switched on my computer and went for a wee. Too sleepy for a shower and too lazy. I sat on the toilet and yawned savagely, enjoying the warm pungent soupy smell of my piss. It felt like a good day.

I made some toast and coffee, lit up and dialled Mary's number. A tiny flicker of nerves fluttered in my stomach, but no more. She wanted me anyway. That much was irrefutable. And she had forgiven me, as she would forgive me anything. So that was all right.

The answerphone surprised me a little. I'd been geared up for a chat. So I chatted briefly to the tape: 'Hi Mary. It's Tanya. I'm back! Call me! Hope you're... well. Bye.' I'd tried to sound bright, but achieved only uncertainty. I tried the mobile. Switched off. Strange. I never left voice messages on Mary's mobile, so I sat and texted: HI! AM BACK! CALL ME! T X

I hesitated with the kiss, but thought she'd be more offended if I didn't bother at all. And besides, you can't see hesitation in a text.

My toast was now cold. I'd planned to eat it while talking to Mary. I'd pictured myself lounging on the sofa, feet up, one leg crossed over the other with my slipper dangling off one foot, flapping it casually in the air; taking a nonchalant bite from my slice of buttered crusty French *bâtard*, one hand holding Mary's chattering apologies, admonishments and forgiveness to my ear. And here she was, not here. Not there.

Still. I had enough to do. Washing. Shopping. Cooking. Eating. Chilling. Where was she?

I got dressed: sloppy, stay-at-home clothes. Doing-the-washing and shopping-at-Somerfield clothes. I checked my emails. There were four or five lengthy ones from Deelishus, Slavey and the rest, which I couldn't be bothered to read. I could imagine what they said. The usual. And a load of adverts and other spam. Certainly nothing worth reading. Nothing to write home about. What was there to write home about? Home. What was home? What *was* there to tell?

What my mother had done. What she had not done. What my mother had. What she had left me with. The knowledge that she heard Ron grab me downstairs one night when I thought he was safe in my mother's bed. The knowledge that she stood on the stairs and watched him rape me. The knowledge that all she said about it was: 'Shut up! It's not as if it's the first time!'

The knowledge that the first time I had been eight years old and this second time, I was barely fifteen.

Ron brought around flowers the next day. He handed them to my mother but looked sidelong at me as he gave them to her. My mother threw them at me and told me to put them in a vase.

The light slashed from the steel knife, blinding me but for the warm wood feel of the handle under my fingers. The crisp chopping thud of the blade on the board and the fresh green stalks of the flowers, smelling like summer and cemeteries. The cut stems bruised dark, weeping greenish ooze from their straight white veins. The pain was clean and dull. I saw and felt on my finger, the red bud blossom to a flower: a bloom of blood.

I cleared out my baggage. Put the bottle of Amaretto in the cupboard with the red wines. Carefully unwrapped the tissue paper from the small piece of Murano glass I'd bought for Mary, a tasteful lilac and blue bottle which would look better on her mantelpiece than those dreadful little pottery people she seemed to collect. I held it up to the light. Gorgeous. I could see the tiny air bubbles swirling up towards the neck. I turned it slowly, wonderingly, pleased by the colours. Lilac drifting into pale blue, like the sky over the sea; summer nights in Saltburn. I wrapped it up again and put it on the coffee table ready to give to Mary when I saw her. I stuffed the washing machine full of my whites, admiring my slim brown arms against the tumble of white cotton. Wait till they saw me! Wait till Mary saw me! I saw my thin tanned arms encircling her pale round body. I turned the machine rumblingly on.

I opened the fridge to survey it. A sad, sparse collection: a foil bag of coffee beans, the carton of UHT milk I'd just opened, butter, a crumpled tube of tomato puree, a nugget of parmesan. A bottle of lime juice and half a jar of sundried tomatoes. No doubt Jamie Oliver would have a banquet here, but not me. Some serious shopping was called for.

Several shopping bagfuls from the car later, when I'd put everything away and swathed my radiators with wet clothes, I sat and rang Mary again.

'Sorry!' Mary's recorded voice, breathless: 'Can't answer the phone! Please leave a message if you like! Bye!' I put down the phone. I frowned down at my watch. Hours had gone by. It was tea time. Even if she'd been out shopping in town, she'd be back by now. Strange. I tried her mobile. No answer. I didn't bother texting again.

After picking at a tea which tasted of nothing, I went into Middlesbrough to see who was out. I kept thinking I caught sight of Mary, but I was mistaken. I got into a crowd of pretty rough dykes, but tagged along for the company. I'm a loner really and I prefer to keep myself to myself but somehow that night I wanted to be with someone. I felt unsure of myself. Not myself at all. So it was tolerable – even essential – to be with a group of people, even if they weren't the type with whom I would normally mix. I hardly looked at the women. Barely window-shopped. I smiled when people talked to me but offered – gave – nothing. I simply didn't have the energy or the inclination. My heart wasn't in it. I wasn't myself at all. Tired from the journey, probably. I got the train home at twenty-past ten. Tried Mary again. No response. Went to bed puzzled and discomfited, with an indifferent book.

32

Mary: Getting back to how it was

I got home from Lindsay's late on Sunday afternoon to find a message from Tanya. My heart sank. I felt queasy but I had to deal with it. I rang her immediately and arranged to go over to see her at her house. In spite of myself, I felt a frisson of excitement.

She opened the door and beamed at me. 'Hi! Long time no see!'

'Whose fault is that?' I retorted.

She looked at me, momentarily taken aback, then she recovered. 'How the hell are you?' She was evidently very well. She looked brown, her eyes and teeth glittering whitely.

'Have a good... holiday?' I asked uninterestedly. I looked around her living room. Nothing had changed. 'Thanks for your postcard, by the way.' I couldn't help but be sarcastic. I felt stronger now. Nothing to lose and everything to gain.

'Oh... er... I didn't think you'd appreciate it... under the...'

'Look Tanya,' I swung round, 'to get to the point... I've met some-one else.'

Her face dropped, then she brightened. 'Oh, Mary! That's nice for you. I wish you the best!'

I frowned at her, finding it difficult to judge her. 'Is that all you've got to say?' I couldn't tell if she really thought so little of me or was protecting herself.

She took a step closer to me: 'Mary... What else can I say? You deserve better.' She looked down sadly. 'I know I haven't made you happy...'

'Oh...' I found myself about to contradict her. 'But you... did!'

'Not in the way you wanted, Mary. I'm sorry...' Her eyes sparkled with the beginning of tears: 'I know I hurt you, but... sometimes how I feel... the depth of my feeling is... scares me. Makes me... So I know I probably can't give you what you want. But I'd like to,' she added softly. 'Oh, how I want to...' she breathed. I felt myself thaw. 'I just... but I got you a present...' She handed me a small package from the table. I pulled off the paper and opened it. A beautiful bottle in her favourite colours, colours that reminded me of Tanya. It was delicately patterned like solid water, like a river of lavender-blue ice.

'I saw it and thought of you. Of the evening we spent walking along the beach when I gave you the piece of glass. Remember?' She looked into my face, testing my reaction to the gift, to her words. I remembered that moment. The time when it had felt like a breakthrough. When we were closer than we'd ever been. She laid her hand on my arm and I felt the familiar charge of electricity I always felt when she was near.

I put my arms around her, cupped one hand in her hair and she looked up at me, her intense deep-set eyes earnest and red-rimmed, imploring, 'I do love you, Mary. I know I don't always show it... I don't know how...' She sobbed into my shoulder, reaching her hand up to my neck, caressing me, her fingers so soft. Something stirred. I melted.

That night, I hadn't wanted to make love. Have sex. I felt soft and open: wounded. I wanted to be close to Tanya again; to make it all right. I wanted to hold her very close in my arms. Have her hold me. We undressed: not sensuously but practically. Somehow I wanted to be honest – and being naked was honest. Close. Nothing between us, just skin to skin, no holds barred. It might be our last time: a farewell. I kissed her damp eyelids one by one. They flickered open and her eyes looked at me with such profound sadness and regret that it wrenched my heart. Our gentle kisses became more pressing. And then it was as it had been before. Only deeper. More honest. A new beginning.

33

Tanya: How to cope

So Mary thought she was in love with someone else. I was not unmoved by the fact. I preferred her to be mine alone but hey, that was hypocritical of me. What's sauce for the goose... is sauce for the gander. And who was I to complain?

I was starting to take a second look at her, plain old Mary. Hmmm. It was a little fillip to my interest in her, and I started to feel that I should make more of an effort to please her. How quaint of me. And so I had a rival then? Never mind, I was competitive. I was willing to take up the challenge. Indeed I thrived upon challenge. Still, whatever the competition, she would always be drawn to me. No matter who she saw, I knew she'd always come back to me. Faithful, loyal, doggy Mary.

I found that the thought of her with someone else titillated me. But the *thought* of her being with someone else was not the reality and it irritated me that she was not so available. She was not at my beck – whatever the hell that was – and not at my call. She always used to be so reliable! I could ring her up day or night, whenever I felt like it and she'd be over in a flash. *Now* there were some nights I had to spend alone, when not even my computer friends could stave off sleep and the black panic that overwhelmed me. The sudden shock of the iron hand that gripped my lungs, or a feather pillow that stopped my breath in the pitch dark. I still woke thinking that I had to play dead to survive. Feel the suffocation and work with it. Surrender to it. The pretty lights swirling through the blackness.

Sometimes I just needed Mary to be there with me. Okay. There – I've said it! Needed her. On occasion.

In Mary's new adulterous days all I got was the answerphone or 'Aww, Tan! I'm sorry! If I'd known you wanted me to come over I wouldn't have arranged to see Lindsay tonight. Aww… can we do something tomorrow instead?'

My teeth would grind.

I didn't want to make her choose. But when push came to shove I was quite sure that she would choose me. I thought. Maybe I would give her a test. I knew how to play her better than anyone; I knew how much to give her and how much to leave her panting for more.

But I took off my hat to her, good old Mary. Good old faithful Mary. I didn't think infidelity was her style at all. Promiscuity, eh? Adultery, huh? What would the old nuns say to that? Virgin Mary, Mary most pure. Very interesting! But we should see how far she'd go. I enjoyed a challenge and a little touch of intrigue – and deception peppered things up for me. The spice of life. At the time, she thought she was in control. I allowed her that for the moment. But we both knew that she needed me. She craved me. She fed off me. I made her. She would die without me. She needed me like she needed to breathe. She needed me like a tiny baby needs a mother. Mother. Makes me shudder. Udder… Mudder… I was not a mother.

Months later. Months of misery. Months of locked doors. Months of my mother telling me that I was lazy. Telling me I was ugly. Telling me I was dirty. Telling me I was fat. Months of me avoiding changing rooms and communal showering after games; of wearing baggy clothes. Keeping myself to myself. Months later and the need to get away, horror trapped and fluttering inside me. The need to get far away from that house. Then the pain that started me running. Months later. The tight belt of fear gripping me, constricting me, making it hard for me to breathe. And all I knew was that I had to go somewhere, anywhere. Time was running out and I wasn't sure how far I could go. Pain searing through me in waves: burning, scalding agony that doubled me up as I made my wavering way to the park. To the quiet. To anywhere out of sight. Anywhere with no one there. To the toilets.

I left it in a black bin-bag. So small, so threatening, trying to cry life. I didn't want it. I left it. In the graffiti-scrawled lavatory. Out of silent, screaming solitude and pain. But I managed; I succeeded. Kept it quiet from the start. So much blood. It slithered hot and naked on the cold tiled floor. I had no blanket. Used my T-shirt. Wrapped it in it, from the cold. So much for love. I left it. There was only a bin bag. I left it there. I had to get rid. I left it in a black bin bag. I didn't want it.

So, no. I'd never wanted to be a mother. Opportunities arose, of course. Oh, great irony. Mother. It didn't bear thinking about. What a mother I would have been! Mother. Mother. Meaningless word. Mother. Mother. Mother. The more you said it, the less sense it made. Mothering didn't come into it. Mother. The name didn't suit me, thank you. Thank you for asking. Thank you very much for asking, but no.

I locked myself in my bedroom. Downstairs, I heard Ron and my mother get back from the pub. I lay curled up on my side in the bed, sanitary towels wadded between my legs to staunch the bleeding; waiting for the pain, now a dull, sore ache, to go. I curled up with my knees tucked up towards my chest, my elbows bent, my head down. Foetal position. Downstairs, my mother and her lover. In high spirits, my mother and the father of the thing.

34

Mary: So many women

Maybe one woman could never provide enough: Lindsay could never provide enough for me. After all, I had a huge investment in Tanya, in our relationship. I'd paid vast amounts into our account and I wanted to be there to receive the interest and benefits.

'Why don't you just chuck that cow?' Clancy asked again. She meant Tanya, of course. In fact this time her reference to Tanya was almost a compliment. She had variations on the same theme: ditch the bitch, ditch the witch, frig the pig, chuck the fuck. She was obviously mellowing.

'Tut!' I was growing tired of giving the same old answer. Invariably I said, 'Because I love her!' Again. It was quite simple.

'Aw jeez, Mare. And there was Lindsay treating you right, making you feel good about yourself...' She was right: having Lindsay in my life had certainly been good for me. It gave me strength and cushioned me against my obsession with Tanya. She wasn't my only option: now I could take her or leave her, to a degree. But still – Tanya held me. There was some powerful magic there that was irresistible and strengthened by our time together and my knowledge of her own past. I didn't want to give up on her. I couldn't let her go. Life at the moment could hardly be better: I had my cake and I was enjoying eating it.

'Isn't it unfair on Lindsay, you shagging Tanya?' asked Clancy, trying the guilt-trip.

'Oh, listen to Mother Theresa!'

'She's dead!' she interjected.

'You – who's so virtuous? You told me you had a harem before you settled down with Clare!'

'Yes, but I know what *you're* like, Mare! You big, daft softy – you'd fall hook, line and sinker for anyone who took any notice of you!'

'You cheeky cow!' I threw a cushion at her, outraged.

For a while I didn't tell Lindsay I was still seeing Tan. I didn't want to hurt her, so I didn't so much lie as simply not tell her. I avoided the issue. I wasn't sure where things were going with either of my relationships. Lindsay was lovely, but she wasn't Tanya. And we had taken no vows of fidelity, so it wasn't as if I was actually cheating on her. With Tanya I was honest and this felt like a new phase to our relationship, moving us on to a more equal footing, with me less dependent on her, less in awe of her. And I think she had a new respect for me.

Now that Tanya was back, the extreme first flush of love I'd felt with Lindsay faded, like the dream it had been, or the memory of a holiday. Lindsay had been good for me. But then, you don't always want what's good for you. She did give me something I'd never had with the other women in my life: confidence in myself. A kind of security. I was grateful for that, and feeling strengthened by it, I could easily move on.

When I was a teenager leaving my mum's house for a date, for shopping, or even to go to school, I could never get out of the door without her picking fault with me: 'You're not going out looking like that, are you?' Or she would grab my arm as I tried to get out of the front door, pinching my flesh with her exuberance and pull a comb through my hair or pick off fluff from my chest or brush off dandruff from my shoulders or turn up my collar or turn down my collar. Always an implicit criticism: I could do nothing right, not even dress myself. Or a justification for her existence: what would I do without her? I couldn't be trusted to look after myself. Where would I be if it wasn't for her making me presentable? And I realised Tanya was a bit like that, although less diplomatic. I'd be all dressed up for a night out and she'd say: 'You look like a bag of shite!' She'd buy me clothes to her taste. I began to be afraid of buying anything by myself. I wanted Tanya with me when I went to have my hair cut because I wouldn't come in for so much criticism if she'd given the instructions directly. But Lindsay? She seemed to accept me for myself. She even complimented me. It made me uneasy.

But Lindsay was not too bright. I'd discovered that she was not... intellectually stimulating. But we were comfortable. We were like an old pair of slippers. No challenge. No excitement. No drama. Still, I needed a bit of slack, some fall-back. As far as my feelings for Tanya were concerned, things couldn't be better. She didn't fill my every waking moment any more – I was confident that she didn't rule my life. And Tanya responded well to the new, less Tanya-driven me. She seemed to make more of an effort, which showed me a new side of Tanya: keen and respectful. Maybe I'd been right after all. Maybe there might be a future there. I took tentative steps to find out.

'Tan... do you mind me seeing Lindsay?' I asked her, snuggled against her chest.

'Huh? Well, of course I mind!'

'You do?' I was startled and sat up in amazement.

'Yeah! There I was – back from Italy, dying to see you again, missing you like mad...'

I frowned at her in disbelief: 'What? Absence really makes the heart grow fonder?'

She nodded. 'And abstinence makes the heart grow fonder too!'

'Aww! Really? But did you *really* miss me?'

'Course I did, you silly tart! There I was, hurrying home to make an honest woman of you... And now I have to share you! How fair is that?' She pinched my nose.

'What d'you mean, "make an honest woman of me"?'

'Well,' she looked at me shyly in a way I'd never seen before, 'I'd had a lot of time to think... and to realise that you were the one I wanted to be with... You know?'

I was gobsmacked. I could only articulate a plaintive 'Aww!'

She went on. 'But... I can get used to this... Since you don't feel the same way...'

'But I do!' I protested, kissing her cheeks, her eyes, her nose, 'Oh, God! I do! Lindsay's nothing compared with you!'

'Prove it.'

'What?' I looked up, mid-kiss.

'If she's nothing to you, then why are you with her?' she asked me frankly, her eyes glimmering with tears.

She had a point. Lindsay was my security blanket and it was time to be a big girl and give it up. Coward that I am, I phoned Lindsay to explain that I hadn't been entirely honest with her – I had a long-term partner who was back after a holiday. There was quite an outcry. She said she had been honest from the start – even about her kids. We talked at length, but my attempts to reassure Lindsay that she was, in fact, everything any woman could want received short shrift. I even rationalised it by explaining that I was insane. She agreed.

'And don't bloody ring me up again when your partner's on holiday or away for the weekend or down the shops for a fuckin' bag of sugar!'

To avoid further unpleasantness and confrontation I just stopped returning Lindsay's calls. My head was fuzzy with distress and anxiety. I had just hurt a lovely woman and, moreover, she was the person who had given me back my self-respect and security. I was free-falling back into Tanya's life and there was no guarantee of the parachute opening. My reserve chute was shot to buggery – I'd made sure of that myself. I was taking a chance on a safe landing in spite of everything. Also, I'm afraid of heights. My head had a fluffy, unreal sensation in it. But thrilling, like taking a huge risk: a Russian Roulette gamble that your life depended on.

A couple of days later, things were fine and I had no worries in the world when my doorbell rang. Clare was standing on the doorstep, her face a thunderous purply pink against her ginger hair. I was very surprised to see her. I looked questioningly at her.

'Can I come in, please?' she hissed. I let her through, wondering what the hell was the matter. What had I done?

She stood in the living room with her hands on her hips, all angles and sharpness. I was wary of her, but I gave her an encouraging nod.

'Tanya,' she said.

I looked blank. So she knew. Clancy had told her. It didn't matter. I half expected Clancy to confide in Clare, if only to reassure her that she wasn't about to run off with me in their fraught and paranoid times. To show that I was no risk. I didn't mind if she knew. I'd just never broadcast it. I was still keeping my vow of silence as my condition of Tanya's love, but the way things were going these days, I was sure we could be a proper couple soon. It wouldn't matter who knew and we could be seen in Middlesbrough together. Invite friends over for dinner. Even live together. Things were going so well.

'It's about Tanya. There's a bit of water under the bridge, and I think it's time you knew. Only I don't want you to tell Clancy, okay? Things are great now. You'd only break her heart if you told her...'

I frowned again. I had no idea what she was talking about.

'Ask her about Red. Ask Tanya about Red.'

I looked blankly at her.

'For God's sake, Mary! Tanya and I were having an affair! I'm Red!' She held up a handful of her red hair and let her hand drop. I looked at her hair. It stayed up in a springy tuft on top of her head. I took particular notice because her words took several seconds to sink in.

'No!' I laughed. 'You wouldn't... do that to Clancy?' I wavered, remembering that Clare had even been so desperate as to try it on with me, her partner's best friend. There was nothing she wouldn't do, then. But Tanya? Would Tanya? No, surely not.

'Mary,' Clare said keenly, 'ask her. Ask Tanya about Red. It's over now, but it went on for about eighteen months. Not long after you got together, actually.'

I stood there and said nothing. My mind reeling. What? What – had I been sharing Tanya with skinny, witchy Clare? All this time? Was I caught in a deceit that had nearly torn Clancy and her family apart? What? Why was Clare here now, telling me this?

As if she'd read my thoughts from my bewildered face she said, 'Look. Things are okay between me and Clancy now. Better than okay! I'm out of it now, but you've been punished enough! I don't want to see Tanya win you back. She needs to get her just reward!'

'Revenge...' I whispered aloud to myself. It didn't make sense.

'If you like. She deserves worse, if you ask me. Nasty, vindictive, de- ceitful. Sociopathic. In fact – a misogynist! She doesn't even *like* women! You've seen how she treats women! If you don't believe me, ask her about Red. Me. Or... how can I prove it? The mole on the in- side of her left thigh, high up near...'

'Stop!' I shouted and covered my ears. 'Stop! Stop!'

'Ask her about Red, is all...'

Clare crept out of the house.

I didn't want to believe it. My brain was reeling. What? I couldn't believe Clare. I didn't trust her motives, but why would she make it up? What did she have to gain in telling me this? Revenge on Tanya? Revenge on me? So – she wanted to split up Tanya and me? Why was she telling me now, when she could have hurt me months ago? A year ago. It didn't make sense. Why didn't it all come to light when Clancy and Clare were having their troubles? I was befuddled. If Clancy'd known, then they would have split up. Clancy. I confided almost everything in her. Clancy, so hurt, so distressed, so full of pain but still there for me, putting herself aside to listen to my fears and my heartache. If Clancy... They would have split up then. One. Two. Three. Four. I paced the room. I waited: one, two, three, four seconds. Gave myself space to breathe.

But Tanya. Red? Tanya. I wouldn't put it past her, come to think of it. I didn't like to think... but... even Christiane... Three weeks away with a woman she says she loves... and she did make that horrible joke about them spending all their time fucking, right before she took off. I would be completely stupid to think that nothing went on... in the bedroom. I'd blocked it out. I was just pleased she still wanted me when she came back, after all. Grateful for her attention, eager for any few moments she was willing to spare me. In her spare time. But Tanya had plenty of time to herself. Plenty of time away from me to mess around. I wasn't her keeper, as she had often so eloquently told me. If I held it up to the cold light of scrutiny, deep down I knew... anything was possible. My ears hummed with fury. I could hear nothing but Clancy's distress and my anger. Things never change. People never change. A huge empty vacuum took up the space where my heart used to be filled with Tanya. Love was a hollow echo.

'Who's Red?' I asked Tanya, tight-lipped.

She frowned at me. 'You are?'

'Tell me about Red.'

'I don't know what you're talking about, love.' Tanya returned to her TV guide. I snatched it away, dashing it to the floor and Tanya looked up in genuine surprise.

'Tell me about you and Clare!' I glared at her and watched her face move from shock through bewilderment to determination.

'Okay. So what do you want to know?' She screwed out her cigarette butt.

'So it's true? You and Clare had a relationship?' I squeaked.

'Hardly. We had sex a few times. If you call that a relationship...'

'How many is a few times? One? Two? Three? Four? Forty? Four thousand?'

'Does it really matter how many times?' Tanya sighed.

'Yes, it bloody *does*!' I shrieked.

'Really? Well, let's say... averaged... twice a week over, say, eighteen months... that's... timesed by four, timesed by eighteen: say...

a hundred and forty-four times, maybe? And *positions*? Do you want to know positions? Missionary, doggy, spoons, 69... with toys, without toys...'

I slapped her across the cheek. Anything to shut her up, her cocky braying voice. The slap rang through the room, rang through my head. She looked up at me, open-mouthed, holding her cheek as if she couldn't believe it. Had to feel it for herself.

'What? What are you doing?' she asked, aghast. I stood trembling, silent. My knuckles were white and fisted, taut by my sides. A moment passed. 'Jeez, Mare! What's your problem? You've been sleeping with another woman! How many times have *you* done it? Do I ask? Is it any of my fucking business? Back off! Stop suffocating me!'

I held my tongue. Somewhere in my brain tiny wires were fizzing, short-circuiting. Clancy. Little, funny, loyal, loving Clancy. Clancy and Clare. The kids: Chloe, Emma, Jamie. Clancy so hurt. And all that time! All that time! Christiane... how many others? How many fuckin' others? Clare! And Clancy distraught, her pain palpable: 'I think there's someone else...' Jesus! And stupid, stupid gullible me. Falling for... it all. Nothing changes. People don't change. You're the only one who can change anything. My brain whirred, swirled, wheeled around in my skull.

Tanya was talking. She's always been good at that. 'Look, Mare, love. I'm sorry... Clare – she threw herself at me!'

For eighteen months, over and over again.

'It's way in the past! And as for you – did it hurt you? Till now? Till she told you? What you don't know won't hurt you. So I wasn't the one who upset you... It's Clare who's the wind-up merchant. She's trying to hurt you. Hurt us.'

My brain had turned to mush. I couldn't think any more. My mind was all full up. Shut down. No room. Closed. There was a closed sign up in my eyes.

'You're so sensitive... too sensitive, darling... Come on, pet... You can't take care of yourself...' I felt it all to be true. A dangerous wind was thundering through my skull, fanning flames in my overheated mind. In my body, I was nauseated and wobbly and couldn't look after myself. I was shivery and frail, a tiny sick child barely able to walk, feeling frightened and needing care. Needing love. I let her lead me to bed, undress me and stroke me. I was as fragile as glass, but I needed to be held. Then Tanya was pushing her hand between my legs. I opened my eyes in bewilderment.

'No...' I said firmly but she pressed on, one knee between my legs. 'No!' I repeated in alarm and struggled to get up. She was kneeling on my thigh and one arm bore much of her weight across my chest and shoulders, so I couldn't move. 'No!' I cried. She bruised me.

'No!' I tried again but her mouth was over mine, her tongue pressing back my tongue while I struggled. And her hand: insistent, jabbing, stabbing. One, two, three, four. Over and over. So rough. And I cried. How I sobbed. And she held me afterwards, telling me how much she loved me and how everything would be all right. And I lay frozen in her arms, staring into the blackness.

'You know me, darlin', you know how I love you,' she whispered, rocking me back and forth. 'You know what I'm like... But see how I love you...' She cradled my molten head, rocking me backwards and forwards.

And I tried to rationalise. Tried to pull explanations out of the red-hot swirl of my brain. But I did say no. I said no. No. No. No. No.

She tried to stroke me to sleep. She called me baby. 'Hush now, baby. It's all right. Shhhhh...' She held me against her warm breasts, trying to mother me. I found no comfort there. Just darkness. I lay rigid against her, waiting. I lay so still that I might be dead. Might be asleep or might be dead. I played dead, but my eyes darted from side to side and my thoughts spattered like hot cinders. I lay still till she left me alone, till she turned over and drifted into innocent sleep.

One. Two. Three. Four. I slipped smoothly out of bed just as I normally do when I go to the bathroom in the night. But this was not a normal night. Nothing normal at all. I stepped lightly down the stairs.

One, two, three, four; one, two, three, four; one, two, three, four – and when I got to the bottom: one, two, three, four paces and I swung into the kitchen and turned on the eye-wincing light. I stood blinking in the brightness like a rabbit caught in the headlights of the truck that's thundering towards her. There was a dull ache in the pit of my stomach or my bruised vagina, throbbing like a memory. This was how it was and this was how it would be. This was the beginning and this was the end.

My hands were filthy. I was filthy. I ran the tap and pressed liquid soap from the dispenser. I lathered the floral creaminess round and round my hands for four seconds, four times, but I'd touched the soap bottle and they still weren't clean. I took the kitchen cleaning cream and squeezed some into my hands, then scrubbed with the vegetable brush. The Cif was lemony and abrasive, but even when I ran clear water over my hands it wasn't enough. I had to wash them again. I scrubbed away at the skin with a scouring pad, but I still couldn't get my hands clean. Desperate, I poured some pine disinfectant on my hands and scoured harder and harder, counting the seconds. Although it made my skin smart and tiny pinpricks of blood appear, it still wasn't clean. Distraught, I could do no more.

I focused on the kitchen wall. Hung on a board and glinting seductively, there were kitchen knives. I fingered the sharp end of the filleting knife. Its sting was so subtle that I didn't know I'd been cut until I watched the blood dripping on to the worktop. 'Plash!' it whispered softly. I stared at the drops, welling like tears. My mouth formed the shapes of the words: scarlet... vermilion... ruby... crimson... I rolled the sounds around my tongue.

One. Two. Three. Four.

'This knife is too-oo big,' said I. I moved on, pointing to the blades of the other knives. My finger left dark smears of my blood. My mark.

'Two. And this knife is too-oo little... Three. And this knife is too-oo-oo hard. Four...'

One. Two. Three. Four. So steely savage and dangerous, knives.

Made me shudder. I sucked the end of my finger, tasting the metallic blood. One. Two. Three. Four. Something knocking at the door. Fe-fi-fo-fum. I smell the blood of a... woman? A dragon? Dragon's blood. Dragon's breath. Wolf's bane. Wolf's breath. I'll huff and I'll puff and I'll blow your house down. Fe-fi-fo-fum. Something nasty this way comes. One. Two. Three. Four. Open up the bloody door.

One. Two. Three. Four. I was chanting over and over again. You can't count on anyone, though. One. Two. Three. Four. Faster and faster. One-two-three-four. My breath came in excited staccato – like adrenalin. Unstoppable. I climbed the stairs.

Who's been sleeping in my bed? And there now she lay so sweetly and so well. Lay on the pillow with her hair spread out like a spider's web, like a trap. Oh, what a tangled web we weave, when first we practise to deceive. Practice makes perfect.

She lies perfectly. Lies. Here she lies. She lies anyway, every way. Liar, liar, pants on fire. It's a sin to tell lies. All liars are sinners. People who sin must be punished. Syllogism. People who lie must be punished.

She's lost her power now and can't hurt me. But silently I'm howling like a damaged beast. Like her Caliban, captive, kept like a beast living off my senses, not allowed to be human. I'm tied to her with something more than passion. Something less than love. She won't let me go and I'm too cowardly to confront her to escape. I've no imagination. I see only one way out.

She's lying so peacefully she could be dead. And here I am, dead already. And *she* looks so untroubled, her dark hair tumbling over the white pillow, her delicate features the monochrome picture of innocence. One arm swept across the bed like a ballet dancer. Or like a mermaid, silver in this moonlight. Washed ashore. And me... washed up. Washed out. Watch out. She sleeps like a baby, needs a nightlight like a baby, cries like a baby, needs comforting like a baby. Poor, damaged baby. Poor dead baby. There's blood on my pillow. And it's mine. For now, I've put the knives away.

I've counted time ticking by. Its rhythm drumming an insistent tattoo, my ears ringing in my head with a song of misery and betrayal. Its tune is like the rush of wind, the sound of a wasted life, of desolation. One hundred thousand. Two hundred thousand. Three hundred thousand. Four... Hundreds of seconds until her breathing has become easy, regular and convincing. My head is bursting. The bony armoured shell of my skull is in danger of erupting, my brain boiling over: a Vesuvius.

Here she is, asleep like a vicious angel of death. Tanya, may she rest in peace. I pick up my stained pillow as I struggle to my knees, my breath catching in my throat and I'm moving in slow motion so as not to disturb the bedcovers. I've been waiting for her to turn over on to her back. Waiting for the small animal snuffle of her breathing as it gets steady in sleep.

And now, it's time. One. Two. Three. Four. Who's that lying on the floor?

35
Tanya: Play dead

Scary Mary. She scared me tonight. I have never seen her so upset. So furious. Filled by the wrath of all her friends, all their histories; the wrath of all her pain and *its* history. I did well to soothe her, to calm her down. Stormy weather. I lay with her at my breast and even let her suckle a little for her comfort. Despite the stirrings it released in me, the flutterings in my womb, the rising of my desire, I didn't want to frighten her with sex again and I stayed calm, loving her, caressing her head, running my fingers through her hair, whispering words as soft as leaves blowing in the trees. I waited until she had fallen asleep, then I moved her head gently from my chest on to her pillow, covered her bare shoulder with the sheet and tucked her in. I kissed her forehead, stroked a strand of hair out of her eyes and then turned and lay a while, staring at the ceiling above my head. Dim and grey, one shaft of light from the street lamp outside tapering across the sheet.

It would be all right. We would be all right. My eyes drifted shut and I gave in to sleep.

Black! ... There's black again and... Oof! Can't breathe... Struggle! There's... no breath... black... pillow... cotton wool... black... breath. Can't... breathe... Know... stop... dead... All the pretty lights. The day-glo pink Mickey Mouse. The purple triangle. Pretty, sparkling things. And black.

More new fiction from Diva Books

The Touch Typist
Helen Sandler

"Funny, witty, moving"
Ali Smith, author of *Hotel World*

Joss is going bonkers. She's being terrorised by her neighbour, ignored by her girlfriend, marginalised by the boss and besieged by mice. It's time to log on.

After getting down and dirty in *Big Deal* (Sapphire), Helen Sandler turns her hand to tragi-comedy in this tale of sanity, secrets and cybersex, developed from a story that first appeared in *The Diva Book of Short of Stories*.

Praise for Big Deal:
"Believe me, it's the deal of a lifetime" *Guardian*
"Groundbreaking... let's hope this is the first of many novels from Helen Sandler" *Pink Paper*

RRP £8.95 ISBN 1-873741-65-0

Breaking Point
Jenny Roberts

Cameron's back!

When Cameron McGill stumbles across a vicious knife attack, the victim begs her to pass on an email address, then slips into a coma. Cam starts to investigate, and meets animal rights militants, local thugs, a mysterious dyke called Beano, the troubled Angel who only wants to get her into bed... and the very unhelpful chief executive of an animal research establishment. Determined to get to the truth, Cam finds to her horror that she has now become the prey.

In this eagerly awaited follow-up to *Needle Point*, Cameron has fallen out with Hellen, and landed up in Hull. More than one person wants to kill her. If only she'd never left Amsterdam.

*"**Breaking Point** is a well-written, fast-moving filmic story and you'll enjoy being taken along for the ride"*
Time Out

RRP £8.95 ISBN 1-873741-58-8

DIVA Books are available from all good bookshops, including
Waterstone's, Borders, Libertas!, Gay's The Word,
Silver Moon and Prowler.

DIVA also has a mail order service on freephone 0800 45 45 66
(international: +44 20 8340 8644). Please quote the following
codes: *Smother* SMO618, *The Touch Typist* TOU650,
Breaking Point BRE588.

For a year's subscription to DIVA magazine, call 020 8348 9967
(international: +44 20 8348 9967). UK £24, Europe £50,
rest of world £60.